Praise for Betsy Tobin:

"A gripping narrative shimmering with psychological depth."
New York Times

"Mesmerizes the reader with its gentle mysticism, carnal themes, and dreamlike qualities... A fine gothic novel which burrows under the skin." *The Times*

"An elegant, haunting novel... meticulously rendered."
Publishers Weekly

"Tobin's neatly measured prose cuts through a tangle of dark and dirty secrets with pearly clarity and precision... Her writing has weight and resonance." *Time Out*

"Wonderful, poignant and gripping... Betsy Tobin has skilfully portrayed life in a 17th-century English village as well as written a compelling mystery." Tracy Chevalier

"A vivid evocation of an ancient volcanic land... Tobin combines the sensuality of Angela Carter with a profound feeling for a violent, unstable and fascinating landscape... this world pulses with subversion and unexpected passion."
Daily Telegraph

"Tobin's novels are dark and bloody, sensual and mythic."
Observer

"A lyrically written epic inspired by the beauty and history of that island, and the rich world of Norse mythology that infuses it..." *Sunday Telegraph*

"Not just a good story, but one of the greatest – beautifully told." *The Times*

"Tobin captures this world in all its complexity... where magic and mystery rise from the currents of nature and not in defiance of it." *Independent on Sunday*

Crimson China

Crimson China

BETSY TOBIN

First published in 2010 by

Short Books
3A Exmouth House
Pine Street
EC1R 0JH

10 9 8 7 6 5 4 3 2

A CIP catalogue record for this book is available from the British Library.

ISBN 978-1-907595-22-6

Printed in Great Britain by CPI Bookmarque

Cover illustration: Jem Butcher

In memory of all those
who perished at Morecambe Bay
on February 5th, 2004

Share the sweet and the bitter.

Old Chinese proverb

February 2004

Sometimes it would be so easy to succumb – to slip beneath the icy surface of her life without a trace. Angie has blundered through the first half of her existence, she thinks drunkenly. Why not cut a fast path through the remainder?

She is nearly through the bottle before she realises that this is what her mother must have felt, the night she drove onto the sands. The thought makes her recoil. She did not empathise with her mother during life. Why should she do so in death? For the first time, she wonders if her mother's blighted spirit has not lodged somewhere deep inside her, like a canker.

She switches off the car's engine and stares out across the vast expanse of bay. One year ago today, her mother had sat in this same spot, contemplating death. She had been diagnosed just before Christmas with cancer of the liver. (Too much bile, Ray had said.) Within four weeks it had spread to her lymph nodes. The doctors recommended that she cease treatment and enjoy what little time she had remaining. This, apparently, had been beyond her.

The sand had swallowed her car like an offering. It could happen in minutes, the police told her afterwards – such was the perilous nature of the quicksand on the bay. A local fisherman had spotted her mother's blue Fiesta lurching across the sand a few hundred yards off Hest Bank. When he'd looked up moments later, the car had vanished. For several days, the coastguard scoured the shores for her body. In the end Angie's mother was declared missing. The police sergeant informed her that without a body there could be no death certificate. Angie had stared at him uncomprehendingly. But her house and her possessions? she'd asked. He shrugged. The law says seven years, he replied. Before that, you can presume nothing.

Six weeks later, after a bad spring storm, the roof of the car had reappeared like an apparition, half a mile out, silted up with mud and sand. The corpse inside was water-logged and barely recognisable. Angie was called to the morgue. The pinched male attendant apologised twice before unzipping the black plastic bag that contained her remains. There was little to identify: the body was bloated, especially the torso, and the skin withered like an old turkey, its bleached surface waxy and riddled with strange bumps. Angie had asked what happened to her skin, struggling to keep her voice steady. The attendant coughed nervously. It's the cold, he explained. The muscles contract and push the follicles up. I'm sorry for your loss, he added. This last word reverberated in the air between them, like a badly plucked string. Yes, she thought. There had been many losses. Right from the start.

The coroner recorded death by misadventure. But Angie knew better. Unable to face the cancer that was slowly eating its way through her organs, her mother had driven out onto the sands at low tide, swallowed a handful of sleeping pills and let nature hurry its course. Perhaps she'd hoped never to be found. That was Ray's theory. Her brother Ray said she'd done it out of spite. Seven years she would have made us wait, Ray said. But the sea spat her back in the end.

Thank God for drink, Angie decides. Over the years she has learned that bad things fall away in the presence of alcohol: guilt, anger, boredom, fear. It's the aesthetics of drink she has always loved: the tinkle of ice cubes in a glass, the pleasing chink of bottle against rim, the amber beauty of the liquid as it tumbles forth obediently, the marvellous heat in the back of the throat. And the melting away of the self in the process. There are few things in life she prefers.

But she likes the sea. That is why she moved to Morecambe after her divorce, into her mother's deserted bungalow. Her mother had bequeathed the house to her: a small, one-bedroom brick and stucco cottage in a suburban cul-de-sac with a long narrow garden at the back that had been her particular obsession. On the night Angie moved in, she had locked the garden door and thrown the key in the back of a drawer, not caring what became of her mother's flowers and shrubs. Over the ensuing months, she had marked the garden's decline with something akin to satisfaction, until it became little more than a dense jungle of weeds.

Now she stares out at the gathering dusk. The tide is set to turn, but it will be hours before the water comes galloping across the bay. Her ex-husband hated the sea, hated the feel of sand in his shoes, the stick of salt in his hair, the endless lapping of waves. He was a terrible swimmer too, something she did not discover until after they were married. Their holidays were invariably of the mountain sort: Snowdonia, the Alps, the Pyrenees. Water did not feature, though she'd sought respite in other forms of fluid. It was a relief to live alone again, to line the empty bottles up along the counter without fear of recrimination.

Outside the night is ugly, just as they said it would be. The beach in front of her is empty, but further down the shore a dirty white van crawls along, snaking its way around rivulets and patches of wet sand. She watches as it stalls briefly, then creeps forward across the sands. A moment later, she hears the muffled roar of engines out to sea. Two quad bikes, laden with hunched figures, come racing in across the flats. They pass the white van, now heading opti- mistically out towards the water. She sees the driver of the first bike gesture towards the incoming tide, but the white van trundles on unheeding towards the fishing beds.

She had not been planning to come. She'd slept badly and woke late, losing much of the day in the process. At half past three she'd driven to the shops and bought a bottle of whisky, and on the drive home, before she'd even realised, she'd turned right at the level crossing and was heading towards the shore. She drove past the far end of the gravel car park, stopping just beyond the battered wooden warning sign, the one her mother had not heeded.

Angie closes her eyes, struggling to shed her mother's memory. The drink takes its toll and she dozes off, dreaming of this same shore, only the day is sunny and she is a child of nine or ten. She skips across the sand to the shoreline, her toes dipping into the frothy yellow edge. Don't wade out, calls her mother. Or you'll be sucked under. She turns to see her mother on the blanket flicking through a magazine, her dark brown hair tied back in a pale yellow kerchief. When she is no longer watching, Angie wades out so that the water rises to her neck. A swell lifts her briefly off the sand, and for an instant she is flying. Then she hears her mother's voice, calling.

Angie wakes with a start, disoriented, her mouth dry. Outside night has fallen. She strains to see the ocean through the darkness, though she can hear the sound of waves close by, together with the patter of rain. Her mother's voice is still in her ear, so real that she half expects her to appear in front of the car. She reaches for the key in the ignition, but as she does she hears the voice again, faint but unmistakeable, torn by the wind. Terrified, her heart flaps wildly inside her chest. She stares out at the blackened night. Why could her mother not stay dead?

She waits, the storm outside taunting her. When she can stand it no longer, she takes a last pull of whisky and steps out of the car, buttoning up her long woollen coat. At once the wind pitches her sideways. She can hear the roar of the tide, the sound merging with the rain and the howling of the wind. She stumbles across the soft press of sand, daring her mother's spirit to call to her again. But when her feet hit the water it is far, far colder than she expected. For a moment she falters. The icy water surges up to her knees, and she can feel the sand sucking at her shoes. She screams into the wind, her voice merging with the memory of the other. She moves forward, sloshing through the waves, crying out again when the wetness hits her groin. She does not stop until the water reaches her breasts, arms floating out in front of her. She feels her body start to sink.

And then she sees a blur of movement in the water: a man's head bobbing out of the waves not ten paces ahead of her. He rises and falls in the darkness, arms flailing, and vanishes beneath the surface just as quickly as he appeared. She scans the waves, aghast. Who in their right mind would swim out on a night like this? Moments later, the man reappears down shore, caught in the treacherous current of the Keer. She hears the hoarse cry of a voice snatched away by the wind. And before she can think, she is pulling her feet free of sucking mud and pushing forward through the water, straining against the waves towards the bobbing figure, now desperately trying to claw his way out of the current's flow.

She manages to come almost abreast with him, but by then the waves are breaking over her head and she knows that if she advances further she too will fall into the tidal current that is carrying him away. The man has seen her now and is gasping words she cannot understand. He thrashes against the water and suddenly his feet have caught the edge of something, for he rises up unsteadily, his arms outstretched towards her, desperate not to fall backwards into the torrent of current. She lunges forward, the water surging for an instant over her head, and reaches out blindly. She feels the clutch of fingers, feels the man's desperate hand close upon her wrist. *So this is death*, she thinks, half crazed with fear. It is not what she imagined.

The water is so cold she can barely feel the man's hand, only the force of his weight as she drags him backwards towards the shore. A huge wave engulfs them both and for a moment they lurch sideways in the dark, floating briefly, before she scrambles once again for a footing. He is naked from the waist up, while her clothes are now a sodden mass. The man cannot stand so she links her arms under his shoulders and pulls backwards with all her strength. Within moments they are staggering out of the waves in waist-deep water, coughing, clutching at each other. When they reach the shallows he falls to his knees. She yanks him to his feet, shouting at him over the wind, for the tide is still racing in and they are not yet safe. She carries on dragging him backwards until they reach the dry ground, where he collapses, gasping and coughing up water. She sinks to her knees, chest heaving, half frozen.

"You bloody idiot!" she gasps. "Another minute and you'd have drowned!"

The man raises his head to look at her, his eyes bewildered. For the first time she takes in his appearance: narrow eyes, black stubbly head of hair, a long thin frame. Chinese, she realises. A cockler. One of dozens who have descended upon the bay this winter. She has seen them once or twice, tumbling out of tightly packed transit vans at low tide. How in God's name did these people get here from the far side of the world?

For the first time, the man speaks, gasping out words in his own tongue. She stares at him uncomprehendingly, then without another word turns and stumbles angrily back towards the car, her sodden coat draped heavily about her knees. When she reaches the car she pulls off the coat and throws it onto the floor at the back, then climbs inside, slamming the door after her. Shivering, she turns the key in the ignition and the car roars into life. The headlights glow eerily: she sees the man lying on the ground some thirty feet in front of the car. Behind him, the waters of the bay come rolling in. He pushes himself up and squints at her, his face a blur of confusion. *Leave*, she thinks. Drive away now. Ahead of her the half-drowned man can only stare, incredulous that she would abandon him to the freezing night.

"Shit," she mutters. "Shit, shit, shit." She opens the car door and trudges back to where he lies. "Come on," she says. "Before you freeze to death."

The man looks up at her uncertainly, so she bends down and grabs his arm, hauling him unsteadily to his feet. She half carries him to the car, and lowers him onto the passenger's seat, swinging his legs in one by one, then shutting the door before climbing in herself. The man has started to shake uncontrollably now, his entire body wracked with convulsions from the cold. She fiddles with the car's heater and turns it on full blast, then turns and rummages in the back seat for anything she can cover him with. She finds an old car blanket on the floor and a moth-eaten cardigan and tucks them around his body.

"We should get you to a hospital. You're bloody frozen. And we should call the police." She is thinking out loud now. She puts the car in gear and starts to reverse when the man grabs her forearm. His grip is surprisingly strong. She turns to face him.

"No," he says. His tone is urgent: it is the first word of English he has spoken.

"No," he says again. Perhaps it is the only word he knows? She puts the car in park.

"No what? No hospital? No police?"

"No." He shakes his head.

With a sigh, Angie drops her head to the steering wheel. A moment later, she feels the weight of his gaze and when she raises her head, the man is gripping his shoulders to stop his body shivering. She sees his eyes sweep across her and alight on the near-empty bottle. Once again he speaks to her in his own language, his voice forming a question. Angie stares at him. Something in his tone makes her uneasy.

"I don't understand," she says after a moment. "Speak English."

The man hesitates, his dark eyes probing hers, and when he finally speaks, his tone is suffused with anger. He nods to her sodden pullover and jeans, then to the bottle, his voice taut with emotion. She does not understand a word that he is saying, but his meaning is perfectly clear.

"None of your business," she says sharply, putting the car back in gear.

She reverses and heads across the pitted gravel car park, driving too fast, the car bouncing violently up and down. She passes the rail crossing and turns right onto the main coastal road heading south. As the road climbs the hill, they see the lights of vehicles further down the shore. Two cars are parked, their headlights shining towards the open sea. Around them four figures are huddled. At once she pulls the car over and halts. Both she and the man stare at the scene without a word. A police car comes racing past them then, ominously silent but red lights flashing, and drives down onto the foreshore where the two cars are parked. They watch as two officers jump out. The figures on the beach begin to gesticulate wildly towards the sea. She turns to him with alarm.

"They're looking for you," she says. "We've got to go down there!"

The Chinese man swallows, then shakes his head.

"No." He gestures towards the ocean. "People," he says in English. It sounds like *purple*.

"What do you mean? What people? Are there others?" she asks, horrified.

He nods, eyeing her.

"How many?"

The man stares at her, his chest heaving.

"How many others?"

"*Tert*," he says.

"Three?"

He shakes his head, then holds up both his hands in front of him. He opens and closes them once, twice, three times, then turns his palms face up. She stares at him.

"*Thirty*? Thirty more besides you?" she asks, incredulous.

The man nods.

"Where?"

He shakes his head, gestures across the entire bay. They both stare at the scene below them on the beach, unable to move. After a few minutes, they hear the engine of a hovercraft out to sea. They watch as its lights criss-cross the bay, flashing eerily across the surface of the dark water. The man murmurs something quietly to himself.

"We have to go down there," she says again. He looks out across the bay, his eyes filled with dread. Slowly he shakes his head.

"No," he turns to her. "*Puh-lees*," he says desperately.

She peers at him. Please? Or police? Is he begging, or warning her? She looks back towards the cluster of cars. Like him, she does not wish to contend with the police and their probing questions. What in God's name would she say to them? Out for a stroll? And she would surely not pass a breathalyser.

"Okay," she says, nodding. "Okay."

He exhales with relief, then passes a hand across his face, while she puts the car in gear and pulls back onto the road.

September 2004

As soon as the plane touches down, Lili feels his presence acutely, like a lost limb. Her dead brother is waiting for her, just as she knew he would be. She walks, dazed with dislocation and fatigue, through a bewildering series of pale grey corridors towards immigration, where she is confronted with a battery of questions about the nature of her stay. All the while she imagines Wen at her elbow, coaxing the correct sequence of words from her that will unlock the doors to this strange country.

The immigration officer is Indian, a Sikh. He frowns at her passport, the folds of his turban ever so slightly askew. Then he looks straight at her and asks if she has relatives in Britain. For a moment she doesn't answer. Does Wen's spirit reside here? Or somewhere else? She looks around, her mind reaching for him. The immigration officer clears his throat, exasperated.

"Family," he says too loudly, as if she hasn't understood.

"No," she replies.

Satisfied, he waves her through. A trickle of sweat rolls down her side. She walks on towards the baggage carousel, and when she reaches it, she has the sudden sense that he is near. She watches, trembling, as her pale grey suitcase trundles past her on the belt.

When she comes through the airport barrier, Jin is there, her hair and clothes completely changed since they last met. Jin wears pencil-thin black jeans and a tightly cut jacket made of shiny black fabric, and her once long hair has been cropped fashionably short, a long slant of fringe hanging over one side of her face. *She is even more beautiful*, thinks Lili in a flash. Jin pushes through the crowd and grabs her in an embrace.

"Lili! You took for ever! I thought they'd kept you!"

Lili smiles and shakes her head. "I made it." She points to Jin's hair and clothes. "But what's happened to you? You look like a foreigner," she jokes. Jin shrugs.

"It's been two years. Did you expect me not to change?" Jin grabs her suitcase and propels Lili through the crowded airport terminal. "You've no idea what it's like here," she adds, pushing ahead through the crowd.

The words float back to Lili, a little ominous, and she realises with a start that Jin is right. Lili looks down at her own outfit: beige trousers, a yellow blouse, wedge sandals and a dark blue raincoat, all chosen with the utmost care at home. Now they seem drab and out of date.

On the bus ride from the airport, Lili stares out the window, feeling as if she is seeing London through the filter of Wen's gaze. That first night she is reluctant to sleep, afraid that if she closes her eyes, even for an instant, her brother's presence will go. Fade, or drift away, like embers on the breeze. Eventually sleep takes her. But even then she dreams of him, and of their childhood together: of endless summer days of heat and dust, of scrambling among piles of rubble outside their village, of bicycle journeys down rutted muddy paths, and watermelon seeds spat in each other's faces. The two of them did not blend easily with other children, who regarded their twinship with suspicion and hostility. From the first they were an anomaly: a brother and sister, born into a culture of children without siblings.

As if this was not enough to mark them out, their survival was a small miracle: only hours old, they were victims of a terrible earthquake that killed their parents, and wiped out nearly half the population of the area. Across the country, newspapers covered the story of their poignant rescue: newborn twins, trapped in each other's arms for twenty hours beneath two metres of collapsed concrete and steel, before a group of ordinary citizens clawed them out with bare hands and pickaxes. To a grief-struck nation, she and her brother became tiny symbols of hope: one small incidence of good fortune amid all the devastation. They were taken in by distant relatives, a childless couple who made nightly offerings to their ancestors for the double blessing. Was it an auspicious way to begin a life? She hardly knows.

Wen had lived in London for a time; he'd said as much in his letter. But the city was expensive in ways she could not possibly imagine. Even a cup of tea was an extravagance, let alone a bed, or a bus ride, or a meal. He'd come to London a month after his arrival in Britain. Those first few weeks he'd spent working in an electronics factory up north, where for twelve hours at a stretch he glued labels onto microwave machines. The work was soul-destroying. After his shift, he would stumble back to a dorm room lined with narrow metal bunk beds and collapse onto a still-warm mattress. *Even the bed was not my own*, he had written. One day, the man on the production line beside him fainted from exhaustion, his face grey, his eyelids swollen with fatigue. He was carried out and within an hour a new man took his place, anxious and bewildered. *I looked at him and saw myself*, Wen wrote.

He had quit the next day and got a bus to London, where he'd slept rough in parks, dodging police and living on air. A loaf of bread could last three days, he'd said. Though the bread was terrible: spongy and flavourless, like eating white moss. With no English, he'd found it impossible to get work. Until one day, a Chinese man approached him on the street. The man offered him a job as a dishwasher in a restaurant: he could share a flat with other immigrants like himself, the man explained, and he could eat for free. Wen was uncertain at first. He didn't like the man's clothing: a cheap but flashy imitation black leather jacket, designer jeans with brass studs. Nor his manner, which was crudely arrogant. But options were scarce.

That was the beginning. One badly paid job had led to another, according to the letter. He'd moved about the country wherever the work led him, sleeping six or seven to a room on bare mattresses laid out like coffins on the floor. The jobs varied: he'd picked apples in Norfolk, packaged chicken in King's Lynn, bussed tables in a restaurant in Hull, though he preferred outdoor work when he could get it. Until one day in early February, he found himself combing the sand for cockles on Morecambe Bay. The work was hard but the money better than he'd made in previous jobs. He was good at it, faster than the others, and more adept at reading the sands. But it was not for the faint-hearted: the winds off the ocean were bitter and the work back-breaking. The massive wooden boards used to tamp the sands and draw the cockles to the surface were awkward and heavy. Wen carried them slung behind his neck like an ox, and by the end of a shift, his shoulders were hunched like those of an old man.

On his first day out, a young woman in his group had broken down and wept. They helped her back to the van, where she sat and cried until the rest of them had finished. *A day's grief with nothing to show for it*, he had written. He felt sorry for the woman, had offered her his last hand-rolled cigarette on the way home. She looked at him, then tore the cigarette neatly in two, handing one half back to him. She did not smoke it but placed it carefully in her pocket. Later, he saw her trade it for a few squares of chocolate with one of the others. *This is what we are reduced to here.*

The letter had been dated the day before he died. He

must have posted it himself, within hours of perishing alongside twenty-two others in the freezing rip tides of Morecambe Bay. Oddly, the faint postmark was dated five days after the incident. When she mentioned this to Jin, her friend only shrugged in response. The letter must have languished somewhere during those five days, Jin had said. Mislaid in a sorting office, or perhaps forgotten at the bottom of a pile. Each time Lili rereads the letter, she feels a tight clench of pain in her gut, as if she is there with Wen inside the story: sleeping rough in a suburban London park, eating stale bread on the street, or freezing on the sands of Morecambe Bay.

And from the moment she arrives, she feels guilty that her own experience in England will be less fraught with hardship. That is the thing about her and Wen, she thinks. We shared everything and nothing. Growing up in their small village, Lili had been all Wen wasn't: a star pupil at school, a devoted daughter to their ageing stepparents, a loyal member of the youth brigade, and the winner of a much-coveted place to study English at a local teacher's college. Throughout their childhood and adolescence, Lili strived for and achieved all that was set out for her, while Wen did the opposite, barely managing to finish middle school before dropping out altogether.

In spite of this, it was Lili who had been plagued by uncertainty and self-doubt, like a spider clinging to the slender thread of her success. As a child, she'd suffered sudden bouts of panic, moments of inexplicable terror, when she would retreat to her bed and hide beneath the quilt. Wen would comfort her during these times, burrowing down beside her and waiting patiently for her fears to subside. Later, she grew out of these attacks, but experienced odd moments of paralysis, when the world around her seemed to tilt uneasily, causing her to question everything she held true. At such times, Lili felt her own history bearing down on her, feared she might be crushed beneath its terrible weight.

Her stepmother attributed these attacks to the traumatic events that followed her birth, a year so calamitous it later came to be known as the *Year of Curse*. They consulted a doctor who prescribed bitter herbal remedies designed to calm the spirit and bolster the heart's *yin*. But the only remedy for what Lili's stepmother termed her "distracted spirit" was Wen. It was Wen who understood that Lili suffered not just the tragedy of her own history, but that of her people. He and Lili had grown up in the distended aftermath of the Cultural Revolution, the chaos and violence of which cast a long shadow over their childhood. And while the nation prided itself on its ability to move forward, the evidence of what transpired lay all around them, from the bludgeoned statues in the local temple, to the disfigured old woman who lived beneath them, who was forced to drag herself about on crude wooden wheels, her legs mangled from beatings suffered at the hands of Red Guards. Each time Lili faltered, it was Wen who would draw her back, clasping both her hands in his and whispering reassurances in her ear. *We are survivors*, he told her repeatedly. And eventually, she came to believe him. In this way, Wen anchored Lili – indeed, he was the only aspect of her life that never wavered.

Until he died. The news of the accident had felled her. That previous summer, she'd begged him not to go: the journey was dangerous and living illegally had its own perils, she had argued. The idea of going abroad terrified her. Though their life was not perfect, she told him, it was *known*. Who could say what he might encounter on the far side of the world, surrounded by a people not his own? But Wen had taken her hand and said: *Fang xin. Relax.* If I stay here, I will suffocate. But you could go to Beijing, or Shanghai, she protested. He smiled ruefully and shook his head. It's not a place I am looking for, he told her. This journey has been coiled up inside me all my life.

She didn't see, but in retrospect perhaps she hadn't wanted to. She'd wanted their lives to run in tandem, like the double yellow lines painted down the centre of the highway. But she and Wen were not the same; she knew that now. The rules and doctrines they lived under, the ones that guided and reassured her, were precisely what had stifled him. I'm like the swallow that flies over the mountains, he explained. I need to escape.

He had phoned her three times since his departure in July. Once from Paris, where he claimed to be standing beneath the Eiffel Tower, and twice from different locations in the UK shortly after he'd arrived. Each time the conversation was brief: he gave few details but assured her he was fine. After the last call, there was a long silence lasting several months, followed by a visit from the local party secretary notifying her of his death. He had drowned, they told her, along with many others. There would be no compensation from either government, the official said, though the men in charge on the night of the incident were likely to be prosecuted.

Two weeks later, the letter arrived without warning. The moment she saw Wen's handwriting on the envelope, Lili felt ill. The sight of it unnerved her. It wasn't just the unhappy timing: the letter seemed to her oddly out of character. It was long and rambling, and filled with tiny details about his life, the sort of things he'd never bothered to disclose in the past. She wondered what had precipitated it. A sudden bout of homesickness, perhaps. Though Wen was not the sort of person to succumb to such emotions. The tone of the letter was reflective, almost sentimental. And in the final lines he had apologised for his departure. *It was painful to leave you*, he had written, *more bitter than you know.* He promised they would meet again soon. Even now, she wonders at his choice of words: as if he'd known that he would soon be proved wrong.

Perhaps it was those last few lines that had incited her to follow him. He had been so certain they would meet again, that she could not deny him this last wish. So within a few weeks of receiving his letter, she had swallowed her fears and resolved to go abroad. She made enquiries, obtained letters of support from prominent local officials and filed a visa application. Most importantly, she tracked down Jin, a former classmate who had gone to England two years before and was now teaching in a language school in

London. She'd been reluctant to approach Jin at first. Though they had been room-mates at university, they had not been great friends. Jin had been one of the boldest girls in her year, and one of the most daring in her lifestyle. She wore make-up, permed her hair, shortened her skirts and dated older men at a time when most girls had only recently shed the dark trousers and shapeless jackets that constituted the party's uniform. She and Lili shared a dorm room with four others, and somehow it was always Lili who was forced to cover when Jin flouted the curfew rules.

She was surprised when Jin responded warmly to her email, promising at once to help her find work. With her fluency in English and teaching qualification, Lili was sure to land a job quickly, Jin had said. Mandarin schools were popping up like mushrooms all over the country. China was the new America, she had written. Everyone wanted a piece of it. But the wheels moved slowly. It was five months before Lili received the visa, and another two months before she had saved enough money to cover her travel expenses. So it was that eight months after Wen's death, she finally fulfilled his promise of a reunion.

That first night, Jin takes her back to her room in a boarding house in Hounslow. When Jin opens the door and turns on the light, Lili is silenced. The room is sparse and depressing: a single bare light bulb hangs from a cracked ceiling, and the walls are covered in badly peeling pale coffee-coloured paper. Jin calls it a studio, but Lili thinks this is far too glamorous a term. There is a double bed, a tiny round table made of white metal, a chipped wooden wardrobe and a small kitchen unit with a sink and a two-ring cooker. The correct word in English is *bedsit*, she remembers. Because the only place to sit is on the bed. But she does not say this aloud. Jin explains that they share a bathroom with five or six others down the hall, which means they must fight their way to the shower each morning. The landlord has installed a timer on the wall, and during peak times, each person is allowed only five minutes. When Jin tells her the weekly rent on the room, Lili gasps, for it is more than two months' teaching wages at home. Jin laughs. Forget about *ren min bi*, she says. We work in pounds now. The pound is our ticket to prosperity.

But I didn't come here to find prosperity, Lili thinks. *I came here to find Wen*.

February 2004

Wen shakes uncontrollably during the drive back to the English woman's house. He has no sense of time passing nor of the direction they are heading, but is relieved when they eventually abandon the coast road. The English woman does not speak; indeed, she almost seems to forget his presence, so preoccupied is she with her own thoughts. She drives recklessly, he notices, too fast for a dark, stormy night. But he is hardly in a position to criticise.

His hands and feet are numb with cold. And each time he draws a breath, pain punches through his chest. But he is alive. He scarcely dares consider the fate of the others. Every time he remembers their stricken faces, he feels his insides lurch. Where are they now? He buries his head in his hands, clinging feebly to the hope that they have somehow been rescued, like him.

He owes his survival to the fact that he was willing to risk

the water. The others refused, choosing instead to walk out
to a high sandbank some distance away, where they assumed
they would be safe from the rising tide. There had been a
brief argument while he'd remonstrated with them. If they
could manage to cross the channel that had severed them
from the mainland, they might be able to find their way back
to the shore, he had argued. But they were already terrified,
and several protested they did not know how to swim, so in
the end he was forced to go alone. He waded out as far as he
was able, then shed his coat and shirt and chose the shortest
route across the channel he could identify in the darkness.
He was a strong swimmer, but the icy water and treacherous
currents proved too much for him. Within moments, his
lungs were so compressed with cold he thought that he
would faint. He managed to claw his way to the opposite
sandbank, only to encounter a second channel a few hundred metres on. It was this second crossing that nearly
claimed him: he had almost given up hope when he saw the
English woman coming towards him in the water.

He glances over at her. Her shoulder-length brown hair
is matted with wet against the sides of her face, and there are
dark circles under her eyes. He is uncertain of her age. Not
young, he decides. Thirty? Forty? He finds it impossible
to judge with foreigners. Her clothes are ordinary: jeans,
a long-sleeved t-shirt and a dark green pullover that now
smells of wet wool. The enormous coat she was wearing lies
in a sodden ball on the floor at the back. It was the coat
he noticed first when she dragged him from the water: made
of heavy black wool, it stretched below her knees and was

buttoned up to the neck. No one in their right mind would attempt to rescue a drowning man in such a coat. That is how he knew.

Her driving makes him nervous. If she was prepared to die once, might she not be willing to do so again? Why rescue him, in order to kill them both moments later? It would not be rational. But then suicide itself is hardly rational, he decides. He closes his eyes, endeavouring to stop the thumping pain in the back of his head. He will have to trust to fate. From the moment he entered this world, his luck has not yet failed him; it is bound to serve him now. He concentrates on quelling the shaking that has taken hold of his body, taking deep breaths of air and exhaling slowly. In his mind he tries to find a place of warmth and stillness. The trembling gradually subsides, replaced by a sharp tingling in his extremities. With considerable effort, he manages to flex his fingers and toes.

The car makes a sudden turn then comes to a halt. Wen opens his eyes and looks at the English woman.

"We're here," she says, turning to him. "Can you walk?"

He nods. She reaches down beneath her feet and retrieves her handbag, then gets out of the car. He opens his door and pulls himself out, nearly falling sideways. The blanket drops to the ground. The woman hurries round the car and grabs him. She reaches down and picks up the blanket, glancing around nervously in the darkness, before guiding him to the front door. The house is a tiny bungalow, set within a terrace of others. It is made of rendered concrete and brick, with a wooden door flanked by barren trellis. Once inside, she closes the door behind him and turns on a light. They are standing in a small entranceway that leads directly onto a sitting room, furnished with a sofa and television and a chunky wooden coffee table that is strewn with glasses and magazines. She leads him into the room and he feels his toes sink into thick carpet. He looks down: cream coloured, with tiny flecks of brown. The woman at once moves to close the curtains and crosses to the kitchen, turning on more lights on the way. Wen looks, feeling faint, as the woman disappears round the corner. She reappears a moment later carrying a bottle of whisky and two glasses. He begins to slip sideways.

"Shit," she says, moving towards him. She manages to catch him with her free hand, lowering him onto the sofa. Then she pours two large glasses of whisky and hands him one.

"Here. Drink this."

Wen stares at the whisky: the first he has been offered in this country. If he drinks it he might be sick. But he does not wish to offend the woman, nor anger her, so he reaches for the glass and swallows a mouthful. The drink burns. But it feels better than he anticipated. Perhaps she is not crazy after all. He takes another large mouthful, while the woman drains her own glass. She turns on her heel and disappears again.

After a moment, he hears the sound of water running. He leans back on the sofa and closes his eyes, nearly succumbing to sleep.

"Come," she says.

He opens his eyes and she is standing over him. He sees that she has changed into dry clothes and towel-dried her hair, and that a bit of colour has returned to her cheeks. In her hand she holds a large red towel and a pair of men's black tracksuit bottoms with a matching sweatshirt. She helps him to his feet and steers him through the kitchen to a small yellow bathroom. She points to a white bathtub, now filled to the brim with steaming hot water. He blinks in disbelief and looks at her. She is no longer crazy; she is a goddess.

"Are you all right?" she asks.

"Yes."

"Can you manage? Alone?" She is staring at him enquiringly, motioning towards the bath.

"Yes," he nods.

"Thank God for that," she murmurs, shaking her head. She withdraws, pulling the bathroom door shut behind her, leaving him alone.

He turns towards the steamy mirror over the sink, staring at his own reflection. He looks like a dead man: his skin is grey and his hair stiff with salt water. He sinks to the edge of the bath and dips his hand in the water. A searing pain runs up his arm, but he resists the urge to remove his hand, and closes his eyes, allowing the heat to rise up his arm and travel through his entire body. After a minute, he hears a knock at the door, and pulls his hand out with alarm.

"Are you okay?" she calls through the door.

"Okay," he repeats.

"Okay then," she says with a sigh. "Just don't… drown in my bath, okay?"

He hears her muttering as he pulls his wet trousers off and sinks into the bath, giving a tiny involuntary cry of pain when his body is immersed in so much heat. He forces himself to remain there for as long as he can, then crawls out and dries himself, pulling on the tracksuit she has given him. His skin has turned bright pink, as if he has been boiled.

When he emerges from the bathroom, she is standing there, glass in hand. Her cheeks are flushed from the whisky, and her hair, now dry, is the colour of chestnuts. It falls in soft waves just past her shoulders. Her features are strong: dark eyebrows, a wide mouth and a long straight nose. Not beautiful, he thinks. But oddly compelling. When she looks at him, her gaze is fierce and unyielding, like a bird of prey — as if she cannot quite believe that he has landed here in her kitchen.

He glances at the bottle on the counter and sees that it is nearly empty. She takes in the tracksuit and frowns slightly, and for an instant he wonders whose clothes he is wearing: does she have a husband or boyfriend? She hands him a whisky. Without hesitating, he tosses it back, emptying the glass in one go. For the first time, she smiles. "You're a quick study," she says. She turns and leads the way back to the sitting room, where he sees that she has made up a bed for him on the sofa. She motions to it. "You sleep here. And me in there." She points to a closed door opposite the kitchen.

"Okay," he nods.

"Okay," she repeats, flourishing the bottle a little

drunkenly. She crosses to the closed door and opens it, disappearing inside with the bottle. He has the briefest glimpse of a double bed, a wooden chest of drawers, a painting on the wall. Then he hears a key turn in the lock, just once.

He sinks down onto the sofa. He is suddenly starving. The woman did not think to offer him food, but he dares not enter her kitchen, and anyway, it is sleep he needs more than anything. He lies down on the sofa and covers himself with the duvet she has given him, closing his eyes. It occurs to him that the sofa is more comfortable than anything he has slept on these past six months. And he had almost forgotten the pleasure of sleeping alone, without the sighs and stirrings of others around him in the darkness.

But he must not think of the others. For there is nothing now that he can do.

September 2004

London, she soon learns, is enormous: a city of endless streets with row upon row of houses that are identical. The street Jin lives on could be any one of thousands. For the first few days, Lili trails after her, struggling to memorise the names of all the roads around the bedsit: Beaver's Lane, Martindale, Hibernia.

"Don't bother," says Jin. "All you need to know are numbers. We live three streets west of bus 237, which will take you to the language school at Sheep Pen. Get off at the last stop, turn left, walk one street south, turn right and the school is at number 57. From Sheep Pen there are buses going everywhere. Bus 18 will take you to Chinatown. Don't take the underground unless you're prepared to pay," she admonishes.

Jin has invented her own codex of Chinese names for London landmarks. Sheep Pen is Shepherd's Bush,

Westminster is Big Ben Clock, Oxford Street is Rip Off Street and Hounslow is Plane City. Even after two years, Lili notices, Jin's English is full of errors and shortcuts, as if she has given up trying to learn the language properly. Her accent, too, remains strong, so much that Lili finds it difficult to understand her when she speaks. Her own English is relatively good, though she has had little chance to use it since she arrived.

True to her word, Jin has found her a part-time job teaching Mandarin at the language school where she works. Lili will teach children, many of whom are overseas Chinese, after school during the week and on Saturdays. The centre can employ her only twelve hours per week, but at fourteen pounds an hour the pay is better than elsewhere, says Jin. And if Lili is resourceful, she can build up a range of private students, who will pay as much as twenty pounds per hour. Jin herself has five such students, whom she sees each week in the evenings after work. In this way, Lili can hope to earn as much as four hundred pounds per week: a small fortune at home.

Four hundred, she thinks. *Life is reduced to numbers here.* In his letter, Wen wrote that he earned ten pounds for each bag of cockles that he picked, and that he could pick up to four in a day. If he worked daily through the winter season, he hoped to save two thousand pounds. His living expenses were low: he paid twelve pounds a week for space on the floor with six others in a run-down house in Liverpool, a pound a day for transport to and from Morecambe Bay and another pound for food. With a bit of luck he could save nearly two-fifty a week. Almost twice what he was earning washing dishes in London. But this is far less than she will earn, Lili thinks, for a fraction of the effort and hardship. Not to mention the risk. Wen never once mentioned the dangers of cockling in his letter, though she has since learned from reading news reports on the internet that the tides at Morecambe Bay are notorious for claiming lives. Whether he was aware of the risks, she doesn't know. At any rate, it would not have mattered: she felt certain he would not have heeded them.

Jin shows Lili where to buy food inexpensively, where to do her laundry and where to find cheap internet access. It feels strange to her, this reliance on Jin, and she must stifle a creeping resentment. She feels as if she is merely passing through Jin's life on the way to somewhere else: she does not know where she is going, only that when she reaches it, Wen will be there. At the end of the second day, Jin takes her to Chinatown for a celebratory meal. When they are finally seated in a tiny restaurant beside a steaming window filled with rows of smoked ducks, Jin gestures towards the room.

"See? Just like home," she smiles, looking around her. The room is filled with Chinese people; there is not a single Westerner present. Lili overhears snatches of three different dialects from the surrounding tables.

"I wonder if Wen ever came here," she muses aloud. Jin's smile vanishes.

"No." She shakes her head. "He would not have done," she says emphatically. Lili is surprised by her vehemence.

Jin never met her brother, so her conviction is puzzling.

"Why not?" she asks. Jin pauses for a moment, frowning.

"Because people like your brother, they live in a parallel world here," she says finally. "Like shadows."

"What do you mean?"

"They are migrants: they move from place to place and never settle. They're always on the run. It's a different life from ours. And believe me, it isn't one you'd want."

The waiter arrives just then with two steaming bowls of noodle soup, which he sets in front of them. Lili watches Jin spoon crushed chilli into her soup.

"How strange to think that you were both here at the same time," she murmurs.

"Not so strange. London's full of Chinese. There are thousands of us here."

"Perhaps I should have come to England with him," Lili says tentatively. Jin pauses and looks up at her.

"Why?" she asks. Lili looks around the room a little searchingly.

"Because... then I could have helped him," she explains.

"Maybe he didn't want your help."

Lili considers this. "Maybe not," she admits. "But in the end he was unlucky."

"Maybe," says Jin. "And maybe he was just foolish," she says with an air of finality.

Jin picks up her chopsticks and snaps them apart while Lili looks on, a lump rising in her throat. She is startled by the harshness of Jin's words, and wonders what lies behind them. Her brother Wen was many things, she thinks. But he was not a fool.

•

The next day Jin goes to work, leaving Lili to face London on her own. She knows at once what she will do. Wen wrote that his second job was in a Chinese restaurant near the river. Not far from the restaurant was a bridge where he often went when he'd finished his shift. The bridge was cast in wrought iron and painted green, and at night it was magnificently lit. He liked to stand in the middle and watch the river flow beneath him. The restaurant specialised in hotpot, he said. So each day he faced a mountain of greasy metal pans in the kitchen. And it was run by a sour-faced Cantonese who docked their wages for the meagre meals he served them. She does not know where the restaurant is, but Jin has given her a map book of London, and she hopes she can find it. After all, she thinks, how many bridges can there be?

She is dismayed by the answer. She sees that it would take her days to walk the length of the Thames, particularly since it does not flow in a straight line, but curves like an unruly serpent. But surely not all the bridges in London are painted green? she thinks. She decides to walk to the closest point of the Thames to Hounslow, and from there follow it east as far as she can manage. She cannot think of an alternative. On the map, the river does not look far from Jin's flat. She must merely keep walking east until she runs into the Thames at a place called Isleworth. But when she emerges out onto the street, she quickly becomes disoriented; walking in a straight line is not as simple as she thought. She must refer to the map book constantly if she wishes to remain on course. Eventually she holds it open in front of her as she walks, checking the names of streets carefully at each intersection.

By the time she reaches Isleworth and the river, she is already tired. But unlike Hounslow, it is very picturesque. Brightly painted old buildings line the shores of the Thames, and a pretty church with spires rises up beside the river. There is nowhere at home that looks like this, she thinks, pausing for a moment to look out upon the swiftly flowing water. In the distance to her right she spies her first two bridges. The near one is low, modern and relatively plain. Though she can see some pale green railings, she does not think it could be the one her brother spoke of. The one behind it, further down river to the south, appears to be a railway bridge, and therefore closed to pedestrians. With a sigh she turns and begins to walk upriver. Two down, she thinks resolutely. Only eighteen more to go.

After half an hour, she passes another bridge, painted red and white. Both sides of the river are lined with parkland here. A gravel path runs beside the water, and for a time she forgets that she is in the middle of a large city. She passes the occasional jogger or cyclist, and a trickle of other walkers, but for the most part she is alone. She and Wen grew up in a small village just outside the city of Tangshan, a three-hour drive south-east of Beijing. A river ran along the outskirts of their village. When they were young, it was clean enough to swim and fish in. But as the region developed, the water became polluted with run-off from factories. Eventually it carried a thick skin of industrial effluent, so dense that birds could alight on it and ride downstream.

The Thames here looks better, she thinks, though not something she would swim in. The late September day is warm and sunny; she has finished the small bottle of water she brought with her and is beginning to get hungry. She follows the path around a bend when suddenly a bridge comes into view. She stops short. It is a tall suspension bridge: graceful, delicately wrought, with two enormous iron spires stationed like guards on either end. The entire bridge is painted green. At once she knows that it is Wen's.

Quickly she checks the map book. She is just beside Hammersmith. She follows a path that takes her up to the bridge and walks out to its centre, just as Wen must have done countless times. From there she has a good view upriver. The tide is low and there are few boats in sight. A small sailboat drifts along lazily in the distance. She stares down at the map book: she does not know which side of the river Wen's restaurant was on, but decides on balance to head towards the centre of London.

Minutes later, she regrets this decision, as she finds herself caught in a series of concrete underpasses with cars whizzing by her in every direction. But she perseveres and eventually emerges onto a high street with shops and restaurants. Hungry, she goes into a small sandwich bar, though once inside, she is bewildered by the display of fillings inside the glass case, most of which she does not recognise. A dark-haired man behind the counter raises a bushy eyebrow at her. Lili flushes and turns away.

She carries on walking, and after a few more minutes she sees a small Chinese restaurant on the opposite side of the road. The sign in English reads *Taste of Spring*, though the Chinese characters across the shop's front say *Fragrant Spring Joy*. She hurries over to it and peers through the window. She sees with disappointment that the restaurant is only a takeaway: inside there are no tables, only a long counter and a few chairs for waiting customers. Besides, she can see from the menu on the door that it does not serve hotpot. She steps inside anyway. A young Chinese man is behind the counter, talking on a mobile in Mandarin. He is tall and lean and clean-shaven. When he sees her, he hastily closes the phone.

"Excuse me," she says in Mandarin. "I'm looking for a hotpot restaurant near here. Do you know of one?" The young man crosses his arms and leans back against the counter, regarding her with a look of bemusement.

"Why?" he asks.

Startled, she hesitates. He is good-looking, the sort of man who knows as much, the sort of man she has always avoided at home.

"I like hotpot," she says finally. The young man laughs genially and spreads his arms.

"We're just a takeaway. Noodles, fried rice, that sort of thing."

"I know. I saw the menu."

"But you only want hotpot," he says teasingly.

"Yes," she replies, the colour rising in her cheeks.

"Stubborn lady," he counters.

Embarrassed, she turns to go.

"Hey," he says. "I was only joking. There's one not far from here."

She turns back to him, her heart racing. He steps from behind the counter.

"Here," he offers, nodding towards the map book in her hand. "I'll show you if you like."

She hands him the book and he opens it on the counter, turning the pages.

"Thank you," she murmurs.

"No worries," he says in English. He glances sideways at her.

"You speak English?" he asks.

"Of course," she replies.

"Not everyone here does," he says, looking back down at the book. "When did you arrive?"

"Three days ago."

"I thought you were new," he says. "From where?"

"Hebei Province," she says carefully. "Near Tangshan."

"And already looking for hotpot? What are you, homesick?"

"No," she stammers. "I..." She breaks off. The young man looks up at her, sensing her discomfort. At once his tone softens.

"Here," he says, pointing to a place on the page. "The place you're looking for is here. Fifteen minutes' walk at most. But be careful. The guy who runs it is a bit of a tyrant. A friend of mine used to work there. A couple of years ago."

She looks at him. A couple of years ago, she thinks. Like Wen. She resists the impulse to ask him the name of his friend.

"Thank you," she says, turning once again to go.

"Hey," he says. "You hungry?"

She pauses, for in truth she is starving. "A little," she admits.

"I'll get you something from the back. You can take it with you." He disappears inside and returns a few moments later with a small white bag, which he hands to her.

"Thank you," she murmurs, embarrassed.

"Spring rolls," he offers with a shrug. "Western style. Made them myself. No charge."

"Do you own this place?" she asks, surprised.

He looks at her askance.

"No way," he says in English. "My mother's cousin owns it. I'm just the hired help. But this is a quiet time of day. So I'm on my own."

"Lucky for me," she says.

"So who are you looking for? Boyfriend?"

Lili blushes and shakes her head. "No one important," she says. "Just an old classmate."

"Do you know people here? In London?"

"A few," she says. "One, actually," she admits.

He laughs. "Well now you know two. My name's Johnny. I'm an engineering student."

"Johnny?" She raises an eyebrow.

He shrugs.

"Zhong Li. But here I'm Johnny."

"Thank you, Johnny," she says. For the third time, she turns to go.

"Hey, Hebei," he calls in English. "What's your name?"

"Lili," she replies with a smile.

He nods. "Come back and see me sometime," he says easily. "I'm here most days."

"Okay." Lili flushes slightly, surprised by her own boldness. Would she have agreed so readily at home?

Johnny is right. The old guy who runs the Golden Phoenix Restaurant is breathing fire at a string of cowed employees when she walks through the door. The restaurant is empty of customers. Four tired-looking men wearing stained aprons are seated at a booth just outside the kitchen. The owner stands beside them waving a lit cigarette and berating them in a mixture of Cantonese and heavily accented Mandarin. Close to the door, a young Chinese woman wearing a tight-fitting black dress sits punching numbers into a calculator. At once she stands and approaches Lili.

"May I help you?" she asks, eyeing her.

"Could I speak with the owner?"

The young woman raises an eyebrow. "If you like. I'll just get him." She crosses over to where the owner stands and speaks quietly to him. The owner looks at Lili across the room, stubs out his cigarette in an ashtray, then walks over.

"Yes?" he says in English.

"I'm sorry to trouble you," she says nervously in Mandarin.

He narrows his eyes slightly. "Go on," he says.

"I was wondering if you could give me some information about one of your former employees."

His eyes immediately register a look of alarm. "Why? Who do you work for?" he asks suspiciously.

"No one," she says quickly. She fishes in her purse for Wen's photo, pulling it out. "I'm looking for this man. His name is Zhang Wen."

The owner frowns at the photo.

"Never seen him."

"He worked here. Last year."

"Last year? I employ a dozen people here. They come and go like salmon. How do you expect me to remember one?"

Lili pauses. "He was memorable," she says quietly.

The old man hesitates. In that instant, she knows that he is lying.

"Who are you?"

"I'm his sister," she says. "His twin sister."

The old man stares at her for a long moment, then points towards a table.

"Sit down," he says. He turns to the woman in the black dress and tells her to bring a pot of tea, then sits down opposite Lili with a sigh.

Slowly he removes a pack of cigarettes and takes one out, offering the pack to her. Lili shakes her head. She waits while he lights the cigarette. The young woman comes hurrying from the kitchen with a pot of jasmine tea and two small cups, which she pours for them. The old man motions for Lili to drink, then takes a long drag from his cigarette.

"Your brother is dead," he says exhaling. "Surely you know this?"

"Yes," says Lili, her voice nearly breaking.

"Then why are you here?" The words are harsh, but his tone has softened.

"I want to know a little more. About him. And his life here, before he died."

The old man nods slowly, frowning. He reaches for an ashtray and taps the cigarette in it.

"I remember him," he says. "In fact, I liked him. I was sorry when he left. He was smarter than most." He inhales deeply from the cigarette.

"How long was he here?"

The old man shrugs. "Three months, maybe four. I don't recall exactly."

"Did he live here? Upstairs?"

"No." He shakes his head. "Your brother lived with his girlfriend. In Hounslow."

"Hounslow?" Lili asks. The information startles her.

"Yeah," says the man with a smile. "He called it Plane City. Said he couldn't sleep for the noise of all the planes going in and out of Heathrow."

Somewhere deep inside, Lili feels something twist.

"His girlfriend," she asks, her voice dropping to almost a whisper. "Was she Chinese?"

The old man nods. "From the mainland. Nice-looking. Bit of an operator. Dressed like she'd been born here."

"What was her name?"

"I don't recall. She picked him up a couple of times. He used to complain that she earned twice what he did. I think she taught Mandarin at a language school in Shepherd's Bush. Sheep Pen, he called it." The old man shakes his head with a smile.

Lili stares at him, unable to speak. *Jin*, she thinks. The old man leans forward, frowning.

"What happened to your brother was terrible," he says quietly. "A terrible tragedy."

She looks at the old man. His eyes are slightly yellow; she sees a small stain on the collar of his shirt.

"Yes," she whispers. "I know."

February 2004

In the morning when Angie wakes, her head is shrouded in pain. She squints at the clock, sees the whisky bottle lying empty on the floor. She peers at it, trying to sift through the events of the preceding night. *Shit*, she thinks. There is a Chinese man on her sofa. Wearing tracksuit bottoms that belong to her ex-husband. Or maybe not. Maybe the man is already gone. And she will never know if he was real, or a figment of her mind, sent to save her from herself. She rolls over and pulls the quilt over her head.

There was a moment in the waves when she thought that they would both die. The fear was unlike anything she'd ever known: enormous, powerful and terrifying. It pierced her like a sharp blade and at once she realised death was not her friend, but her enemy. How stupid could she be? And yet she'd saved a man's life. She is not religious, does not even believe in God. But perhaps something greater than herself sent her to the bay last night.

Yesterday had been a bad day: the first anniversary of her mother's death. She'd woken with a sense of dread, and had stumbled through the day feeling oddly out of place and time. She does not remember making a decision to drive to Hest Bank, only that she ended up there. *Christ*, she thinks now. *I have to go out there. And talk to him. It would help if he could speak back.* His inability to communicate irritates her. How hard can it be to learn a language? Slowly she rises and moves about her room as noiselessly as possible, finding some clothes. She is desperate for the loo. Perhaps he is still asleep and she can get to the bathroom without having to face him first. She turns the key in the lock and eases the door open as quietly as she can, peering out.

The Chinese man is sitting on her sofa, the bedding she gave him neatly folded in a pile to one side. The TV is on but he has muted the sound. When he sees her, he rises at once to his feet, his eyes filled with uncertainty. She comes out of the room. He nods to her nervously, then glances at the TV and quickly moves to turn it off.

"Don't," she says quickly. "It's okay." She sees for the first time the images on the screen. He is watching a local news channel, and the picture is of Morecambe Bay. She walks slowly towards the TV, staring at the images. Police cars, ambulances, yellow tape, a string of bodies laid out upon the sand, covered in pale white cloth. She turns and looks at the man.

"I'm sorry," she says. He nods grimly. She reaches over,

turns up the volume and sinks down onto the sofa. A reporter is speaking: eighteen bodies have been found, but five more are missing. She listens for a moment, then turns to him.

"They're looking for you," she says. "You," she repeats, pointing to him.

He swallows a little nervously, and nods.

"Do you speak English?" she asks.

He holds up two fingers close together.

"Little," he says.

"Do you understand me?"

He shrugs. "Little," he repeats.

She takes a deep breath and lets it out, remembering her full bladder. She rises and walks through the kitchen to the bathroom, closing the door behind her.

The bath is full of cold water. She reaches down to pull out the plug, watching the water slowly ebb as she relieves herself. What in God's name is she meant to do with him? Should she ring the police?

"Are you hungry?" she asks a moment later.

His eyes widen, and he nods.

"Please," he says.

She crosses to the refrigerator and looks inside: a sagging grapefruit, a bottle of salad dressing, three tired tomatoes and some out-of-date milk. Dismayed, she realises she will have to go out for food and she can hardly take him with her. So he will have to stay.

She looks into the sitting room: he is seated on the sofa, his eyes locked onto the news report. Poor bastard. She picks up her handbag and keys, then returns to the sitting room where he is waiting.

"I'm going out," she says. "To buy food. To eat. Stay here. I won't be long."

The man's eyes widen briefly.

She buys more food than she has eaten in a month. Orange juice, bread, eggs, bacon, potatoes, chicken, cheese. She adds rice and soy sauce as an afterthought. At the till her eyes land on the rack of newspapers: the story is all over the headlines. She picks up two different papers and throws them on the counter. The shop assistant, an older woman with badly hennaed hair, clucks at the headlines.

"Terrible, what's happened," she says. "Someone should've warned them. Imagine dying out there in that freezing water!" The woman looks up at her for confirmation. Angie cannot meet her eye. She stares down at the food, a lump forming in her throat. It is all she can do to nod.

When she opens her front door, she does not know what she will find. Perhaps he has fled, along with half her things. A part of her would be relieved. But he is there, seated on the sofa just as she left him, the TV still on. *Where would he go?* she wonders. He jumps to his feet as she enters and immediately moves to help her with the bags. She unpacks the food while he watches. She turns to him after a minute.

"You're making me nervous," she says.

He blinks, uncomprehending. She points to the sofa.

"Go watch TV," she orders. "I'll call you when it's ready."

"Okay," he says, retreating quickly.

She turns back to the food laid out in front of her.

"Okay," she mutters to herself.

He eats ravenously: she thought she had cooked masses but it is not enough. She too is hungry, has not eaten properly in days. They finish the breakfast and then she makes several slices of toast, which she puts on his plate. She hands him a knife, a plate of butter and a jar of honey.

"Toast," she says pointedly.

"*Toe se*," he repeats.

"Yeah, something like that," she says. "I use butter and honey, but you can eat it how you like," she adds, not really caring whether he has understood.

He watches her spread butter and honey on her toast, then does the same. After six slices, he finally indicates that he has had enough.

"For someone so thin, you can't half eat," she comments.

He regards her uncertainly. She sighs.

"You're going to have to learn English or I'll go mad," she says, picking up both their plates and moving towards the sink. At once he leaps up and crosses to help. She looks at him and laughs.

"Okay," she says, indicating the dishes in the sink. "They're all yours."

"Okay," he replies.

She goes back to the TV, switching channels to try to find more coverage, and scanning the newspaper stories. Eighteen men and two women were dragged out of the bay last night.

Only two were still alive. It is uncertain how many more are missing. The Chinese had ventured out at dusk so as to work under cover of darkness, because of recent disputes with local cocklers. She has a flash of memory then: a battered white van crawling across the sand. Her stomach lurches. *I saw them,* she thinks. *And I did nothing.* But neither did the others, she remembers, those coming in from the beds. So the blame does not sit on her alone. And anyway, she thinks, I saved him. But how many more could she have saved?

Just then she hears the sound of breaking glass from the kitchen. She jumps up and crosses the room. The Chinese man is staring at the floor where he has dropped a tumbler. He raises his eyes to her and she sees fear in them. At once he drops to his knees and begins to gather up the pieces.

"*Dui bu qi,*" he says in Mandarin.

She goes to the cupboard under the sink and takes out a dustpan and broom.

"It doesn't matter," she says. She lays a hand on his arm, and he looks up at her. His jaw is set in a grim line and there is a remote look in his eye. *What exactly has this man endured?* she wonders.

"It doesn't matter," she repeats slowly.

He takes a deep breath and nods, just once.

As she finishes sweeping up the glass, the telephone rings. The sound startles her. The Chinese man eyes her to see what she will do, and for a moment she is paralysed. The phone rings six times, seven, before she finally picks up the receiver.

"Hello?"

"Angela?" A male voice comes down the line. Tony, she thinks. Her boss.

"Tony."

"Are you okay?" he asks. She glances at her watch: it is past eleven. She is two hours late.

"I'm fine," she says quickly.

"So are you coming in?"

"Actually, I'm not well."

"What kind of not well?" His voice is sceptical. Angie hesitates.

"Some sort of food poisoning." It is the first thing that comes to mind.

"Food poisoning? From what?"

She looks around the room uncertainly. Her gaze settles on the Chinese man, who is watching her closely.

"Bad takeaway," she says. "Chinese," she adds. She has to stifle a laugh.

"Well, I'm a bit snowed under here. Can you make it in?" He is asking, but his tone is one of irritation. "Angie?"

"Yeah. Give me half an hour."

She goes back into her bedroom to change into work clothes. So this is how it goes, she thinks. The business of life. There is no stopping it. Here she is, going through the familiar rhythm of it all, dressing for work, combing her hair, making excuses to her boss. And yet things have altered, she thinks. There is a complete stranger on her sofa. She finishes dressing and returns to the sitting room, where the Chinese man is still watching TV. She takes up her handbag and keys and turns to him.

"I have to go now," she says. "To work," she adds.

He nods anxiously.

"Okay."

"Make yourself at home."

He looks at her quizzically, has clearly not understood.

"Stay," she says then. "You can stay. I'll be back later." Their eyes meet for a moment. She taps her watch. "Later."

The Chinese man nods. "Okay," he replies.

She moves to the door, but at the last minute she turns back to him with a frown.

"I'm not in a position to save anyone," she says. "Least of all myself."

September 2004

It takes hours to walk from Hammersmith to Hounslow, but Lili wants to etch the journey in her mind, for she is searching for a way into Wen's past. She is numb with disbelief that Jin was sleeping with her brother. How could she not have known? And why would Jin keep it from her? When she finally arrives at Jin's flat, dusk is falling. Jin is already home from work, boiling dumplings on the small stove, and greets Lili unsuspectingly when she enters. Lili sinks down onto the bed and kicks off her shoes. She watches as Jin drains the dumplings and pours them into a small red bowl.

"What did you do today?" asks Jin, sitting down beside her on the bed. In her hand she holds the red bowl and a pair of chopsticks. The smell of soy sauce and black vinegar fills the tiny room.

"I went to Wen's restaurant. In Hammersmith."

Jin turns to her with a frown. "Why?"

"To find out more about his life here," Lili replies. The silence stretches out between them. Jin stirs the dumplings slowly round in her bowl with the chopsticks.

"And did you?"

"Yes," Lili says in English. The way she says it makes Jin freeze, her chopsticks halfway to her mouth. Lili looks around the room, trying to imagine Wen in it. After a moment's hesitation, Jin pops the dumpling into her mouth.

"I walked home from Hammersmith. It took me three hours."

"Why didn't you get a bus?" Jin asks.

"Because I wanted to know what his journey was like," she says slowly, "when he came home each night to share your bed."

Jin stops chewing and turns to her. Their eyes lock for an instant, then Jin sighs and sets the bowl down on the table.

"Don't stop on my account," says Lili. "You've never done before."

Jin turns to her. "Why don't you just ask me?" she says in a weary voice.

Lili looks at her: there are so many things she wants to know. But she doesn't want to hear them from Jin. What she really wants is for Wen's life to happen again, so that she can be a part of it.

"Why didn't you tell me?"

"Because he told me not to."

The words land like a punch. For a moment, Lili cannot speak.

"You didn't own him," continues Jin. "He had a life that was unconnected to you."

"But *you* are connected to me," counters Lili.

"I was connected to both of you. In the end." Jin picks up the bowl, popping another dumpling into her mouth. Lili watches as she chews.

"How did you meet?"

"He came to the language school to find me, not long after he arrived."

"How? I don't understand." Lili frowns.

"You *told* him I was here. Don't you remember?"

Lili stares at Jin, trying to focus her memory. So much has happened during the interim. Perhaps she did mention Jin to her brother. But surely it was only in passing, she thinks. *I have a friend in London.*

"But I knew nothing then of how to find you," says Lili. A part of her does not wish to believe anything Jin says.

Jin shrugs. "You knew enough. Anyway, he was resourceful. He asked around, found out the address of the school, and one day when I finished work, he was waiting for me outside. I'd met him once before. At college. You must remember. Even so, I walked right by him that day."

No, thinks Lili. *I don't remember at all.* And then a picture forms in her mind of a sunny afternoon in early spring. She is playing volleyball with a group of friends when she looks up to see Wen standing just outside the gates, watching her. She drops the ball and runs over to him, throwing her arms about his neck in greeting. She drags him through the gates and onto the court, introducing him to each of her friends in turn. Jin is the last to nod her greetings.

"Anyway, he remembered me," says Jin. She stands up and rinses the red bowl in the sink, then sets it upside down on the drainer before turning back to Lili.

"And one thing led to another," she continues.

"How long?" asks Lili. "How long were you and he… together?"

"A few months. Maybe longer."

Long enough to grow accustomed to each other, thinks Lili. She is suddenly bitterly jealous. "Why did he leave?" she asks.

Jin turns away. "He hated London. He thought he could do better elsewhere. I told him he was lucky to have me, and this flat. I paid the rent. My salary was more than twice his. Anyway, we argued. And he left to find his fortune elsewhere. That was the end of it."

"And after? Did you see him after he left?"

"No," she says. "He called me twice. It was harder than he'd imagined, I think. Though he never said. And then, for a long time I heard nothing. Until the day I saw his face in the newspaper." Jin's voice drops to a whisper. "I couldn't believe it at first. I couldn't believe that it was real."

"Well, it was real. Wen died that night."

"Yes," says Jin. She looks up at Lili and their eyes meet. "I'm sorry if I deceived you," she says slowly. "But in the end, it makes no difference."

Jin moves to the sink and fills a glass of water. As she raises it to her mouth, Lili sees the slightest tremor in her hand.

"Were you in love with him?" she asks.

Jin turns back to the sink to refill the glass.

"No. Love was not a part of it."

Lili frowns. She cannot see Jin's face. But even if she could she does not know whether she would find the truth there. Jin turns and crosses to the bed, picking up her coat and handbag, before turning back to Lili.

"I have to go. I have a student waiting. We can talk later."

"Okay," says Lili.

After Jin leaves, Lili lies face down across the bed, listening to the faint sounds of life around her. She hears the low hum of the television next door, and the sound of the shower running in the bathroom down the hall. She struggles to conjure a picture of Wen in this place, and for the briefest instant, imagines him entwined with Jin on the bed where she is lying. But the image jars her. Wen was no stranger to women; she knows this. Indeed, they were drawn to him, for he had a kind of transparency that was rare in a man. He was completely without guile. But neither was he weak. He had a kind of inner strength that women found reassuring. Lili looks around the room. Knowing Wen was here does not bring her any closer to him. Instead, he seems to drift even further away.

At length, she rises and crosses to the counter. She's eaten nothing but the spring roll since morning and is suddenly starving. Jin has left some dumplings for her, and Lili boils a pot of water and drops the dumplings in one by one with a pair of chopsticks. She looks down at the water, waiting for the dumplings to rise. As she does, her eyes alight on a battered black canvas suitcase beneath the bed. Without knowing why, she goes over to the bed and sinks to her knees, dragging the suitcase out from underneath. She unzips the lid and looks inside: some old jumpers, half a dozen paperbacks, and a thick brown envelope with an elastic band around it. She hesitates only for an instant, then reaches for the envelope. Inside is a sheaf of papers and correspondence: letters, visa documents, bank and travel receipts. She glances through them quickly, careful not to disturb the order. Near the bottom is an envelope with Jin's address in Hounslow written on the front. When she sees it, her heart begins to race, for the handwriting resembles Wen's. She pulls out a single sheet of folded notepaper; two photos drop into her lap.

Wen looks up at her, smiling. He wears jeans and a black t-shirt and carries a dark green satchel over his shoulder. The day is sunny, and in the background is the London Eye. The expression in his eyes is relaxed and good-humoured. The other photo has fallen upside down. When she turns it over she draws a sharp breath. Wen is completely different in this photo: his face more angular, his expression troubled. Wen and Jin pose together in front of a statue of a large bird that sits atop a tall stone column. The day is cloudy and in the background Lili can see an endless stretch of ocean. They appear to be standing on some kind of pier. Jin has both arms linked through one of his, but Wen's hands are thrust deep into the pockets of his coat. Lili stares at the photo: there is something unyielding in Wen's stance, as if he is resisting. Jin wears a smile of satisfaction, but Wen stares angrily at the camera. Clearly they are not in London. They are somewhere on the coast, but where?

Lili opens the folded sheet of paper, and sees at once that it is a note to Jin hastily scrawled in Wen's handwriting. Her eyes sweep quickly to the end, but curiously, there is no signature. The note says only: *I am sorry to call upon you once again. I hope this will be the last time.* She stares at the paper, struggling to make out the note's meaning. What is it he was after? And why is it the last time? She looks again at the photos, this time laying them side by side. At once she sees the differences. Wen's hair is considerably longer in the first photo. And in the second, his complexion is slightly darker than she remembers. She peers closely at this second photo. There is also a small mark above his left eye, which does not appear on the first photo, perhaps a scar. She realises that the first photo is very like the Wen she knew. The second is of a different person – older, and altered in ways she cannot grasp. She stares down at them. Jin said that she and Wen had been together a few months. But these two photos could not have been taken within the same space of time. Lili looks again at the envelope: the date has been smudged, but the letter has been posted from Morecambe Bay.

February 2004

When she goes to work, Wen is left alone in her house. She obviously trusts him, though he is not sure why. He is not the thieving sort, though she has no way of knowing this. Perhaps she does not care if he steals from her – maybe her possessions hold no value. For the first time, he allows himself to look at her belongings. It was not poverty that took her to the bay last night, he decides. At least not by his standards. The house is comfortably furnished, though everywhere he sees evidence of neglect: peeling paint in the bathroom, a broken light in the hallway, stains upon the carpet in the sitting room, the front panel of a drawer missing in the kitchen. She has a long garden out the back, but it appears overgrown and unused. When he peers through the glass door, he sees a large ceramic pot tipped upon its side, the plant it once contained withered to dry stalks.

More crucially, her house does not feel like a home. It is cold, as if lacking some key element of vitality. He remembers a proverb that his stepmother used to say: *if there is light in the soul, there will be harmony in the house.* After a few minutes, he realises there is not a single photo in sight. Puzzled, he searches through her things, opening drawers, leafing through papers on the counter, but he finds no evidence of her family, or any connection to the world. He moves into the bedroom, looks inside the small closet, then crosses to a chest of drawers standing in the corner. He opens the top drawer and sees that it contains her underclothes: a pile of frayed knickers and a tangled assortment of bras in different hues. He stares at them transfixed for a moment, but feels a sudden sense of shame when he remembers they are Angie's.

He starts to close the drawer when he sees the corner of a tarnished silver frame at the back. It holds a faded snapshot of a woman flanked by two young children: a boy of perhaps ten, and a girl half that age. Neither child is smiling. The woman wears bright red lipstick, a short navy-blue dress and a bouffant hairdo. Her head tilts slightly to one side. The boy scowls at the camera, his hands thrust into the pockets of his trousers, and the girl fixes her gaze on the photographer with an intense scrutiny. Wen realises the girl is Angie, and suddenly the similarities between the child and the woman become glaringly obvious, as if the passing of time has happened at a stroke. He stares at the photo, wondering about the girl trapped inside. All the while Angie stares back at him accusingly, until he stuffs the photo in the back of the drawer, feeling as if he has violated her some-how.

He plants himself upon her sofa, scanning the channels for more reports on Morecambe Bay. Eventually he sleeps. When he wakes, dark is falling outside. Hungry, he goes into the kitchen and looks inside the refrigerator. Her food is strange to him: cheese, yogurt, a bag of salad. Discouraged, he returns to the sofa and watches a game show where schoolchildren vie for prizes by completing tasks of strength and stamina. There are two teams of four. Five of the children are white, two are brown and one is black. The colours of modern Britain. Not one of the children is Chinese. *Because we are invisible here,* he thinks. After the show finishes, a local news report comes on. A young woman stands upon the sands close to the spot where they set out last night, gesturing to the ocean behind, the wind whipping her dark hair about her face. He does not under-stand what she says, but after a moment, a series of photos flash up on the screen: passport pictures of those who died. Wen freezes, the horror of last night flooding back to him. One by one, the people he worked with appear in front of him. He had not been digging fish in Morecambe Bay for very long, so he could hardly number these people among his closest friends, but their faces now seem utterly familiar. He sees with relief that Lin is not among them.

For the first time, he allows himself to think of his friend. He first met Lin picking apples in Norfolk in the autumn, and when the harvest had finished, they had come to Morecambe together seeking work. Though they usually worked in the same team, yesterday they'd been bundled into different vans on the long drive from Liverpool. Lin's van had parked about a quarter-mile further west than the one he'd been travelling in, and the visibility had been so poor that he'd seen nothing of the other group once they were out on the sands. Angie told him that more than a dozen cocklers had survived, and that a few more were still unaccounted for. He can only hope that Lin is among the survivors. The reporter concludes the story and the screen changes to a commercial. Wen slumps back against the sofa, feeling drained.

A quarter of an hour later, he hears a key in the front door. Angie stops just inside the door and looks at him.

"You've not moved an inch, have you?" she says.

He rises and nods hello to her, uncertain of her meaning. She takes off her coat, hangs it on a hook by the door and walks by him into the kitchen.

"I thought I hallucinated you," she remarks as she passes. He takes a few steps towards the kitchen, watches her take a bottle of whisky from beneath the sink and pour herself a generous glass. She drinks a third of it in one go, looks over at him and holds the glass up.

"Drink?"

He shakes his head.

"Suit yourself. Are you hungry?" She gestures putting something in her mouth.

"Yes," he nods. "*Puh-lees.*"

"Can you cook?"

He hesitates. She opens the refrigerator and pulls out a

pack of chicken, then reaches up to the cupboard for a small bag of rice, before turning back to him.

"You," she says, pointing at him. "Cook? Food?" She holds up the rice, gives it a little shake, and points towards the cooker.

"Yes," he says. "Little."

"A little," she corrects.

"A little," he repeats.

"Thank God for that," she says with a sigh. "'Cause I'm knackered." She bends down and removes a frying pan from the cupboard and hands it to him, walks past him into the bedroom and closes the door.

He stands uncertainly holding the pan for a moment. He places it atop the cooker and picks up the packaged chicken: two breasts, sealed in plastic on a white tray, for a price that would buy five times as much at home. He is not entirely sure he understood her meaning. But he is hungry, so he rummages in the cupboard and drawers and finds the soy sauce and some onions, a knife and a wooden cutting board, and begins to skin and bone the chicken, cutting it into pieces. The door opens and she walks past him in a dark blue dressing gown, still holding the glass, now empty. She pauses to refill it, then disappears inside the bathroom. After a moment, he hears her running the bath. He does not know any English people, so has no basis for comparison. But her actions seem strange by any standard.

He is not a bad cook. In fact, these past few months he'd taken over much of the meal preparation, as he was more experienced than the others: men whose wives had looked after them at home. No one wanted to spend more than a few pounds a week on food, so he was forced to be resourceful, scouring the shops for items that had been heavily discounted. Mostly they lived on homemade dumplings, instant noodles and rice, occasionally buying cheap sausage or pork belly to go with it. He has not eaten chicken since he left London. He finds some oil in the cupboard and stir-fries the chicken with the onions and soy sauce, and prepares the rice the way his stepmother taught him, cooking it halfway, then turning the heat off and allowing it to steam itself from the bottom up.

When the food is ready, he goes to the bathroom door and presses his ear against the panel. He can hear nothing. Perhaps she has fallen asleep, he thinks. After a moment, he raps softly on the bathroom door. At once he hears the slosh of bath water from within, and after several seconds she opens the door. Steam wafts over him, mixed with the flowery scent of shampoo.

Her face is flushed and her hair slick with wet. She wears the blue dressing gown, hastily closed so that he can see a broad slice of moist cleavage. She takes a deep breath and sways ever so slightly.

"Yes?"

"*Puh-lees*. Eat." He motions to the table where the food waits. She looks at the food, then back at him.

"Blimey. You weren't kidding." She crosses to the table and sits down, and after a moment's hesitation, he joins her. She picks up the fork and takes a bite of the chicken.

"Not bad," she says. "Much better than I could do." She

turns to him and leans in close. "Good," she enunciates heavily, nodding.

He gets a brief whiff of whisky mixed with soy and onion.

"Thank you," he says.

"No, *sank you*," she replies, a slow smile spreading to her lips.

They continue eating, and when she has finished, she lays down her fork, leans back in her chair and crosses her arms.

"So what now? We get married?" She throws back her head and laughs.

Wen smiles uncertainly. She is drunk. And she has clearly made a joke. But he has not understood it. Still, he should humour her. She stops laughing and looks at him, leaning forward.

"What. Are. We. Going. To. Do." She pauses in between each word. "With you," she adds, pointing at him.

He takes a deep breath. This time he has understood. Maybe not the words, but the meaning. He lowers his eyes to the empty plate in front of him. He knows that he should offer to leave, but he has no idea where he would go. He does not even know where he is. He raises his gaze to hers: she is frowning at him. They regard each other for a moment.

"I think," she says slowly. "That you should stay. Here," she adds. "With me."

Wen looks at her. He has understood three words: *stay*, *here* and *me*. He does not know precisely what she is offering, but it seems worth the gamble. And he does not really have an alternative. Even if he was prepared to contend with the police, the thought of returning to ill-paid jobs and sleeping eight to a room now seems impossible.

"Okay," he says.

She nods. "Okay," she repeats.

He does not know where he is going, but for the moment, his journey has brought him here.

•

The next morning after she leaves for work, he writes a letter to his sister. It is the only letter he has written since leaving China, and he dates it three days previously. He cannot risk telling her the truth: the letter might be intercepted by the authorities en route. When she receives it, she will think it was written the day before he died. He is not certain what the outcome of his present situation will be, but he wishes to set down his life to date. He owes that much to his sister, particularly if he is going to disappear off the face of the earth.

It takes him most of the day to write the letter, and in the end it runs to several pages. He describes his experiences in England, leaving aside a few key details. His affair with Jin he does not share with her. His sister has always been conservative in such matters; for all he knows she has never slept with a man. And Jin is not the sort of woman she would have chosen for him – he knows this even without asking. Though the two were room-mates at university, they were very different in their characters. But he was drawn to Jin from the moment he first met her. He admired her strength and her independence, though he sensed that she was cold-hearted. When they eventually became lovers, he was surprised by the contradictions in her nature. Jin was fiercely self-reliant, but over time, became increasingly demanding of him. He could see, after a few months, that she was falling in love with him. This, more than anything, accounted for his decision to leave London.

He finishes the letter with a cryptic message, urging his sister not to lose heart over his absence. *It was painful to leave you*, he writes. But after a moment's hesitation, he promises they will meet again soon. In the absence of truth, he wishes to furnish her with a small degree of hope. For now, it is the most that he can do.

September 2004

Lili does not speak to Jin of the photos or the note. She hardly wants to disclose that she has been through Jin's things. But the atmosphere between them the next morning is strained. Lili is due to start work at the language school, so she catches the No. 43 bus with Jin. On the way, Jin explains that the school's owner, a Hong Kong Chinese woman called Fay, is keen to open branches in other parts of London. For now, the school is located in the lower ground floor of a terraced house ten minutes' walk from Sheep Pen.

The house is owned by Fay and her English husband Robert, who live upstairs. Robert, says Jin, is a balding accountant who brays like a donkey when he laughs. Last year, he drank too much at the school's Christmas party and made a pass at her in the hallway outside the bathroom. Jin shrugs when she relates this tale, as if such behaviour from middle-aged English men is to be expected. But Lili is secretly appalled.

Fay herself is a plump fifty-year-old who speaks Mandarin with a southern accent. She is short and wide and wears a tight-fitting charcoal mini-skirt with a black silk shirt. She takes Lili to her office, a tiny room on the first floor with a paper-strewn desk and one small window. She asks her to fill out some forms, then hands across a folder of class lists and lesson plans. While Lili looks over the latter, Fay lights a cigarette and sits back in her chair.

"Jin told me you were good with children," she remarks.

Lili does not recall ever discussing children with Jin. What's more, she knows little about them. Her only job since leaving university has been teaching adults.

"I like children," she says tentatively.

"Do you have experience teaching younger ones?" Fay asks.

For an instant Lili considers lying. But that would be too much like Jin. "No," she replies. "I'm afraid I don't."

"It doesn't matter," says Fay, waving smoke away. "You'll learn quickly. Don't expect too much from them. The parents will be happy if they can say *please* and *thank you* by the end of term. It's often just a form of babysitting."

"Oh." Lili frowns.

"The important thing is that the kids leave here with a smile. So their parents sign them up again."

At this Fay throws back her head and laughs. Lili sees

a dark pocket of silver fillings. Fay reaches down to the bottom of her desk and pulls out a jar of brightly coloured sweets.

"I always give them one of these at the end of class," she says holding up the jar. "But you'll find your own way. Just keep them happy."

"I'll try," says Lili.

Fay eyes her for a moment. "Where did you say you were from?"

"Hebei. Near Tangshan."

Fay narrows her eyes. "Tangshan," she murmurs. "Why do I know it?"

"The earthquake," says Lili. "Nineteen seventy-six."

"Yes, of course. I'd forgotten. Before your time, I expect."

Lili swallows. *No*, she thinks. *We were there, Wen and I.* But Tangshan and Sheep Pen seem a million miles apart.

"Yes," she answers.

Fay takes one last puff, then stubs the cigarette out in a jade ashtray, before exhaling. "Jin said you'd be perfect for this job," she says, standing up.

"Thank you," Lili replies uncertainly. She realises that she no longer trusts Jin or her motives; she feels as if she has stepped from sunlight into darkness.

She will teach two afternoons a week at the school, as well as Saturday mornings. And on Thursdays she will teach at a private school in Notting Hill that has introduced an after-school Mandarin club. Fay gives her a map showing the school's location. This will be her first class, as she is due to start there the following afternoon.

"Get bus 31 from here," says Fay. "You'd best go there now and find it, so you don't get lost tomorrow."

"Yes, of course," says Lili. She has never been to Notting Hill, but she has seen the film. She imagines it is full of charming bookshops and cafés. That evening, when she tells Jin about the school in Notting Hill, her friend looks at her askance.

"Notting Mountain?" she says in Mandarin. "Full of rich people. I thought Fay gave up that school."

"Why?" asks Lili.

Jin shakes her head dismissively. "Too much trouble."

"It sounds okay," ventures Lili.

"Spoilt kids. Rich parents. You'll see. No one wants to teach there."

"Oh," says Lili, dismayed.

"But who knows?" says Jin. "Maybe you'll find a rich husband."

"Is that what you want?"

Jin shrugs. "There are worse things."

The next day, Lili arrives twenty minutes early at the school. She walks around the area for ten minutes, then returns to the school's entrance and presses the intercom. For a moment no one answers. Lili surveys the building: an imposing three-storey red-brick mansion, secured behind heavy black iron gates. At the top of the front stairs, a video camera points directly at her. The buzzer sounds and she pushes open the iron gate. At the door she is met by a carefully groomed woman with silver hair, who introduces herself as Mrs. Russell, the deputy head. The woman motions her to follow and they begin a winding journey down a series of twisted corridors. Lili hurries to keep up: from behind, the woman's hair looks like a helmet. She wears a pale blue wool suit and cream-coloured tights, and as she walks her thighs brush against each other audibly. The school is decorated in bright colours and the walls are filled with artwork and posters for upcoming events. Behind the closed classroom doors, Lili can see children in yellow and green uniforms seated around small tables. Their faces are flushed with tiredness and they sprawl in their seats, like limp flowers.

Mrs. Russell comes to an abrupt stop at the door of an empty classroom. "This is where you'll be each week. I hope you have a good memory, because after today you'll have to find your way here on your own."

"Yes," says Lili. She looks for a number on the classroom door, but sees none.

"I don't know if they told you, but you're the third teacher we've had. I told the language school that if you don't work out, we're going to cut the Mandarin Club and do karate instead." She pauses and frowns. "Karate *is* Chinese, isn't it?" she asks. Lili feels the colour rise in her cheeks. The woman gives a brisk shake of her head. "Anyway, as long as you understand the position." She pauses again and scrutinises Lili. "You *do* speak English, don't you?"

"Yes," says Lili. "I have advanced qualification in English," she adds hastily.

The older woman sighs. "The last teacher didn't, I can tell you. You can't handle these children if you can't communicate with them, I promise you that. Now today you've only got four. Normally you'll have seven, but two are ill and one is away. So that's lucky for you. The youngest is only nine. We originally set a minimum age of ten, but her father is especially keen. You'll see. It's a complicated situation. I'm sure he'll explain in due course. Any questions?" She stares expectantly at Lili.

"No," says Lili quickly.

"Good. 'Cause I've got to run. The children will be here in a few minutes. Bring them down to the front entrance afterwards, and they'll be collected by their parents or carers. Make sure they all go with someone they recognise."

"Yes, of course," says Lili.

She watches from the doorway as the silver-haired woman strides off down the hallway, the noise of her tights becoming more and more faint. Lili returns to the classroom and unpacks her teaching materials. Her heart is racing. Apart from the immigration officer at Heathrow, the silver-haired woman is the first English person she has spoken to here. With relief, she realises she understood most of what the woman said. After a minute, she hears a general stirring in the hallway, and soon the corridors are filled with chattering children fumbling with coats and bags. Lili positions herself so as to see them better. There are one or two darker-skinned children, but the vast majority are white. To her, they look like movie children: clear-eyed, fresh-faced, each with perfect teeth and skin. *Rich white children*, she thinks, remembering Jin's words. *Who lack for nothing*.

After a few minutes, a young heavy-set teacher with long curly hair and shiny skin comes marching down the hallway with a small clutch of children in tow. She pauses at the doorway, smiling brightly, and ushers the children inside.

"Here they are," she says to Lili, by way of introduction. There are three girls and a chubby boy, who is hurriedly stuffing the remains of a chocolate muffin into his mouth as he approaches. Two of the girls are tall and blonde and confident-looking. They carry matching Hello Kitty backpacks, and as they draw near, one of them whispers something to the other and the latter smirks. The youngest child stands behind the others. Lili sees with surprise that she is Chinese, and extremely small for her age. Her shiny black hair has been cut in a blunt fringe that nearly over-hangs her eyes, and her green and yellow uniform seems to swamp her tiny frame.

"Hello," says Lili. The four children stare at her mutely.

"Good heavens! She won't bite! Go on then, say hello," says the teacher in a thick Scottish accent.

"Hello," say the two older girls in unison.

"I'll leave them with you, if that's all right," says the teacher with a smile. Without waiting for an answer she turns and goes, leaving Lili alone with the children. She nods to them.

"*Ni hao*," she enunciates carefully in Mandarin.

Once again the children stare at her. The boy frowns.

"We don't understand," he says. Lili smiles at him.

"I thought you had a Mandarin teacher already," she says.

"She was useless," says the boy.

The class does not go well. The two blonde girls chatter ceaselessly, the boy nearly falls asleep, his head draped across the desk, and the little Chinese girl refuses to utter a word. Lili tries without success to engage them in a series of word games, but the hour drags. Towards the end, she suddenly remembers that she purchased a pack of biscuits on the way here. She stops mid-sentence and fishes them out of her bag, and the children immediately lean forward with interest. She opens the pack and offers it round.

"Can I have two?" says one of the blonde girls.

"Yes, of course," says Lili.

The boy stretches out a pudgy hand and grabs a second biscuit. When the pack reaches the Chinese girl, she takes one.

"Would you like two?" asks Lili.

The child shakes her head. "No thank you," she says.

Lili turns to the class.

"Do you know how to say *thank you* in Chinese?" she asks.

"We never learned that," says one of the blonde girls defensively.

"Then I will teach you," says Lili. "*Xie xie ni*," she says slowly. The children stare at her. She repeats the phrase again. After a moment, the Chinese girl speaks.

"*Xie xie ni*," she says.

Lili smiles at her. "Your pronunciation is very good," she says encouragingly.

"Figures," says one of the blonde girls. She rolls her eyes at her friend.

Lili looks at the Chinese girl, who seems to shrink under her gaze. She turns to the other children.

"Don't worry," she says. "Soon you will all be speaking Chinese."

"Are we done?" asks the boy abruptly. A small crumb of chocolate has lodged in the corner of his mouth.

"I'm sorry?" says Lili. She glances at the clock on the wall. The class is due to end in five minutes.

"The hour's up," he says, rising halfway to his feet. "My mum'll be waiting outside."

"Oh," says Lili uncertainly. "Yes, of course."

At once the other children stand up and begin to stuff their things into their satchels. Lili leads them out of the classroom, but once in the corridor she pauses, unsure of her bearings.

"It's this way," says one of the blonde girls, striding ahead down the corridor.

When they reach the main door, a couple of parents are waiting just outside. The two blonde girls skip to the side of a well-dressed woman in her forties who nods quickly to Lili.

"I'm taking both of them," she says efficiently, turning away.

The boy walks over to a short young woman with badly dyed red hair and wearing low-slung combat trousers.

Lili sees a tiny silver stud in her nostril.

"I thought Mum was coming," he says with a trace of accusation.

"Do I look like your mum?" says the young woman in a thick accent.

The boy shrugs and walks down the steps. The young woman raises her eyebrows at Lili and turns to follow him. Lili wonders where she is from: Poland perhaps? Or Hungary? London is bursting with Eastern Europeans, according to Jin. She also insists that white immigrants are first in line for all the best casual jobs. But watching the young woman follow the sullen boy down the street, Lili does not envy her.

She turns back to the Chinese girl and smiles.

"My dad's late," says the girl apologetically.

"No problem."

"He's *always* late." The girl pulls an exasperated face.

"That's okay." They stand there for a moment, eyeing each other, and Lili realises with dismay that she has forgotten to ask the children their names.

"What is your name?"

"May," replies the girl. Lili smiles.

"That's a lovely Chinese name."

"It's the name of a month. In spring."

"You are right. It is that too. But in Mandarin, it means *beautiful*."

"Yeah, I know." May kicks at the ground with her shoe. Lili glances up the street. There is no sign of the child's father.

"My mother named me after her favourite time of year," says May after a moment. "But then she died," she adds.

"Oh," says Lili. "I'm sorry."

"It's okay. She wasn't my real mother. My real mother was Chinese."

"What happened to her?"

"Which one?"

"Your Chinese mother," says Lili.

May shrugs. "I don't know. They found me in an alley."

"Oh," says Lili, silenced momentarily by the girl's bluntness.

"You're from China too, aren't you?"

"Yes."

"What's it like there?"

"It is very different to here."

"Different how?"

"Well. The people there are all Chinese."

"But I'm Chinese."

May is staring at her. Lili falters. She owes the child a better answer, but she is completely at a loss. Where would she begin?

"How old are you?" she asks instead.

"I'll be ten in a few months. But I'm the smallest in my class," May says, as if it is an oversight on her part.

"It's okay to be small," Lili says. "Maybe better than being big."

May studies her with a frown, weighing up the truth of her words.

"I'm sorry! So sorry!"

Lili turns to see a tall, red-haired man rushing along the pavement, calling to them. He climbs the steps two at a time, coming to an abrupt halt in front of her.

"The traffic was murder," he exclaims.

"You're late," says May accusingly.

"Sorry, darling," he exhales, reaching out and laying a hand on her head.

"The other kids went home ages ago."

He flashes her a brief frown, then turns to Lili.

"Are you the new Mandarin teacher?"

"Who else would she be?" says May quietly.

"Yes. I am Lili."

"Hello. Adrian. May's father." He thrusts out his hand and Lili takes it. His fingers are long and slender. Lili sees a tiny tuft of strawberry hair peeking out of the triangle of his shirt.

"She is a good student," says Lili, indicating May. "She learns very quickly."

Bored, May has begun to hop up and down the steps on one foot. Adrian too glances at May. He takes a deep breath and runs a hand through his pale ginger hair.

"Well, it's in her genes, I guess. I don't speak any Chinese, so I thought it would be good for her to learn."

"Yes," says Lili. "Of course."

"May's adopted. From the mainland."

"Yes. She told me this."

"And she's *very* excited about learning Mandarin, aren't you, May?" He looks at her hopefully. May hops up the last two steps and comes to a halt abruptly in front of him.

"Can we go home now?" she asks.

"Yes, of course," says Adrian. May hops down the stairs. Adrian turns back to Lili. "It was good to meet you. I guess we'll see you next Thursday."

"Yes," says Lili. "Goodbye, May," she calls.

May raises a hand in a sort of wave but continues hopping on one foot out the school gate and onto the pavement.

"Bye," says Adrian with a small shrug of apology. He hurries down the steps and follows May out onto the street.

February 2004

For three days, Angie goes to work, leaving Wen alone in her house. She has no idea what he does to occupy himself in her absence. But he leaves virtually no imprint. When she returns at the end of the day, the house is exactly as she left it, almost as if he ceases to exist when she is gone.

Several times she has experienced an unsettling moment at work when she is suddenly convinced that he is a figment of her imagination; that the events that night on the bay were nothing more than a drunken dream. And each evening when she walks through the door, her heart beats a little faster in anticipation of what she will find. But he is always there: sitting on her sofa, wearing the same black tracksuit, his hands resting uncertainly at his sides, his eyes trained on her. And each time what she feels is relief.

With remarkable ease, they slip into a sort of rhythm. Every night after work, she stops at a local supermarket and buys groceries and a small bottle of whisky. Once home, she pours a drink, slips into a hot bath and emerges to eat whatever he has concocted out of her purchases. On the third night, she hands him a carrier bag containing a packet of mince, a tin of tomatoes and a small package of spaghetti. Wen looks inside the bag.

"Bolognese," she explains.

Wen pulls the ingredients out of the bag, eyeing them with uncertainty, and places them on the counter.

"*Bo lo nay*," he repeats, frowning.

"Italian," she says. "From Italy. Spaghetti with meat sauce. Okay?"

Wen shrugs. "Okay," he replies gamely.

"Fabulous," she says, disappearing into the bath.

When she emerges forty-five minutes later, she finds that he has boiled, then stir-fried the spaghetti together with the mince. She watches with interest as he drains the tin of tomatoes, chops them roughly and adds them to the pan. After another few moments of stir-frying, he turns to her tentatively, holding the food out for her inspection. He watches as she leans down and inhales its fragrance.

"Perfect," she says, raising her head. "Spot on."

Wen looks at her and smiles.

After they have eaten, Wen does the washing-up, while she settles herself with the whisky in front of the television. Eventually he joins her on the sofa, and though he does not understand much of what he sees, he appears to find it entertaining.

They watch in silence, and occasionally he steals a glance

at her. He sips one glass of whisky to her three or four. When the bottle is nearly finished, and her brain is sufficiently numb, she nods to him, stumbles into her bedroom, closes the door and pitches off the edge of consciousness into sleep. It is all, she decides, remarkably easy.

•

On the fifth day, towards the end of the afternoon, her boss Tony leans back in his chair and regards her with an arch look.

"What's going on?" he asks. "With you?" His tone is friendly but suspicious.

She hesitates, feeling her stomach start to churn.

"What do you mean?"

"*You* know." He rises from his desk and walks over to where she sits, stopping in front of her.

"No," she says, looking up at him. "I don't."

"Something's changed. You've changed," he continues. He raises an eyebrow in a vaguely suggestive manner. Instantly she feels irritation. She reaches down and grabs her handbag under her desk.

"I changed my shampoo," she says tersely.

"Angie," he admonishes. "I'm not an idiot. I see things."

"What kind of things?"

"I don't know. It's just a feeling. You seem different."

"Don't be fooled," she says. "Nothing has changed, Tony. And I am exactly who I was." They eye each other for a moment, then he turns and walks back to his desk.

"Okay," he says placatingly. "Okay. I just thought..."

He allows his voice to trail off suggestively.

"You thought *what?*" She meets his gaze and holds it challengingly.

"Nothing," he says, looking away. Angie looks at her watch, then begins stuffing things into her handbag.

"I'm off, if that's okay. I'm tired."

"Stay," he says suddenly.

She looks up at him with surprise. He shrugs.

"We'll... go for a quick drink."

She shakes her head.

"Not tonight. Sorry. Thanks, anyway."

"Okay," he says, frowning. "Suit yourself."

On the drive home she agitates. He is right, of course. Something has changed. Slowly, almost imperceptibly, she has altered in response to Wen's presence. It is not deliberate. Or at least, not consciously so. Two weeks ago, she could not see the point of living. Her life jolted along a featureless road beyond which she no longer cared to see. Now, suddenly, her fate has been yoked together with that of a complete stranger from the far side of the world. The very fact that such a thing could happen, that it *did* happen, has taken her completely by surprise. She had thought that she was beyond surprise. It is an enormous relief to discover that she is not.

Mercifully, Wen's presence has freed her from the burden of herself. But now Tony's words have somehow disturbed the course of things. She had begun to look forward to the end of each day, to facing the array of choices at the supermarket, to the reassuring weight of the tumbler in her hand, to the lingering hot bath with the sound of Wen tinkering in the kitchen just beyond the door. These are small things, but she realises she has anticipated them with something akin to pleasure. Now Tony, with his smarmy look and insinuating tone, has somehow snatched this from her. For nothing has *really* changed, she thinks with dismay. The circumstances of her life may have altered – but she herself is fundamentally the same.

At the shop she stalks through the aisles, feeling the familiar flood of anger rise within her. Its reappearance startles her. Where has it been these past few days? Oddly, she had not marked its absence. Now she realises it was there all along, simmering just beneath the surface of her life. Anger has been her companion for as long as she can remember, stamping itself indelibly on her childhood and adolescence, and scarring her marriage from its earliest days. Angie stands motionless in the vegetable aisle, wondering why she thought she would ever be free of it.

A woman pauses just beside her, waiting politely for her to make her selection. Angie grabs a bag of potatoes and a head of iceberg lettuce, then moves to another aisle where she picks up a packet of pork chops, then crosses quickly to the spirits. Instead of one bottle of whisky, tonight she buys three. After all, she thinks grimly, it's the weekend. She pays for the food and drink and once inside the car, cracks open a bottle and takes a long pull of burning liquid before starting the engine. She drives with the open bottle wedged between her thighs, and by the time she reaches her house, she has downed almost a third of it.

When she walks through the front door, she comes abruptly face to face with Wen. Angie stops short. He looks down and sees the open whisky bottle in her hand, then looks back up at her. For the first time, she sees the dark flash of accusation in his eyes. She brushes past him and goes into the kitchen, tossing the bag of food onto the counter and reaching for a tumbler. Wen follows her into the kitchen and stands watching as she fills the glass. She takes a long drink and turns to him.

"What?" she demands.

He purses his lips, then turns away.

"Fuck off," she says, going into the bathroom.

When she emerges from the bath some time later, she sees that he has chopped all three ingredients and stir-fried them together. The iceberg lettuce has wilted into pale green spittles and the long slivers of pork look like grey worms. In spite of herself, she bursts out laughing.

"Jesus Christ! Don't you know how to do anything but fry?"

He eyes her silently for a moment, his chest rising and falling, his anger almost palpable, an even match for her own. They stand facing each other, and it is as if they have been stripped of everything but their fury.

He gestures to the dish with a wooden spoon, speaking to her in Mandarin, the tone of his voice barely controlled. He is holding the spoon so tightly she can see the whiteness of his knuckles through the translucent membrane of his skin. Wen finishes speaking and Angie feels a terrible sinking deep inside.

"I'm sorry," she whispers.

He nods, just once.

•

Later, when they have finished eating, he gets up to clear away the dishes and she lays a hand upon his arm. "No. Let me."

He looks down at her hand upon his wrist, and instantly she removes it, the blood rushing to her face with embarrassment. He goes and sits on the sofa while she does the washing-up, and when she has finished she picks up the remains of the bottle and her glass and follows him into the sitting room. She plants herself next to him, and refills her glass. For the first time, she feels nervous in his presence. She raises the glass to drink, and is startled to see her own hand tremble ever so slightly. He is watching a travel programme, but when she raises the glass to her lips, he turns his gaze to her instead, his eyes sliding down to the amber liquid, then back up to her face. She feels a sudden surge of fear.

"What?" Her voice is barely more than a whisper. He holds her eyes for a long moment, and she feels a tremor pass through her. She sets the glass down and places her hands on her knees.

"Look," she says, swallowing. "I drink too much. I'm sorry. But that's the way it is." Her voice sounds hollow, as if the words themselves are empty of all meaning. He regards her uncertainly, measuring her.

"I drink," she says slowly, "because otherwise I will go mad."

Wen's expression darkens with effort as he struggles to decipher her words.

"Or maybe," she adds, "the madness makes me drink. Either way, I'm fucked if I do, and fucked if I don't." She looks up at him. "Do you understand?"

He nods his head slowly.

Her eyes drift away, flick past the television, the pile of magazines on the coffee table, the faded stains on the carpet, and settle on the neatly folded pile of bedding on the floor. She thinks of Tony's raised eyebrows, his insinuating comments, and her response. Nothing has changed.

"Look at me," she says with a small snort of disgust. "It hasn't even occurred to you to come into my bed." She gives a brief, grim laugh, and takes another drink of whisky.

"Maybe you're not that way inclined," she continues, talking to herself. She turns and scrutinises him. "Are you that way inclined?"

He regards her uncertainly. Perhaps it is her imagination, but in that instant he seems to recede slightly, to draw back from her, and the realisation hits her like a slap. It has happened so quickly: this sudden shift between them. Now she is the one struggling to stay afloat.

"You're afraid of me, aren't you?" she says, her voice incredulous. "Shit-scared. Afraid I'll chuck you out. Or top myself. Either way, you'd be in trouble." She pauses for a moment. "Well you're wrong. I don't know why exactly. But I'm not going to do either. Okay?"

She turns to him for a response. He gives a brief nod.

"Okay," he says.

She takes a deep breath and lets it out. "But what I'd really like," she says, her voice wavering slightly, "this night, is not to be alone. Do you understand?" She looks at him for confirmation. "I do not want to be alone," she repeats slowly, her voice trailing into nothing. She is swimming in drink now. Or is it nerves? She feels her head rush drunkenly and looks away. Her words float around her in the room; part of her would like to snatch them up and run away.

Instead, she rises and crosses to the bedroom, leaving the door wide open behind her. She walks over to the closet and begins to strip off her clothes, her back to the door. After a few moments, she sees Wen's reflection appear in the mirror. He stands motionless in the doorway to her bedroom, his arms hanging loosely by his sides. She freezes for a moment, then pulls the last piece of clothing off and lets it slip from her grasp to the floor. Wen's eyes flicker briefly to the pile of clothing at her feet, then back to her face. They stare at each other in the dim glow of the mirror for what seems like an eternity. And then he steps into the room.

September 2004

Lili and Jin do not speak of Wen, but he hovers like an unseen presence between them. Lili cannot banish the photos from her mind, nor the idea that Jin may have travelled to Morecambe Bay to see him in the weeks before he died. The thought preys on her, and she secretly resolves to find her own way there. Her knowledge of British geography is hazy, so she buys a road atlas from a newsagent in Sheep Pen. She knows the country is an island, but sees at once that its shape is amorphous, like a giant squid, with London rooted firmly in the bulging south, and other cities flung like ink spots around the periphery. Scotland perches precariously atop England, a huge expanse of land with relatively few interruptions. Wen once told her that he longed to see Scotland: Western men with bushy beards, he had joked, wearing women's skirts and playing pipes upon the hillsides. But as far as she knows, he never travelled north of Morecambe Bay.

With some difficulty, she locates it on the atlas, two-thirds of the way up the western seaboard, not far from Liverpool. The bay is vast, stretching far out into the Irish Sea. She had not realised how close Ireland was – had never thought that Wen's body might have drifted to another country altogether. She continues leafing through the pages of the atlas until she finds the nucleus that is London. She sees that the city is surrounded by a fat blue circle of roads, with a web of motorways extending north and west, one of which eventually leads straight past Morecambe Bay.

It couldn't be easier, she thinks, tracing the long blue line that curls upwards from Birmingham towards Lancaster with her finger. She will have to find a way.

On her day off, she spends the morning doing laundry and revising her English. Apart from the old woman who works there, she is the only one in the laundromat. She notices that people do not remain there while their clothes are washing: instead, they come and go at intervals, some not even bothering to fold their newly cleaned clothes, but quickly stuffing them in sacks and carting them away, as if they cannot bear to linger, even for a minute. The people who come are a jumbled mix of colours and ages, but they all seem slightly put upon by the drudgery of the task, rather than resigned to it. Perhaps if they scrubbed at life hard enough, she thinks, they would not be saddled with its more menial jobs. After an hour, Lili tires of the place and decamps to a café across the road. But she finds the atmosphere inside little better: the slightly rancid smell of bacon grease and stale cigarette smoke oppresses her, as do the leering glances of a knot of workmen at a nearby table.

That afternoon, she takes a bus to Hammersmith, for she has quietly formed a plan, and that plan involves Johnny. But when she arrives, she finds that the area is not as she remembered. The bus lets her off at an unfamiliar cross-road, and she immediately walks in the wrong direction. In the end it takes her more than an hour to find the takeaway where Johnny works. When she finally sees Taste of Spring she feels a surge of relief, as if the next hurdle in her journey to Wen has been overcome.

She walks tentatively up to the plate glass window and peers inside: Johnny is behind the counter, serving a dark-skinned teenage boy wearing a hooded sweatshirt and baggy jeans.

When she pushes open the door, Johnny doesn't notice her at first. She watches as he hands the boy a white plastic bag containing a small polystyrene container.

"Hey," says the boy. "You got any chopsticks?"

"Sure," says Johnny. He hands a pair of disposable wooden chopsticks over the counter.

"Can I get some more?" asks the boy.

Johnny fixes him with a look. "How many?"

"Like, six or seven?"

"For one dish of fried rice?" In that instant Johnny sees her, and a slow smile spreads across his face. He nods to her over the boy's head.

"Yeah," says the boy.

Johnny shakes his head. "Help yourself," he says with a

shrug, grabbing a huge fistful of chopsticks and handing them across the counter.

"Hey, thanks," says the youth appreciatively.

"No worries," says Johnny. Lili steps to one side as the hooded teenager brushes past her, then walks up to the counter.

"So, Hebei," says Johnny in English. "What's wrong? You tired of hotpot?"

Lili laughs.

"I thought you forgot me," he continues in Mandarin.

"Impossible," says Lili.

"Excellent," says Johnny. "You're just in time. I'm off in ten minutes."

He takes her to a nearby Starbucks, and though Lili blanches at the price of coffee, she doesn't let it show. They sit in leather armchairs by the window. Johnny tells her that his family is from Shanghai, and that he has been in London studying for almost three years.

"No wonder," she says. "You seem so accustomed to it all."

He laughs. "Only in comparison to you," he replies. "Believe me, I'm still just as much an outsider. I don't even need to open my mouth. They can tell just by looking." He glances surreptitiously around at the other customers, as if they are adversaries.

"But now I do it too," he adds with a shrug. "I've got so I can tell who was born here and who wasn't."

Lili looks at the people sitting around her: two young Muslim women with headscarves huddled over hot chocolates, a blonde woman wearing horn-rimmed glasses and a business suit working on a laptop, and two middle-aged men in anoraks who are deep in conversation in a language she doesn't recognise. These people could be from anywhere, she thinks. She turns back to him.

"How?"

"The people from here look like they *deserve* to be here," Johnny says easily. "Like it's their entitlement. The rest of us look as if we are scrambling to find a way in."

He takes a sip of cappuccino, and a small fleck of foam remains on his upper lip. Lili's eyes are drawn to his mouth: his lips are beautiful, full and perfectly formed. She considers reaching out and dabbing at the fleck of white with her napkin. She forces her gaze away.

"You don't look like you are scrambling," she remarks, stirring her coffee with a wooden stick.

"Well, I am," he says. "We all are. The good news is," he adds, "there are so many foreigners here, we almost outnumber them." He flashes her a grin.

He is too handsome, she thinks suddenly. *And too confident.* Not like Wen, who had a quiet self-assurance. She cannot help but compare them. Her brother's looks were unremarkable, but he had something that drew women to him like swallows to a nest. She was fourteen when she first noticed, barely into puberty. One day, two girls followed her and Wen out of school, nudging each other, their eyebrows arched knowingly. They looked straight past her, as if she wasn't there, and boldly asked Wen if he would help them with their homework. Lili often did Wen's homework for him, so she was surprised when he readily agreed. After that she grew used to approaches from other girls, could discern at once the predatory look in their eyes. And though it grated on her each time, she eventually learned to steel herself against them. It helped that Wen did not attach himself to any one of them. He ranged freely across them, always coming back to her in the end.

"Hey, Hebei," says Johnny in English. "What's up?"

She looks at him, startled.

"I lost you for a moment," he says in Mandarin.

"I'm sorry," she says, blushing. "Everything is so new," she adds a bit feebly.

"No worries," he says in English.

She wishes this were true. For she does have worries.

"Do you have a car?" she asks suddenly. Johnny raises an eyebrow.

"My uncle does," he says. "Where do you want to go?"

"To the seaside," she replies.

•

Later, they go for dinner in a crowded pizza house, where Johnny orders a large pitcher of beer to wash down their meal. Afterwards, he takes her hand and walks her to a small park. When they reach an empty bench, he pulls her down beside him and into an embrace. His kiss is tentative at first, but quickly takes on urgency when she responds. She feels his hands searching out her softer places, and feels herself stirring, a little reluctantly, somewhere deep inside. But almost at once, a part of her seems to detach and float away, as if this second self is above her looking down. A sudden thought alarms her: perhaps Wen is watching too? Instantly, she pulls back from him. Johnny struggles for breath, as if she has winded him.

"Hey," he murmurs, leaning forward to nuzzle her ear. "What's wrong?"

"Nothing," she says quietly. "We should go." He draws back and looks at her a long moment.

"No worries," he says then.

It is only the second time she has kissed a man. Unlike most of her classmates, she managed to avoid any romantic entanglements at university. The first time was only four weeks after Wen's death, when she went out to a bar with friends and drank too much in a bid to forget. That man was another young teacher she had known vaguely for a few years. Towards the end of the evening, he had taken her outside and led her down a dark alley, where he had pressed her ardently up against a wall. His movements were clumsy and unpractised, and she was unwisely tempted to laugh. That night she had allowed herself some drunken licence: she was twenty-eight years old, had lost her only blood relation and had never been with a man. But she had stopped short of having sex. Even so, the next morning she woke with a creeping sense of self-hatred. The teacher rang and she refused to see him. In the weeks that followed, he plagued her, calling constantly and waiting outside her building after work. In the end he wrote a letter asking her to marry him, which she sent back along with her refusal. It was about this time that she admitted to herself a truth that she had known all along: men made her uneasy. And the only one who didn't was dead.

•

A few days later, Johnny rings to say his uncle has agreed to let him borrow the car the following day. But when he hears where she wants to go, his tone alters.

"Hebei," he says, uncertainly. "I was thinking maybe Brighton."

"Lancaster is only three hundred kilometres," she says. "If we start early, we can be there by lunchtime." In truth she has only guessed at the distance. But Jin has told her that the highways in the UK are as smooth as glass, and that cars can travel at alarmingly fast speeds compared to home. Since buying the atlas, the desire to get to Morecambe Bay has threatened to devour her. She wants to run her fingers through the water of Wen's grave and feel its bitter chill. She will walk there if she has to.

"Please," she says to Johnny, a note of desperation creeping into her voice.

"Okay," he says after a moment.

After she hangs up the phone, Lili wonders what she will have to offer in return.

The next day he collects her from Hounslow Station at eight in the morning. Inevitably, they lose their way getting out of London, and in the end the journey takes more than five hours. After three hours, they stop for petrol at a service station just past Birmingham. By then Johnny's good humour is wearing thin, and Lili wonders whether she has overstepped his kindness. When she sees the price of fuel she is horrified; the bill comes to nearly forty pounds.

"So much money," she says, her eyes widening. "I didn't know." She reaches in her purse, wondering whether she has even brought that much.

"It's okay," says Johnny, waving her away. "My treat," he adds in English.

She watches a little uneasily as he pays at the counter.

He suggests they go for coffee, so they drive to another part of the service area. It is built like a shopping mall, filled with shops and restaurants of all kinds, as if it is a destination in its own right. Outside the car park is nearly full, and inside there are throngs of people milling about. It had not occurred to her that petrol stations could be so elaborate, nor provide so many services; at home they usually consisted of a single pumping station. She insists on paying for the coffee, and when they are finally seated opposite each other, Johnny crosses his arms and fixes her with a look.

"Okay," he says. "Now is the time."

"The time for what?" She smiles nervously.

"The time for you to tell me your story," he replies. "The one you've not been telling me."

Lili hesitates; her eyes drift around the café. Across the aisle, an enormous woman wearing pale blue stretch trousers wedges her massive frame into a booth. Her short dark hair looks artificially curled and her face is bright red with exertion. Lili frowns at the women's bulging thighs. She has seen more obese people these past two weeks than in her entire lifetime. She turns back to Johnny.

"I had a brother," she says finally. "He died in Morecambe Bay."

Johnny frowns.

"You mean this year? In February?"

She nods. He leans back, clearly surprised, and draws a breath.

"I'm sorry," he says then. "I didn't know."

Lili shrugs. A lump rises in her throat. Beside her, the woman in pale blue trousers bites into an enormous cheeseburger. A large dollop of ketchup squeezes out and falls onto the table, but the woman does not notice.

"I should have told you earlier. I just wanted to go there, and see."

Johnny eyes her for a moment.

"So this trip," he says slowly. "It's about you and him."

"I'm sorry."

He looks away for a few moments, scans the other people at the tables around them, then finally turns back to her.

"So am I."

They drive on and the atmosphere between them is strained. Lili keeps the map book open on her knees and as they approach Lancaster, she directs him on a series of roads leading towards the coast.

When they finally reach the broad promenade overlooking Morecambe Bay, she feels almost ill with anticipation. Johnny pulls into a disabled parking bay and stops the car, turning to her.

"Now what?"

Lili stares out at the water: it is high tide now, the waves rolling in at even distances. The day is overcast, and the wind whips along the seafront. As she looks around she sees nothing that is familiar; no sign that he was here. This place is completely strange to her, and she wonders how that possibly could be. A creeping sense of disappointment steals over her, and she resists it with all her might.

"Drive on," she says impulsively. "Go further up the shore."

Johnny pulls the car out and drives further north along the shore for a few minutes.

"Here," she says finally. "Stop here!"

He pulls over and parks the car. Without waiting, Lili jumps out and begins to walk down towards the water, until her feet crunch against pebbles and sand. She carries on walking until her shoes are almost in the surf. Ice cold water washes inside them, startling her with its chill. She reaches down and plunges her hands into the water. When she straightens she sees a lone male figure behind her up the shore. *Wen*, she thinks fleetingly. But it is not Wen, of course. It is Johnny. She looks back towards the endless grey of the ocean.

They order pasta in a café across the road, just as a line of dark clouds comes sweeping across the bay. Lili picks at her spaghetti while Johnny wolfs his hungrily. When they have finished, he pushes his plate to one side and takes out a pack of cigarettes, lighting one.

"Smoke?"

She shakes her head. He takes a deep drag and exhales.

"How long was he here?"

"In Morecambe Bay? A month or so. Maybe two. Not long, I think."

"Was he illegal?"

Lili nods, watching his eyes narrow slightly with judgement.

"Wen was different," she says earnestly. "He wasn't like the others."

"Different how?"

"He didn't come here to get rich."

"It's no crime to be rich," says Johnny.

"I know. But he wasn't after money."

"Then what did he come for?"

Lili falters, searching for the right words.

"He was restless. Things weren't good for him at home."

"In what way?"

"He needed to go abroad. To see other places, to see other ways of... being."

"We all wanted that."

"Wen wanted it more."

"Why?"

"I don't know. It was like he was looking for his place in the world." She shrugs a little self-consciously and glances over at the next table, where an older couple sit chewing in silence.

"Did he find it?"

Lili shrugs. "I don't know. But that's why I came to London. To find out."

"How?"

"By looking for him."

Johnny looks at her askance.

"His spirit, I mean. I know he's here. But I can't find him."

Johnny raises an eyebrow, then leans forward to tap ash onto his plate.

"Maybe he doesn't want to be found."

Lili shakes her head.

"You don't understand. Wen and I were twins. In ancient times we would have been left to die at birth. They would have called us ghost spouses."

"He was your twin?"

"Yes."

Johnny leans back in his chair, regarding her. "Like two halves."

"I guess so."

"So what does that make you now?"

Lili swallows. "Broken."

As they rise to go, it begins to rain, and they are forced to run the brief distance back to the car. Once inside, Johnny turns to her. "Are we finished?"

She nods. He turns the car around and heads south down the coast road. After a few minutes, they pass a long pier jutting out into the bay. At once, her eyes alight on a stone statue halfway down the jetty.

"Wait! Pull over, will you?"

Johnny pulls the car into the side of the road and puts it in park.

"I'll just be a moment," she says, jumping out. She dashes down the jetty towards the statue, pausing just in front of it. An enormous stone bird stares down at her. Without a doubt, the photo of Wen and Jin was taken here. Lili stands staring up at the bird, wondering why Jin has lied to her a second time. After a minute, she returns to the car.

"Okay?" he asks.

She nods.

They head out of town and as they hit the motorway, the weather deteriorates. Johnny is forced to slow his speed. Darkness falls early due to the storm, and soon they are both straining to see through the windscreen. Johnny looks increasingly tired, running his hand every minute or so through his short cropped hair, as if struggling to stay awake. Lili too feels exhausted, both from the journey and the emotional energy it has cost her. She dozes off just past Birmingham, waking with a guilty start when Johnny pulls off the motorway into a rest area. He parks the car in a deserted area and switches off the engine. She turns to him, and a shot of apprehension runs through her: she barely knows this man, nor whether she can trust him. She feels her chest tighten. Johnny rubs his face in his hands.

"*Ta ma de*," he swears through his hands. He lowers them and looks at her. "I need to sleep."

"Okay," she says, her voice faltering a little. She is flooded with relief as he climbs into the back seat and stretches out across it, balling his jacket into a cushion. He closes his eyes and gives an enormous sigh, and within moments is asleep.

Now Lili herself is wide awake, staring out into the deserted car park, watching the rain run in tiny rivulets down the windscreen. The night Wen died the weather was similarly bad, according to the news reports. She wonders whether it was the waves that finally overcame him, or the freezing cold. She feels guilty that she is now warm and dry, as if she should be out there somewhere, battling the elements, just as he was forced to.

With dismay, she remembers that she had meant to look for cockles on the beach, or at the very least, buy some in a local shop. She has never seen a cockle, much less eaten one. Wen said in his letter it was easy to spot the tell-tale pockmarks in the sand just after the tide had gone out: that when you raked the sand they lay like buried treasure just beneath the surface, their pale white feet pointing downwards. Once he had pocketed a few small ones and later pried them open with a kitchen knife. They had the taste and texture of salty elastic bands, he had written. Perhaps steamed with ginger and spring onion they would be palatable, but the English ate them cold from polystyrene cups with only a small squeeze of lemon, and this he could not fathom.

A sharp knock on the window startles her, and Lili looks out to see a tall figure looming in the darkness. She glances anxiously towards the back seat, but Johnny is still fast asleep. Slowly she lowers the window, and is relieved to see a man in a police uniform. He leans down to speak to her.

"Everything all right here, miss?"

"Yes."

"You're not allowed to stop here overnight."

"We do not stay the night," she says nervously. "My friend is tired."

The policeman cranes his neck forward to look at Wen in the back seat.

"I can see that. Is he the one that's driving?"

"Yes."

"Has he been drinking?"

"Drinking?" repeats Lili.

"Yes, miss. Alcohol. Has he had any alcohol tonight?"

"No. No alcohol. Only water. And Coca-Cola," she adds, wondering whether it is a crime to drink Coca-Cola while driving.

The policeman eyes her, weighing up her words.

"This is a rest area?" she asks.

"Yes, it's a rest area. But it's not for sleeping."

"Oh," she replies. "Of course. I will tell him."

"Thank you."

She watches as he returns to his car. Johnny is stirring now, awakened by their voices. He sits up and looks at her, bleary-eyed.

"Who was that?"

"Police," she says.

He looks askance.

"Why?"

"He says you're not allowed to sleep here."

Johnny shakes his head, swearing under his breath, and climbs over into the front seat.

He starts the car and backs out of the parking space.

"Do you want to stop for coffee?" Lili asks.

"I'm fine," he replies, lurching into forward. "I just want to get home."

They reach London just after ten o'clock, and she is relieved when he does not offer to take her to her flat, dropping her instead at Hounslow Station. After she steps out of the car, she bends down to say goodbye through the open window. She wants desperately to thank him, to convey to him how much it meant to her to see the place where Wen died, but she knows that gratitude is not what Johnny needs right now. His hands are gripped tightly on the steering wheel, and his eyes linger slightly to one side of her.

"I'm sorry," she says finally. "I didn't mean to deceive you."

Johnny's hands flex open and closed on the wheel. After a moment he nods. Lili turns to go.

"Hey Hebei," he calls out.

She turns back to the car and bends down again. This time he meets her gaze.

"Let me know when you stop looking."

February 2004

Early the next morning, Wen wakes beside her sleeping form. She breathes deeply, her body turned away from him, the bedcovers flung back almost to her waist. Her dark brown hair is fanned out across the pillow like a tangled halo, and her bare shoulder looks stark and vulnerable in the grey light of dawn. With care he eases his body back from hers. But he dares not rise, as he does not wish to wake her. Right now what he needs is time.

Last night her actions took him completely by surprise. Until then, he had found her behaviour unpredictable and bewildering: her manner had seemed flint-like at times, almost brittle. But after a few drinks, the shell of her exterior fell away; she relaxed, became light-hearted, though he still found her changeable. Yesterday morning, when he came out of the shower, she'd stopped short and stared at him for an instant, before carrying on with what she had been doing. Oddly, it was the first time he had felt male in her presence. Their relationship had been defined by culture and circumstance: they were not man and woman, but Chinese and English, desperate and despairing.

But with hindsight, perhaps a part of him had anticipated their pairing. He knows enough of women, knows the changes that occur when they've made up their minds. Even without the aid of whisky, she had altered in the past few days. Shifted in her bearing, in her treatment of him somehow. He'd felt it happen gradually, like the slow movement of a weather vane. One moment pointing one direction: the next, swinging silently towards his own.

The alcohol terrifies him. He has never known anyone drink the way she does. Quietly. Privately. And with steely determination. As if she is locked in a nightly battle with the bottle. His stepfather liked to drink, could down bowl after bowl of *bai jiu* until his eyes watered and his lips shone. But his bouts of drinking were infrequent: like most people, he could not afford to indulge with any regularity. Alcohol, like everything else in their lives, was a luxury. Used to mark an occasion. It was not a way of survival. He wonders how she came to be this way. And whether many English people are the same. At once he dismisses this thought. He may be alien to this culture, but he can still recognise someone who is quietly perishing within their own life.

He turns back to survey her body. Was making love to her different from the other women he has known? They came together like a warm rush of tides: almost melting into one another. He was deliberately gentle at first, alarmed by her fragility, afraid that she might somehow break apart in his arms. But her urgency soon overcame him, for she seemed hungry for physical contact, starving even. Within moments, she had moved to bring him inside her, and they had remained locked together, coupled like animals, for what seemed like hours. He struggled not to come too soon; to give her what it was that she needed. Even afterwards, she kept him inside her, until his body had signalled exhaustion and withdrawn. By then she had fallen deeply into sleep.

He runs his eyes along the broad arch of her back. Her skin is the palest of whites. It seems almost translucent, like the inner membrane of an eggshell. His own skin seems tarnished by comparison. He has never been particularly drawn to the physical features of Western women. But there is something pure about her skin that fascinates him. She is heavier than he is, her figure more abundant than his own. Her breasts are generous, her hips wide and curving, the globes of her bottom large and rounded like heavy melons. When he first took her in his arms, her flesh was warm and thick and yielding, nothing like the angular tautness of the women he has known. Chinese women were built like songbirds in comparison: slender-boned, with relatively little fat or muscle to pad them out. A trait he had always liked in the past. But now he wonders why.

She smelled completely different too. That had taken him by surprise. Maybe it was the drink. Or what she ate. But it was entirely unfamiliar. He had buried his face in the hollows of her neck, underneath her arms, between her breasts, everywhere he could in an effort to capture the scent of her, to somehow make it his own. Inevitably, her mouth tasted of whisky, but his mind struggled to reach past that, knowing that if he didn't, he would not find his way into her essence. He needed desperately to know this woman, to make sense of what was happening. For him, last night had not been about sex – in spite of the fact that he had not slept with a woman in many months. He had grown accustomed to celibacy since leaving London and Jin, had almost revelled in it. But last night, though his body was desperate for release, his mind was all the while engaged in feeding her, understanding what it was that she required.

She rolls over and sighs in her sleep, one arm flung over her head across the pillow, her hand curling towards him. He shifts closer, studies her fingers. With a start, he realises that her fingernails resemble those of his sister: broad and relatively flat, with a tiny sliver of pale moon across the top. He has always thought that women's fingernails were like snowflakes: infinite in their varieties. He wonders how he could have missed hers earlier. His own nails are blunted and badly torn from cockling; they have only just begun to repair themselves. But he realises that, given the chance to grow, they would eventually look like hers. This strikes him as significant – the first point of physical convergence between them – perhaps the only one.

She stirs, breathes in deeply, exhales and opens her eyes. For the briefest instant she does not seem to know him. Then her face seems to cloud with turbulence, though whether it is anger or fear, or something else altogether, he cannot tell. Instinctively, he reaches out a hand and gently places his palm upon her cheek, as if to siphon away her feelings. He moves to take her in his arms, pulls her to his chest and cradles her as tightly as he can. They remain wound together for a long time, perhaps an hour or more, until she has drifted once again into sleep. He too falls off the edge of consciousness, lulled by the warmth of her body next to his, and he dreams that they are entwined like seaweed, floating together in a vast warm sea.

When she next wakes she is newly calm, as if he has stilled something within her. They do not speak, but once again she moves her hands across his body, and urgently manoeuvres him inside her. This time he lets himself go, takes his pleasure without thinking, and it is over quickly, both of them slick with sweat and desire. When they have finished, she perches on one elbow over him.

"Come," she says.

She takes him by the hand and pulls him through the kitchen to the bathroom, where she leans down and runs the tap, while he relieves himself in the loo.

They bathe together, something he has never done before, and he marvels at the fact of it. He sits behind her, her ample body pressed back against him, and he soaps her ivory flesh until he feels himself grow hard again. He positions her on top of him and comes into her from beneath, and she settles herself astride him comfortably, her breath coming in audible gasps. Afterwards, he buries his face in the wetness of her hair and the furrows of her neck, and realises that the scent of her is no longer strange to him. She turns her face to him.

"Hey," she says, in a voice thickened by desire. "What are you doing in my bath?"

Later she cooks him breakfast in her dressing gown, the first meal she has prepared for him since the morning after the accident. He tries to talk to her, to converse as normal people would, but each time his English fails him. He resolves to learn her language before he does anything else, for without language here he is nothing. When they have finished eating, she disappears into the bedroom and comes out a moment later wearing jeans and a sweater, clothes different from the ones she has worn before. She comes over to him with a smile.

"It's Saturday," she explains. "I don't have to work."

Nearly a week has flown by since the accident. A lifetime ago. Since coming to England, he has worked steadily regardless of the day. They did not have days off, only occasional times when work was not available for some reason, and when this happened everyone grew anxious and irritable. They did whatever they could to fill the time, rolling back the mattresses in their accommodation and playing cards or sometimes *mah jong*, if a set was available. When they were working they would lose track of time altogether, had no sense of days or dates for weeks on end. They had no weekends, no holidays. The only day that mattered to anyone was pay day.

Ironically, the accident had happened on the biggest holiday of the Chinese calendar: the eve of Spring Festival, the start of the lunar New Year. When they set off from Liverpool that afternoon, the mood had been decidedly glum. At home their families would be gathering around tables for festive meals, boiled sweets hidden inside dumplings, the start of fifteen days of celebration. Originally, there had been talk among them of a small party after they finished work, but these plans were quickly shelved when they'd been told they would be leaving later than usual, owing to disputes with local fisherman, who had set fire to their catch the day before. We'll go out late tomorrow, the gangmaster had told them. At dusk. After the locals have gone home. We don't want any more trouble.

During the long drive from Liverpool, the atmosphere in the van was unusually tense, everyone anticipating the angry shouts and reddened faces of the men who had attacked them the day before. They all realised what lay ahead: they would be expected to cockle under cover of darkness, with only the headlights from the vans to help them see. Cockling was difficult at the best of times, but doubly so at night, and in foul weather. When they'd first reached the fishing beds, the conditions hadn't been so bad, but the weather had quickly deteriorated, and soon the wind was whipping around them in savage gusts. Wen had lowered his head against the cold and worked steadily, trying hard not to dwell on the fact that halfway across the world his people would be celebrating.

He still remembers the moment of utter panic, of sheer terror, when they realised the tide had risen higher and more swiftly than usual – had in fact surrounded them, closing them off from shore.

His mind flies to Lin. Where is he now? At home his wife

and children will sprinkle ash across their threshold to catch his footprints, searching for a sign that he is with them, for after seven days the soul of the deceased must find its way home. But if Lin is truly dead he is a *shui gui* now: a water ghost, doomed to remain at the scene of his death until his spirit is released by someone else, a new victim. Wen looks down at his hands: scratched and scarred, they are the hands of a survivor. He is here and he is alive, but is he whole? Perhaps a part of him, like Lin, remains trapped beneath the waters of Morecambe Bay.

"Wen?" Angie is staring at him, her expression creased with concern. He raises his head, takes a deep breath. She takes a step forward and places a hand upon his arm.

"Are you okay?"

"Yes."

"I think we should go out." She nods her head towards the outside.

He frowns. He has not left the house since she brought him here. He has no shoes, no coat, no money, no passport. He looks down at his clothes: he is still wearing the black tracksuit she gave him the first night. She follows his gaze.

"Don't worry. We'll fix you up." She goes back into the bedroom and returns a minute later carrying a pair of rubber flipflops, some white socks and a large green anorak.

"Here. This will do for now."

He takes the things from her, but does not put them on, for he is not certain he is ready to face the outside world. But he does not know how to express this to her, to explain why he is reluctant to return to living.

"Okay?" she asks.

"Okay," he answers tentatively.

The drive takes nearly an hour, much of it on a vast highway. The day is cold and sunny, and as he looks out the windscreen, he begins to relax a little. He feels as if he is seeing England for the first time, through eyes that are somehow different. When they finally arrive, he sees that she has brought him to an enormous shopping complex just beside the motorway. The car park is crowded and she circles a few times before she finds a spot. She switches off the engine and turns to him, reading his uncertainties at once.

"Don't worry," she says. "We're miles from home. Here," she adds. "Put this on."

She hands him a bright red woolly hat. He pulls it on his head, then looks in the mirror. The hat looks ridiculous, and they both burst into laughter. But she is right; he is unlikely to be recognised wearing it.

They go to a large department store where she buys him jeans, shirts, underclothes and trainers. He blanches at the prices when he sees them, but she tells him not to worry. In all she spends nearly two hundred pounds. Twenty bags of cockles' worth. Or more than a week's wages at the restaurant. He cannot help but make these calculations: the numbers follow him everywhere. She pays with a credit card, as if this amount of money is nothing to her, and he realises that this is another enormous difference between them. No matter what his circumstances, he does not think he will ever treat money with such casual indifference.

Afterwards, they go for lunch in a restaurant. He orders a hamburger, the only food on the menu he has heard of, but when it comes he is dismayed. The meat is grey and flavourless; the bread it sits upon stale. A thin slice of pale pink tomato and a withered leaf of green lettuce sit sadly to one side, next to a pile of chips that look like fat fingers. His appetite vanishes; he finds that he can only nibble at the food. She has ordered something in a bowl with red beans and bits of meat in thick tomato sauce, which she eats only half of in the end. He is relieved when she eventually suggests they go. Once out of the restaurant, he starts to head towards the car park but she catches his arm.

"Wait. There's one more thing." She pulls him along the row of storefronts until they find a shop that sells books. Inside he trails along behind her through the aisles until she pauses in front of one section. She runs her fingers along the shelf and finally pulls out a fat plastic wrapped box, which she places in his hands.

"Here. You'll be wanting this."

He looks down. The cover says *Easy English for Beginners*. The box contains a book and a stack of eight CDs. Is such a thing possible? he wonders. To learn a language from a box? He thinks of his English teacher at school: Wang Laoshi, a short prim woman with thick glasses and hair pulled so tightly in a bun that you could see her scalp. Teacher Wang would rap sharply on her desk with a ruler whenever she was irritated or impatient. English, she had said, was like a giant crane that would lift China out of poverty. His marks were consistently low, while his sister came top of the class.

After each exam, Teacher Wang would frown at him with exasperation. "How is it that the same seed produces such a different flower?" she would ask.

"Okay," he tells Angie. She hears the hesitation in his voice.

"Please. You must try."

"Yes." He struggles to erase the doubt from his voice. He wants to reassure her, to let her know that he will do his best. But most of all, he wants to reassure himself.

It is almost dark by the time they reach her house, and he feels an enormous sense of relief as he passes through the front hall into the sitting room that has become his home. He watches as she puts the clothes they have bought him in the bedroom. His eyes drift to the corner of the sitting room, where the bedding he has slept on this past week sits in a carefully folded pile. She comes out of the bedroom and her eyes follow his to the bedding. She stops short, the colour draining from her face.

"I didn't mean..." She pauses, her voice unsteady, and motions with one hand towards the bedroom. She takes a deep breath and calms herself.

"You can do what you like," she murmurs. She walks into the kitchen and reaches down under the sink for the whisky, then pulls a glass down from the shelf and fills it. He follows her into the kitchen, sees her hands tremble as she lifts the glass, and wonders again what beast has taken hold of her, and why. She takes a large drink, nearly half the glass, then turns to him, her expression vaguely defiant. They stand staring at each other for a long moment.

"Okay," he says then.

"Okay," she replies.

They have reached some sort of agreement, but he does not know what it signifies.

September 2004

The day after her trip to Morecambe Bay, Lili does not see Jin until the evening. But from the moment she wakes, the image of Jin and Wen in front of the statue smoulders inside her. She knows that Jin is withholding information from her. What she needs to uncover is the depth of her deception. That night when Jin returns home from teaching, Lili is at the counter making a mug of instant noodles. Jin greets her matter-of-factly, drops her bag on the floor, and flops backwards onto the bed.

"I'm exhausted," she says, throwing an arm over her eyes to shield them from the bare light bulb overhead. After a minute, she lifts her arm and squints at Lili.

"Where were you yesterday?" she asks pointedly. "You were out all day." Lili picks up the mug and moves to the tiny round table, sitting down in a chair opposite the bed. She feels her heart begin to race.

"I went to Morecambe Bay."

At once Jin sits up, her expression stunned.

"Why?"

Lili stirs the steaming mug of noodles slowly with a spoon. She speaks in a carefully modulated tone.

"Because I wanted to see it for myself. The place where Wen died. Didn't you?"

Jin shakes her head.

"No," she says. "Not at all."

"So you never went there?" Lili presses her. "Not even before?"

"Before what?" Jin frowns.

"Before his death. To visit."

"He didn't want me to visit," says Jin coldly. She rises and goes to the counter, rummaging in the cupboards. Lili watches her. *Is it just this one, small thing that Jin conceals?* she wonders. *Or something far bigger?* Jin finds a packet of biscuits and takes one out, popping it in her mouth.

"So what was it like?" she asks, chewing. She leans back against the counter, her long legs stretching out across the floor. Lili pauses, choosing her words with care.

"It was strange. And unfamiliar. Like travelling to another planet."

"Of course it was unfamiliar," Jin says with a snort of disdain. "What did you expect?"

"I don't know. Some sign that he was there, I guess. I wanted to feel his presence. But I couldn't."

"You need to let go of him." Jin's voice is laced with disapproval.

Lili frowns. She knows that she will keep Wen with her always. Why shouldn't she? Surely that is her right? He was her twin: her *shuang bao tai*.

"He was my twin," she ventures defensively.

"No," says Jin. "He was more than that."

Lili feels the blood rush to her face.

"You're one to talk. You slept with him for months! And now it's like he never existed. You don't even mourn him properly," she says bitterly.

"No. Perhaps not. Not like you, at any rate. You've been mourning Wen all your life."

"What do you mean?" Lili asks uneasily.

"That's why you never dated anyone at university. Why you stayed a virgin all these years."

"Don't be ridiculous!"

"He was never going to be yours," says Jin bluntly.

Lili stares at her in complete disbelief.

"It wasn't like that."

"Well, let me tell you something about your precious brother. He was massively in debt to the snakeheads. It would have taken him years to pay them off. But I'll bet he never told you that."

"Wen had no secrets from me," says Lili guardedly. "I knew he'd gone to snakeheads to arrange his passage to the UK."

"And do you know what he offered them as security?"

Lili stares at Jin, the question hanging in the air between them. She feels as if she's being dragged into a dark tunnel. But it is too late. In front of her, the mug of noodles slowly congeals; the smell makes her feel ill.

"You," says Jin, in a quietly triumphant tone. "He offered you. And your precious chastity. So I wouldn't save yourself for his sake. Because he would never have done the same for you."

Lili struggles to make sense of her words. There is a hot ringing in her ears. In front of her, the noodles begin to blur. She rises a little unsteadily, and without a word, she grabs her handbag and jacket and pushes past Jin out the door. Jin calls out to her, her tone suddenly contrite.

"Lili, wait!"

But Lili is already halfway down the darkened hallway. She can hear Jin calling her name again, but soon she is out on the dark pavement, running along the road towards the high street. She doesn't stop until she reaches the shops, where she stands in front of the newsagent, staring down at the plate glass window. Behind her, buses lurch along the busy road. Jin has lied to her in the past, more than once. But this time she may be telling the truth.

Lili knew that Wen had run up debts, though he had never shared the details with her. When he first went to the snakeheads, she questioned him about how he would repay them. He told her not to worry, said that England was awash with money – it would come quickly and easily. He could earn enough to repay his debts and buy a house upon his return. A house that they could share, he had said, perhaps with a garden where they could grow their own vegetables, like the one their stepmother had kept before she died. He had seemed so optimistic, and Lili had wanted so much to believe him. The idea of the house delighted her: a place where she and Wen could live for ever, free from the demands of the outside world. A haven. She desperately wanted to believe that such a place existed.

But it didn't. She knows that now. How naïve she had been. Jin was right. She had saved herself all these years for nothing. Wen was gone. And now she was alone.

She looks at her watch. It is nearly ten o'clock. She has no desire to return to Jin's flat. And nowhere else to go. She turns and sees a bus crawl forward to a stop just in front of her. It lurches to a halt and the doors open, disgorging a string of tired-looking passengers. With a start, she sees that it is a No. 9, the bus she takes to Hammersmith. It is a sign, she thinks. She leaps on board without another thought, and the doors close behind her.

Half an hour later, she arrives at the takeaway where Johnny works. A small knot of apprehension has formed in her stomach. She pauses just outside the window, uncertain what she will say. Inside she can see Johnny serving two young blonde women. Lili understands at once that they are flirting with him, casting knowing glances at each other and laughing at his jokes. Suddenly she feels as if she is seeing him for the first time; that his lean frame and chiselled good looks are something she should covet. She watches as he hands a white polystyrene container to one of the blonde girls and takes her money, his easy smile causing an abrupt pang of jealousy. He glances through the window just then, and she sees a brief flicker of disapproval cross his face. She waits until the two girls have pushed past her out the door before stepping inside and moving forward to the counter. Johnny picks up a damp cloth and slowly wipes the surface, eyeing her.

"Hey," she says with a nervous smile.

"Hey," he replies cautiously.

"I guess you weren't expecting me."

"You guessed right," he says. He folds the cloth methodically and lays it to one side, then leans back against the counter behind him and crosses his arms.

"I came to apologise. For yesterday." She waits for his response. Johnny frowns slightly, then shrugs.

"Apology accepted," he says evenly.

"There's something else," Lili continues nervously. She looks down at the pale brown linoleum floor: a long crack runs the length of the room.

"Go on," says Johnny.

"It wasn't just about him," she says, raising her eyes. "It was about you, too."

Johnny stares at her for a long moment. She feels her face flush.

"Okay," he says in English. His tone has softened slightly, and Lili feels a rush of relief. She smiles.

"Maybe we can go for a drink later," she says tentatively. "When you get off."

Johnny looks down at his watch, then back up at her. "It's your lucky day," he says.

•

They go to a nearby pub, the first Lili has been to since arriving in London. It is large and dark and strangely quiet, with a dozen people scattered about and a snooker table at the rear. They slide into a dark red booth off to one side that smells of old cigarette smoke and sour lager. Lili looks around, her spirits dampened by the drab room.

"Beer?" Johnny asks.

Lili hesitates. She is going to need something stronger.

"Could I have whisky?" she asks.

Johnny's eyebrows shoot up.

"Sure," he replies. She watches as he approaches the bar and orders, returning a minute later with two small glasses of whisky. He hands her one and slides into the booth opposite her.

"*Gan bei*," he says.

Lili picks up the glass of amber liquid and takes a small sip. The whisky burns on her lips. Then she takes a deep breath and drains the glass, feels it rocket down her throat to her stomach. Johnny looks at her with surprise.

"I was only joking," he says.

"I wasn't," she replies.

He gives a slow smile of realisation, then picks up his glass and drains it. Lili reaches for his glass and stands up.

"I'll get the next one," she says.

Three drinks later, they decide to return to Johnny's room in Ealing, catching a No. 11 bus just outside the pub. The bus is crowded and they are forced to stand. As the bus rounds a corner, Lili leans into him and Johnny thrusts a hand into the back pocket of her jeans, causing her insides to clench with desire. She raises her face to his, studies the sparse patch of whiskers on his chin, and thinks that after four whiskies things do not seem so very difficult. She is a fish being carried along on the tide, certain now that she wants this, certain that it is the right thing for her to do. She should not remain a virgin any longer – not another second, not another minute, not another hour. Even Wen would not want her to die an old maid, she thinks. But the sudden thought of Wen makes her head reel. She squeezes her eyes shut; she must not think of him now.

The house Johnny shares with other Chinese students is in a run-down neighbourhood: a terraced house of brick on a row with many others. When they enter, they walk straight into a small, dank sitting room, dark except for the flickering light of a television set. A clutch of young men are ranged across a battered dark blue sofa and they raise their eyes curiously to Lili as Johnny waves and pulls her past them into the tiny kitchen beyond. Behind her, she hears them titter with laughter.

"Don't mind them," he murmurs into her ear. "They're just jealous," he adds with a grin.

She has only the briefest glance of the kitchen as he pulls her along: a harsh fluorescent light, chipped white formica, dull brown tiles, and a sink piled high with dirty dishes. A tiny corridor leads off the rear of the kitchen, with a door at the end. Johnny pulls her through the door into the room beyond and quickly shuts it behind them. She looks around at his room: small, sparsely furnished, with a threadbare dark green carpet and a double mattress on the floor in the corner. Opposite the wall is a cheap white desk piled high with books and papers. The bed is a tangled mass of pale green sheets. Johnny's clothes are strewn about the room.

"Sorry about the mess," he says apologetically. He reaches down and turns on a lamp beside the bed, and begins to gather up the clothing hurriedly. Watching him, Lili feels a creeping sense of dismay, as if once again her purpose has been blighted by the shabby reality of the room. But she is determined to finish what she started, so she reaches out and grabs hold of his shirt. Johnny turns around, reading her meaning instantly. He tosses the clothes he has gathered into the corner, and pulls her to him. Gratefully, she surrenders herself to his embrace: his mouth is warm and urgent upon hers, the smell and taste of whisky mixing with his own unfamiliar male scent. She feels his hands roam across her body, pulling at the confines of her shirt, moving up to the front of her bra, then sliding down inside her jeans. Lili allows herself to be carried along by the wave of passion that has engulfed them. It all happens so quickly that she is amazed – amazed that it takes no time at all to undo a lifetime of chastity. Within moments, they are both naked and lying down on the mattress, Johnny poised on top of her, his knees thrusting her thighs apart, the hard part of him probing her darkest place. He enters her quickly and decisively, seemingly unaware of her inexperience, though at the last instant she gives a little cry of pain and surprise. Johnny pauses, looking down at her with confusion.

"Lili," he whispers in the half-light. "*Zen mo le?*"

For a moment she cannot speak. Johnny pulls back.

"Are you all right?"

She looks up at him, at his too-handsome features, and

wonders how she came to be in the bed of a stranger on the far side of the world. But then she remembers that her life is not what she had once imagined; that it is full of sharp edges and unexpected turns and moments of surrender.

"*Bie ting*," she says, pulling Johnny in deeper. *Don't stop.*

•

Hours later, when she wakes, the room is cold. Johnny's arm lies draped across her waist: she can feel the dead weight of it pressing on her belly. She eases out from under him and turns to look at his face. Asleep, he looks younger somehow, and exposed. They had made love twice before he had gathered her in his arms and succumbed to sleep. She lay awake for what felt like hours, the wetness of him between her thighs. Now she wonders whether she is somehow changed. She ponders this; decides she does not feel any different. Perhaps chastity is nothing but an empty myth. A feminine ideal that has no basis in reality. At any rate, part of her is relieved to be free of its burden.

She considers her situation: she cannot remain here with Johnny in a house full of young men. Nor is she anxious to return to Jin's bedsit, where the atmosphere is bound to be even worse than before. She will have to find her own place to live, she decides, regardless of the cost. Perhaps Fay can help. She eases herself silently out of Johnny's bed and begins to dress herself as quietly as possible, but inevitably he stirs, rolling over sleepily.

"Lili?"

"I have to go to work," she says. "I'm sorry," she adds.

Johnny raises himself up on one elbow and looks at her with a quizzical smile.

"For what?"

Lili freezes, uncertain of her answer. She does not know what her feelings are for Johnny; indeed, she does not know whether she feels anything for him at all. From the first she has deceived him, and last night was no different. Johnny watches her closely; he seems to sense her discomfort.

"Hey," he says with a smile. "No worries. I'll see you later."

"Okay," she replies gratefully, slipping out the bedroom door.

March 2004

The dawn no longer frightens her. Angie used to dread the sickening, sober start of each new day. But now, even before she opens her eyes, she knows that Wen is there, can sense the warm weight of him next to her upon the mattress, can hear the steady rhythm of his breath. His presence is like a charm: one that soothes and calms and wards off evil.

It had been different with her husband. For a time in her first year of marriage, she fooled herself into thinking she was fine. But it wasn't long before she realised that she was struggling to suppress the darkness in herself, and the realisation that her husband did not wage such battles only made it worse. She could not explain to him the sheer effort required each day to live: he would not have understood. The fact of this drove a wedge between them, and over time, she filled it with drink.

The marriage ended badly. One night they argued in a

restaurant. For some months he'd been pressing her to start a family, a prospect that terrified her, though she could not articulate why. She only knew that her response was both visceral and instinctive. Struggling to explain, she reached a hand out to refill her wine glass and he had placed his own over the bottle, stopping her. Furious, she lost her temper and stormed out of the restaurant. She got in her car and drove home too fast, veering out of control near an embankment and running straight into a tree. She was knocked unconscious, and when she came to she was in hospital, her husband at her side.

He was sorry, he told her. They would wait to start a family – he could see she was not ready. Half an hour later, a young male doctor appeared, clutching a clipboard with test results. When he saw her husband, he told them at once how sorry he was for their loss. Angie stared up at him, confused.

"I thought you'd been informed," the young doctor stammered. "You lost the baby in the accident."

"What baby?" asked her husband.

There was an awful moment when both men turned to her, as if she was privy to some great deception.

"I don't understand," she said.

"You were twelve weeks pregnant," the doctor explained, colouring. "I assumed you knew."

Angie shook her head slowly.

"How could you not know?" her husband asked in a shocked voice.

How indeed, she thought? Her periods came and went –

she'd never tracked them. She'd been on the pill since she was seventeen, though drink had made her sloppy these past six months. Sensing their discomfort, the young doctor hastily made his excuses and left them alone. Her husband stared at her, his expression veering from bewilderment to betrayal.

"How could you not have known?" he asked again.

•

The marriage foundered in that moment. Afterwards, her husband could barely bring himself to speak to her. He was so angry that two days later, when she was discharged from hospital, he'd already moved his things out of their flat. Her immediate reaction had been relief. She felt no sadness at the end of her marriage, though she mourned the loss of the baby she'd never known was there. She wondered if she was lacking some vital piece of chemistry: a maternal gene, perhaps, that would have enabled its detection. It would not surprise her, given her own mother's inability to mother.

As a child, Angie had been afraid of the dark – terrified of an unnamed beast that lay in wait for her beneath her bed. By the age of eight, she woke nightly in tears. Unable to cope, her mother took her to the doctor and demanded sleeping pills. When he refused, her mother found a private clinic, but this time she went alone. The unsuspecting doctor nodded sympathetically when she spoke of her prolonged battle with insomnia, and wrote her a six-month prescription. Each night, Angie's mother carefully chopped a pill in half and ground it to a powder, mixing it with chocolate syrup. The pills did not stop Angie's nightmares. But she slept through the night, waking each morning exhausted by the demons that held her fast.

By adolescence, she'd grown out of such fears. But it wasn't long before a new beast appeared. This time it did not lurk beneath her bed, but crawled right inside her. Eventually she discovered that alcohol subdued it. Drink became her safeguard, and her reward for getting through another day. Angie had never been afraid of death; it was life she found terrifying. When she dragged Wen from the bay that night – frozen, half-drowned, terrified – it was the fear that she recognised, the fear that she was drawn to.

•

Several weeks after Wen's arrival, her brother Ray telephones her at work. She has not heard from him in six months, and at once his voice drags her back in time.

"It's me," he says. "I've got the papers through. Can we meet?"

She feels the familiar tightness in her gut.

"Angie?"

"Yeah?"

"What about tomorrow night? I'll come to you," he offers.

"No," she says quickly.

"When?"

"Give me a few weeks."

There is a long pause on the line. She knows that he does not wish to press her.

"We can finish this, Angie. Draw a line beneath it."

He speaks of their mother, and of her terrible, vengeful

death. A death that implicated them both somehow, though she is not sure how or why they came to be the guilty ones.

"I know."

"So name a day."

"I can't, Ray. Not right now."

He sighs. Again there is a silence. When he speaks his tone is tentative, conciliatory.

"Are you okay?"

They both know he is breaking the rules. Their relationship is based on circumspection, on the understanding that they will not delve too deeply in each other's lives. Ray does not question her drinking, while she ignores his tawdry affairs and unorthodox business dealings. This has been true ever since their youth, ever since they first held secrets from each other.

"I'm fine," she replies.

"Okay. Let me know when."

"I will."

She puts down the phone. She is not ready yet. Not ready to mix the past with the present, nor to expose Wen to the wider world. She is certainly not ready to introduce him to the remnants of her family.

October 2004

Before her afternoon class, Lili knocks on the door of Fay's office. Fay calls out for her to enter, then motions for her to sit. The older woman lights a cigarette and leans back in her chair, her knees bulging inside her black tights, while Lili explains her purpose.

"Housing is a big problem in London," says Fay, exhaling. "The biggest, in fact. But the further out you go, the cheaper it gets."

"Oh," says Lili. She wonders how far out Fay means. Beyond Heathrow? Or maybe south, as far as the coast?

"We don't have room here to put up teachers, if that's what you're thinking," says Fay flatly.

"No. Of course not." Lili colours.

"I thought you were staying with Jin," Fay adds.

Lili hesitates. "I don't want to trouble her any longer."

Fay takes a deep drag on the cigarette, eyeing her.

"What you need," she says exhaling, "is a boyfriend."

Lili frowns. "Why?"

"To move in with," explains Fay, waving the cigarette in the air. "You're young. And pretty. Shouldn't be too difficult." She leans forward with a knowing smile. "English men love Chinese girls," she says confidingly. "As long as you know how to play the part."

Lili looks at her, uncertain of her meaning. Fay shrugs.

"We can all play the part if we need to," Fay says matter-of-factly. "It's called survival."

•

After her meeting with Fay, Lili resigns herself to the possibility of sleeping at Jin's flat that evening. It could take her days to find her own room. So she might as well make the best of things in the meantime. She takes the bus from Sheep Pen to Notting Mountain, as it is the day of her after-school class with May and the others. Today, she resolves, she will try to make the class as fun as possible, and make sure to learn their names properly. She stops at a shop and buys two packets of chocolate biscuits, just in case. All the time Fay's last words are ringing in her head. She has never thought much about survival in the past. Now she thinks of little else.

After two wrong turns in the corridors, it takes her several minutes to find the classroom. When she finally arrives, May and the other children are already waiting for her. There are two new children, a boy and a girl, who are seated in the front row, while the others lurk restlessly in the chairs behind.

"Hello," says Lili. "I am sorry to be late," she adds.

"Were you lost?" asks one of the blonde girls with a raised eyebrow.

"The school is very big," says Lili apologetically. Actually it is not so big, just a baffling series of twisting corridors and stairways, but she feels she must say something to explain. The two blonde girls exchange a quick smirking glance, then turn back to her.

"So what are we doing today?" says one of them. Lili takes a deep breath. *Surviving*, she thinks.

"Please, could you tell me your names?"

Ten minutes later, she is none the wiser. Their names are hopelessly confusing. One of the girls has a name she has never heard before, but which sounds a little like the word imagine. When she tries to repeat it, the entire class bursts into giggles. The new boy is called Jacob, a word she finds almost impossible to pronounce. Even more alarmingly, the fat boy is called Thaddeus, while the blonde girls are called Freya and Olivia. She makes each of them write their names down on a sheet of paper, then keeps it in front of her, but the letters seem to dance about on the page, mocking her with their difficulty. Of the six names on the list, only May's is comprehensible. She finds the fact of this depressing.

Still, they manage to get through the rest of the hour without incident, and the chocolate biscuits ease the last ten minutes. After class, Lili walks them in a line to the school's front door, where she dispenses with them quickly enough. All except May, who is left waiting with her once again. May looks at her a little sheepishly.

"He promised to be on time today," she says.

"It's okay. Did you like the class?" May shrugs.

"I'd like it better if the others weren't there."

"Oh." Lili frowns.

"I'd learn faster too," adds May. "If it was just you and me."

Just then Adrian comes rushing up along the pavement.

"Sorry," he calls out. "Very sorry. I meant to be on time today."

He comes to an abrupt halt on the steps, and lets out a sigh.

"You're late." says May.

"I apologise," he says pointedly.

"Anyway, did you ask her?"

"Why should I ask her? It was your idea," May says grumpily. Adrian smiles and colours a little, turning to Lili.

"We were wondering if you would like to come to dinner," he says. "At our house."

"You were wondering," mumbles May.

"Tonight?" asks Lili.

"Unless you're busy, of course," adds Adrian hastily. "Then we could make it next week. Or the week after. We just thought it would be nice. To get to know you better." He shrugs.

"You thought it would be nice," says May quietly, stubbing at the step with her shoe.

"We both thought it would be nice," says Adrian, shooting May a glance.

"Yes," says Lili. "I am free. Thank you."

May raises her eyes and looks intently at her, as if she is trying to divine whether Lili is telling the truth.

"Excellent," says Adrian.

He explains that they live twenty minutes' walk from the school, in a small industrial building that used to house a printing shop. On the way he chats with Lili, explaining that he is an architect, and that the house is a little unusual by London standards. When they arrive, she sees it is tucked away in the corner of a small garden square, the entrance almost hidden. Lili steps inside a long narrow corridor with a low ceiling and a series of square skylights, with rooms leading off to the left. May disappears into the first one, which has a sliding wooden door. Lili catches a glimpse of a bed on stilts with a small wooden slide running to the floor, and a vast array of soft toys piled up underneath, before May pulls the sliding door closed, shutting off her view.

Adrian leads her down the hallway to the kitchen, which is large and airy and modern, with a square glass table and four chairs in the centre.

"We converted the building ourselves ten years ago," he explains. "My wife and I. It used to be a printworks."

"What happened to her?" Lili asks.

"She died of breast cancer. It was very fast. Less than four months after we got the diagnosis." He breaks off and shrugs.

"I'm sorry," says Lili.

"It seems a long time ago now. My wife was fortunate enough to have three years with May. We adopted her from the mainland when she was six months old."

"Six months," murmurs Lili. "So young."

"Yes. We were lucky. It can take years to get a Chinese baby, but in our case it all moved very quickly. Like clockwork." Adrian smiles.

Lili does not quite understand. Like clocks?

"Where did she come from?"

"Shanxi Province. An orphanage there."

"You went there?"

"Yes. Well. Very briefly. We collected her from there and then flew to Guangzhou to apply for her passport. It took about two weeks altogether."

"So fast," murmurs Lili. Two weeks to travel to a strange country, find a child and make her your own.

"Sian and I had hoped to take her back when she was older," he continues. "To visit the orphanage. But..." He stops and shrugs. "May doesn't really remember her now. But Sian adored May. She had so much more mothering to do. I think that was the hardest thing for her: that she was given a chance to be a second mother to this child, and that somehow she was failing her by dying."

Adrian stops short then, just as May comes into the room. May looks from Adrian to Lili. The last word hangs heavily in the air, threatening to swallow them all.

"You're talking about me, aren't you?" says May.

"I was just telling Lili how lucky you are: you had two mothers who loved you, not one."

May stares at him for a moment. "What's for dinner?" she asks.

"Pasta," he replies.

May frowns. "Don't you think she wants Chinese food?" May nods her head at Lili.

"I don't know. Why don't you ask her?" says Adrian.

May turns to her.

"I like pasta," says Lili quickly. "Italian food is very popular in China now."

May studies her. "Do you know how to use chopsticks?"

"Of course," Lili smiles.

"I just learned. But I'm not very good."

"Maybe I can help you," says Lili.

"See?" says Adrian to May. "I told you."

An hour later, they are drinking red wine and eating spaghetti with chopsticks. Lili shows them how to eat noodles in the Chinese manner, placing one end of the noodle in her mouth and sucking up the rest, which brings peals of giggles from May.

"I get told off when I slurp!" she cries.

"Not any more," says Adrian. "At least not when you're at home," he adds.

"So people do not eat noodles like this here?" asks Lili.

"No!" shouts May. "It's mega-rude to slurp!"

"Mega?" Lili asks, uncomprehending.

"She means very," explains Adrian. "Well, it's quite rude, at any rate."

"Everything is different here," says Lili. "Many things seem the same, but they are not."

"You're not different," says May. "Not different from me."

Lili smiles, and exchanges a quick glance with Adrian, who raises an eyebrow.

"Thank you," she says to May.

"Where do you live?" asks May.

"I stay with a friend in Hounslow," says Lili. "But I am looking for a room to live in."

May opens her eyes wide and looks at Adrian, who sets down his chopsticks and frowns at her slightly. May begins to hop up and down in her chair.

"May," he says doubtfully.

"We have a room!" she cries.

"I don't think she would be interested," murmurs Adrian.

Lili looks at him enquiringly.

"It's very small," he adds.

"We used to have an au pair," says May. "From Poland. She was horrible!"

Adrian shrugs. "She was pretty dreadful," he concedes.

"She never washed her hair! It was really greasy! And there were white things in it!"

"May! Too much information," he admonishes with a frown. He looks at Lili.

"It didn't work out," he explains. "I thought it would be good for May, but —"

"She was useless," interrupts May. "All she ever did was watch TV on the sofa and eat crisps."

"Not one of my better decisions," admits Adrian with a sigh.

"It must be difficult," says Lili. "Being just one parent."

Adrian glances quickly at May, who has suddenly grown quiet.

"We manage," says Adrian, smiling. "Don't we, May?"

May nods earnestly, her eyebrows knit together. At once Lili regrets her comment.

"Do you want to see the room?" asks May suddenly.

Lili looks from the child to her father uncertainly. Adrian hesitates, his expression guarded.

"Well," he says slowly. "May would certainly learn more Chinese if you lived here."

"Come on!" May jumps up and grabs Lili's hand, pulling her down the hallway.

The room is up a tiny flight of stairs halfway down the corridor. May scrambles up the stairs ahead of Lili and dashes into a small room at the top, dancing about expectantly. Lili pauses in the doorway. The room is indeed small, perhaps ten feet by eight feet, with a sloping ceiling fitted with a levered window. A single wooden bed with a pale blue duvet sits in the corner, opposite a small chest of drawers. Beside the bed is a cast-iron bedside table with a reading lamp, and on the floor is a brightly coloured circular rug. May's eyes follow Lili's around the room.

"Do you like the rug?" she asks. "We bought it at Ikea. I chose it!"

"The rug is very nice," says Lili. Indeed, she thinks, the room is perfect. Much nicer than anything she could afford, she is certain. Adrian appears on the stairs behind her and she turns to him expectantly.

"Well?" he asks. "What do you think?"

"The room is wonderful," says Lili.

"Well, I don't know about wonderful. But we did try to make it look cosy, didn't we, May?"

"Does that mean you'll stay?" asks May, hopping about excitedly and grabbing Lili's hand. Lili pauses. She would love to live in this room. She turns back to Adrian, her eyes hopeful.

"I'm sure we could work something out," he says quietly.

"Thank you," she says.

They agree that Lili will live for free in the room in exchange for tutoring May in the evenings and collecting her from school on the two days she is not teaching.

"I can't really afford to pay you," Adrian says to Lili, refilling her wine glass. "Money is a little tight right now."

"No," insists Lili. "To live in this room is enough. Much better than any room I could find."

"How long are you planning to stay in London?" asks Adrian.

Until I find Wen, she thinks.

"I do not know," she says evasively.

"But you aren't planning to go back any time soon?" he asks cautiously. "It's just that, for May's sake, too much change can be difficult."

"No," says Lili quickly. "Not soon. I will stay for one year. At least."

Adrian relaxes visibly.

"Okay," he says, raising his wine glass in a sort of toast. "One year it is."

March 2004

How long will you stay in Britain? asks the man on the CD. *I will stay for three months*, replies the woman.

When he first arrived in England, Wen had no notion of how long he would remain. Two years, three years, five? His future did not stretch beyond a brief horizon. But now, the life he left behind in China seems impossibly distant, as if he is peering at it through the wrong end of a telescope. As if it is someone else's altogether. He has no idea whether he will find his way back to that life again.

It is very cold outside today, says the woman. Wen repeats her words mechanically. He has spent most of the day listening to *Easy English For Beginners*. In Unit One the man and woman discuss a variety of topics: school, housing, weather, transport. Wen struggles to follow their dialogue – not least, because nothing in his experience relates to it. The woman on the CD is a student from Italy: she flew to London from

Rome and took a train to Brighton, where she lives in a dormitory with others and attends morning classes at a language school. In the afternoons, she and her friends go to the beach or visit nearby places of interest.

They do not need to work, apparently. So they must be rich, Wen concludes. *I love to go shopping by the pier*, says the woman. Wen practically chokes on these words. Would he ever use them? He hits the power button, silencing the woman, and thinks of the English he has learned since he first arrived in Dover last year. Though he can barely hold a conversation, he has built up a highly specialised vocabulary during his time here. He compiles a mental list, dividing the words into neat categories of experience. Words relating to fishing: *cockle, tide, quicksand*. Those having to do with money: *wage, tax, fee, bribe*. Words of anger learned from locals: *bastard, fuck off, chink*. Words relating to his status: *illegal, police, deport*. And since the accident, a new string of words: *death, drown, survivor*. Each day he understands a little more of what Angie says, though her conversation bears little resemblance to the dialogue on the CD. Especially after she's been drinking.

Still, he must try. He wishes he could jump forward in time: if he worked hard, a year from now he could be fluent. To speak English easily and correctly: to be able to joke, debate and flatter. What entitlements would this bring? he wonders. Would he feel as if he belonged? He would still be illegal. And he would still owe money to the snakeheads that brought him out of China. And he would still look Chinese. So the answer is no. It is not just English he must wrestle with. There is much more about his life here that doesn't fit.

But inside this house – with her – he has achieved a sort of harmony. Even with the barrier of language, he no longer feels out of kilter. He and Angie exist in a sort of bubble, free from the constraints of either culture. How has this happened so quickly? he wonders. Is it the fact that they lie entwined each night, skin to skin, and taste each other's fluids? Or is it something that goes beyond nakedness? A place of doubt that each has glimpsed inside the other. In truth, he doesn't know. But if he can achieve this here, with her, surely it must be possible in the outside world. If that is what he wants – right now he doesn't know.

Something else is happening. His own culture is receding, like an outgoing tide. He feels increasingly estranged from his people, a process that started long before the accident. From the moment he left China, he sensed that he was different from other illegal Chinese. His reasons for leaving set him apart. It wasn't desperation that drove him abroad. Nor would he have called it opportunity. It was more akin to hope. He was searching for something that lay outside the boundaries of his experience. In another time, perhaps he would have been an explorer, or a wanderer. Or possibly a sage. But such avenues were not open to him, so he took the only route that was. He made a giant leap into the unknown, a leap that nearly took him to the bottom of the sea.

When he first made contact with Old Fu, the snakehead recruiter who organised his passage to the UK, the old man sat him down in the courtyard of a small tea house, lit a cigarette and scrutinised him from head to toe. Wen remembers how his heart raced as the snakehead looked him over. He had not anticipated any difficulty: was this not a straightforward business arrangement? But in retrospect he realised it was the first of many tests.

After a minute, Old Fu hawked loudly, spat onto the ground and asked him a series of questions. Was he prepared to work hard and to suffer? To endure privation for months on end during the long journey overland? Was he strong, both in body and in mind? Would he break easily under pressure? Old Fu weighed his answers carefully, as if he were interviewing him for a job. After all, Old Fu explained, spreading his hands, he was making an investment. As with any investment, he needed to gauge the level of risk.

Old Fu was in his late fifties. He had nicotine-stained teeth, a pot belly, and wore a brown plaid jacket with a foreign cut that had nevertheless seen better days. His steel-grey hair was like a coarse brush, and his eyes were ringed with tiredness. As he lit a second foreign cigarette, he leaned back in his chair and relaxed, and Wen understood that he had cleared the first hurdle. Old Fu explained that he had been in business many years, describing himself as something of an economic pioneer. He had started out trading textiles in the late eighties to Czechoslovakia, but after a decade of exporting handbags, he had graduated to human cargo. The risks were higher, he explained, but so were the profits. At one point, the old man leaned forward and tapped his lighter on the wooden table for emphasis. He was like a Wall Street broker, he said: he traded in human futures. And in all his years transporting people, he added proudly, he had yet to lose one.

The price was 35,000 US dollars. "Take it or leave it," Old Fu declared. "There are plenty more like you," he added with a shrug. Wen asked about the method of payment. Five thousand must be paid up front, said Old Fu, the balance by his relatives once he had arrived safely in England. Wen stared down at the bloated tea leaves nestled in the bottom of his cup, pondering his response.

"I can get the five thousand," he said finally. "But the rest is a problem."

"Borrow it."

"From who?"

Old Fu shrugged. "Whoever. Family. Friends."

"My friends are labourers. They have nothing. Less than nothing."

"Your family then."

"I have no family."

Old Fu leaned back in his chair and narrowed his gaze in disbelief. "No family at all?"

"We were orphaned in the earthquake."

"We?"

Wen hesitated, his heart sinking. "My sister and I."

"Ah. So you have a sister."

"Yes. But she has no money to speak of."

"Is she married?"

"No."

"How old is she?"

"Twenty-seven."

Old Fu raised an eyebrow. "And single? Why? Is something wrong with her?"

"My sister is fine," Wen said testily. "She's particular, that's all."

"If the water is too clear, the fish will not thrive," replied Old Fu elliptically.

"What's your meaning?"

Old Fu shrugged. "That your sister may need to be less choosy in future."

"Why?"

"She's not the sort of collateral we're used to. But in the absence of anything else, she'll have to do."

"You can't use my sister as collateral!"

"Then borrow the money. Go to a moneylender."

"And pay treble the interest? Why can't I work off my debt in Britain?"

"That's not the way we do things."

Wen stared at him, frustrated. He had not expected the old man to be so hard-nosed. But these were snakeheads, he reminded himself. The only thing they understood was money.

"I'm honest. And a good worker. I'll work harder than the others," he offered.

"Why should I make an exception for you? I've got a dozen other people waiting for transport."

"Because I'm good for it."

"Then you've no cause for concern, have you?" said Old

Fu. He leaned forward and stubbed out his cigarette. "No collateral. No loan," he said firmly.

Wen hesitated, his thoughts spinning. In his mind he was already bound for Britain. He would have to find a way.

"Her name is Mei Ling," he said finally. "Zhang Mei Ling. She's a schoolteacher."

"Where?"

"Tangshan No. 35 Middle School." Wen lied without hesitation, giving Old Fu the first thing that popped into his mind: the name of his old school.

"Fine."

"But if you lay a hand on her I'll kill you," he said.

"Honour your debt and we won't have to," said Old Fu.

As they rose to leave, the old man leaned forward and placed both hands on the table. "Don't think for a moment that you can evade us once you get to Britain," he said intently. "Our organisation is like the long tail of a dragon. No matter where you go, we will find you."

Over the ensuing weeks, throughout his negotiations, Wen was careful not to give them any information that might lead to Lili. She would be shocked to learn of his plans to go abroad; she would be even more appalled if she knew he had involved her in his dealings. Most importantly, he needed to protect her. Though he had every intention of making good on his bond, he did not want to put Lili at risk, however remotely. She was young, attractive and unmarried: a valuable commodity in today's China, where men outnumbered women by far, and kidnappings were not unheard of. Though Old Fu seemed reasonable, snakeheads were little better than gangsters. He knew they could be vicious in their dealings if they chose.

He had a few years' savings to put towards the deposit, and borrowed the remainder from an old classmate, promising a twenty per cent return as soon as he had cleared his bond. Up until the time of the accident, he had made his payments to the snakeheads faithfully each month, setting aside a portion of his wages for himself and turning over the rest to his contact in the UK, a young Fujienese who went by the nickname Little Dog. Little Dog was something of a mystery to Wen: he was small and slight but nonetheless menacing in a way Wen could not quite pinpoint. He tracked down Wen on the first of each month, regardless of the day, and was always accompanied by a couple of thugs, who lurked behind and let him do the talking. Wen had heard a rumour that Little Dog was the wayward son of a Fujienese tycoon, but didn't know if it was true. What he did know was that Little Dog was clever, well-spoken and seemed to anticipate his every move. Even Chen, his gangmaster at Morecambe Bay, seemed intimidated by Little Dog, warning Wen not to underestimate his power and reach.

To date, Wen had worked off a third of his bond. But he had another two years to go before it would be clear. What this meant now, he didn't know. In the eyes of the world he was dead. He fervently hoped that Old Fu and Little Dog would swallow their loss. But if they were resourceful and chose to dig deeply, sooner or later they might find their way to Lili. This was his biggest fear.

None of this did he disclose to Angie. It was not just the

limitations of his English that prevented him from doing so: he did not wish to disturb the fragile balance of their existence. He and Angie lived solely in the present. She did not ask questions, nor did she give answers. He understood a handful of truths about her: she needed silence in the mornings, could sidestep problems with ease if she chose to, used a grim humour when she felt uncomfortable, and drank to subdue her fears. She was fiercely private and self-reliant to the point of stubbornness. She was also damaged, though he did not understand how or why. And the fact of this made her oddly compassionate towards others.

Apart from this, he knew no details of her life. Her work, her family, even her age remained shrouded in mystery. And she had asked him nothing about his own. That they each had a past was understood; but it remained closed, like the lid of a coffin. It was as if the events that night on the bay had robbed them of their histories. Perhaps, he decided, this was for the best.

So now he was a man without a country, a language or a name. Sooner or later, he would have to confront the question of his lost identity. He'd been stripped of his passport by the snakeheads during the long journey overland, and been told his papers would be returned once his bond was paid. He had a small sum of money stashed in a bank account in London in Jin's name. She had agreed to this when he left London: it was not safe to keep the money he earned with him, and neither did he wish to send it home, like most of those he worked alongside. So he had made periodic deposits into Jin's account, whenever he could manage. The sum he'd saved was not enormous, though it might be enough to buy a new passport on the black market. But to gain access to the money he would have to make contact with Jin, and the prospect of this unnerves him.

He finds it difficult to think of Angie and Jin in the same moment, as if the presence of one somehow erases that of the other. His affair with Jin had been deeply physical at first. After months of privation during the long journey overland, his need for a woman was all-consuming, and he indulged himself greedily. She too had seemed inexhaustible in her desires, and he wondered at the time if she would have behaved the same way at home. Perhaps, he had thought, coming to England had set her free from the constraints of their culture, a culture that still prized virtue and modesty for unmarried females.

But after a few months, the flame that had consumed them gradually burned low, and for Wen at least, extinguished itself. He sensed that it was the same with her, though she refused to admit it. Those last few weeks, her lovemaking developed an angry edge. One morning shortly before he left, he woke to find that she had bitten him the night before: he lay in silence next to her and examined her toothmarks on his arm. It seemed to him the marks were not emblematic of her love, but of her bitterness. He was slipping away from her, even while she lay in his arms, and she knew it.

The day he told her he was leaving, she had been strangely calm. She sat at the small metal table in her room and smoked a cigarette while he spoke, exhaling through her nose. But when she leaned forward to tap the ash into a chipped mug in front of her, he saw her hand tremble ever so slightly. By then he had already begun to store his savings in her account, and she agreed to allow him to continue. That he trusted her completely with his money was implicit, and she lived up to his belief in her, keeping meticulous accounts of their respective savings over the ensuing months. He sent her emails whenever he made a deposit in her name, and he always received a polite, but brief, acknowledgement. He called her only twice after leaving London, both times within the first month. After that he sent only the occasional email, mostly to let her know he was moving on.

Now he looks over at the phone on Angie's counter. He pictures himself dialling, and tries to imagine the sound of Jin's voice on the other end of the line, but he cannot. How could a simple piece of plastic reach across the two halves of his life, from the past into the present, from death by drowning to life in Angie's house? Instead, he goes and finds his coat and shoes, takes some change from a bowl in the kitchen, finds a spare set of keys, and for the first time since the accident, ventures out alone.

He walks towards the coast, knowing instinctively which direction to turn, for one thing cockling has taught him is how to smell the ocean. Though he grew up some eighty kilometres from the Bohai Sea, he had not set eyes upon it until he was ten, when he stowed aboard a lorry bound for the port city of Tanghai. The lorry was driven by an old school friend of his stepfather's, who had stopped by on his way through town. The two men had sat reminiscing for an hour in the front room, and Wen had been sent out to buy a large bottle of beer and a bag of sunflower seeds from a nearby stall. Later, Wen overheard the man say he was bound for the coast, so he crept out to the lorry and hid beneath a pile of burlap sacking. Two hours later, when the red-faced driver found him stowed away, the man swore and clouted him so hard about the ear that it did not stop ringing for the entire journey home. Upon his return, Wen's stepfather had given him a second beating. But later that night, his stepmother had quietly placed a bowl of dumpling soup in front of him in reconciliation. She sat down opposite him with a troubled look.

"Were you running away?" she asked.

Wen shook his head. "I wanted to see the ocean," he explained.

She sighed then and he could sense her relief. "And did you?" she asked.

"No. At least, I don't think so. We stopped at the municipal docks. I saw only buildings, and grey water."

"I'm sorry."

"I wanted to get to Beidaihe. To the place where Chairman Mao had his villa by the sea."

"Ah. Beidaihe is further north."

"They say the beaches there are made of golden sand. And the rocks along the shore are shaped like crouching tigers."

"That is what they say," she mused.

"Have you been?"

"No. I haven't had that pleasure."

"I'm sorry if I disgraced you."

"To long to see the ocean is no disgrace." She smiled at him, as if she knew that he was destined to go, as if her hold on him was only brief. "Perhaps you saw more than you realised," she added. She patted his hand then and stood, carrying his empty bowl to the sink. At the time he was uncertain of her meaning, but the words stayed with him long after.

•

Now Wen carries on walking towards the coast, where he knows there will be a high street and shops, and hopefully an internet café. Angie has no computer at home, a fact which surprised him at first, as he'd assumed every English household would have one. But he has come to understand that Angie defies normality in more ways than one, and now nothing about her would faze him.

It takes him longer than he expected to reach the sea. When the vast grey waters of the bay finally appear, he stops dead. The stench of briny air is overwhelming, clogging his lungs. He stands motionless, his eyes fixed on the white caps in the distance, the memories of that night flooding back. Perhaps he shouldn't have come, he thinks. Perhaps he will never be able to face the sea and its ghosts again.

He does not know how long he remains there, standing on the pavement. An old man walks by, his back hunched with age, but does not appear to notice him. It is only when the purple light of dusk begins to settle on the bay that Wen turns and heads north along the coast road, heading for the high street. He walks for several blocks without success, until he eventually decides to enter an empty shop selling flowers to enquire. He rehearses the words in advance but still panics when he utters them. The shopkeeper, a barrel-shaped woman in her late fifties, frowns with incomprehension. But after three tries her eyebrows lift knowingly, and she directs him further into town.

Fifteen minutes later, he finally reaches the internet café. The neighbourhood looks familiar, and the idea that he may stumble upon his former co-workers, or even worse, his gangmaster, preys upon him. He has worn the red woolly hat as a kind of protection, but however much he wishes, it will not make him invisible.

The café has a small scattering of young people. He pays a bearded cashier for a half-hour and finds a monitor at the back. But once seated, he is reluctant to continue. He had not thought this far ahead, had not considered what sequence of words he should write to bring about the truth. He sits for ten full minutes without touching a single key. A thin-faced youth at the back coughs and looks pointedly in his direction: Wen does not know how to decipher the young man's glance. Is it sexual or racist or merely bored? He has no idea, and suddenly he has never felt more foreign than he does right now in this room full of English people.

He takes a deep breath and logs onto his email. A rash of messages come through, one by one. He scans them quickly, reading past what is mostly rubbish. His eyes alight on one near the bottom. It is from Jin, and when he clicks on the message, three words come up. The message says simply: *Is it true?* It is dated four days after the accident. He sits and stares at the words for a long time. In her knowing way, Jin has seen right through his deception. And for the first time, he feels truly ashamed. He should have died out there that freezing night, along with all the others. The answer to Jin's email should be yes.

But it is not, so he sets about composing a reply. It takes him several attempts. By the time he is finished, the bearded cashier is glancing repeatedly in his direction, for he has overrun his half-hour by five minutes. He takes one last look at the message and hits the send button, then rises and walks out of the café without a backward glance. Suddenly, and without fanfare, he is back among the living.

He walks home slowly, pondering his options, and it is already dark when he finds his way back to Angie's house. He comes through the front door and she is there, seated on the sofa, her features rigid. Her hands are wrapped tightly around a glass, and when he steps into the room, one glance is enough to tell him he has erred. He stops short and their eyes meet across the silence. He sees her chest rise and fall, and sees her swallow with relief.

"I'm sorry," he says. "I go out." He motions with a thumb towards the outside.

"Yes," she replies, her voice unnatural, as if she is squeezing the word out of her throat.

"What time is now?" he asks.

"It doesn't matter." She sets the glass down carefully on the table in front of her and rises. He takes a step forward but the chunky wooden coffee table is still between them, preventing him from taking her in his arms the way he knows he should. Instead, he extends a hand across to her, and she looks at it a moment before reaching out her own. He gives her fingers a reassuring squeeze, for in the absence of words, he must rely on touch. Finally he pulls her around the table to him and folds her closely into an embrace. He can smell the whisky on her, mixed with her own scent, and he wonders whether she will ever be free of drink.

"You went out," she says accusingly, her voice a low growl laced with humour.

"Yes," he whispers into her hair.

"I thought you'd gone," she adds. This time the humour is gone, and her voice has thinned.

"No," he says. *I would not leave you*, he thinks. *Not like that.*

October 2004

The day after she has dinner with Adrian and May, Lili moves out of Jin's bedsit in Hounslow. That afternoon, Lili is packing her things when Jin returns from the language school. When Lili tells her where she is moving to, Jin raises her eyebrows.

"You work fast," she exclaims. "Don't tell Fay," she adds, flopping onto the bed and kicking off her shoes.

Lili pauses and looks over at her. "Why not?"

"She doesn't like it when we fraternise with students."

"I'm not fraternising," says Lili defensively. "I'm tutoring his daughter."

"Whatever," Jin shrugs. "Sounds like it's the dad who wants tuition," she adds suggestively.

"It's not like that," replies Lili. "The girl is Chinese. Like us. But she's confused."

"And you're going to rescue her?"

171

"She doesn't need rescuing. She needs –"

Lili stops short, unwilling to continue. What May needs, of course, is mothering. But she daren't say that to Jin. And anyway, that is far more than she is in a position to provide. "I don't know what she needs," she says finally. "But I can teach her about her culture. And help her make sense of who she is."

"If she was raised *here*, by an English father, and speaks only English – then English is her culture," says Jin staunchly. "She's certainly not Chinese."

"Well, she can learn," says Lili.

Jin snorts. "Some things can't be taught. Anyway, better you than me. I get my fill of English kids at school."

Lili looks up from her suitcase, surprised by her friend's tone. Jin does not meet her gaze, but rises from the bed and crosses over to the kettle, filling it with water. Lili closes the lid of her suitcase and locks it. She suspects that Jin is secretly envious of her good fortune: to be given free housing in a nice part of London is not a small thing and Jin knows it. When she has finished packing, Lili arranges her bags by the door and puts on her coat. She wants desperately to ask Jin about the letter beneath the bed, but cannot bring herself to. Perhaps later, she decides. When they are no longer on top of one another. She turns to go and Jin stops her.

"Hey," says Jin. "Those things I said the other night... about Wen."

"It's okay," says Lili quickly.

"No. I shouldn't have said it. I was angry. Wen loved

you. He would never have done anything to put you in danger."

Lili stares at Jin. Though she knows this in her heart, a part of her feels enormously relieved.

"Wen and I spent the first nine months of our existence wrapped in each other's arms," she says slowly. "I used to think that we could never be separated." She pauses, choosing her words with care. "Now I know that I was right. Because a part of me died with him that night."

Jin stiffens. She gives a small shake of her head.

"You've lost a great deal, but you are stronger now than you were, Lili. Believe me. In that sense, Wen did you a favour."

"By dying?" Lili's voice is incredulous.

Jin opens her mouth to speak, then decides against it. Lili waits for her to say something. The kettle boils and Jin reaches for it, filling a mug with hot water. "He would not wish you to feel this way," she says finally, her voice subdued.

"No," replies Lili. "I suspect not. But it's not for him to say any longer."

Lili reaches down and picks up her bags. Jin looks up from the mug, and their eyes meet across the room.

"No," says Jin.

"I'll see you at school," says Lili.

•

She takes the No. 237 bus to Sheep Pen, then changes onto a 94 for Notting Mountain. As she is struggling to lift her enormous suitcase onto the second bus, her phone rings in the pocket of her coat. She lets it ring as she drags the case through the crowded bus, conscious that her ring tone is drawing looks from those around her. It is Fei Xiang, a famous Taiwanese pop singer, and she had meant to change it after she arrived in London. She flops down into an empty seat, wedges the suitcase between her thighs, and pulls the phone out of her pocket just as it stops ringing. She sees the caller is Johnny, and feels a surge of relief that she has not answered it. She has not spoken to him since the night they slept together; indeed, she has tried to distance herself from the events of that night altogether. What she did was necessary; she knows that now. But it does not make her proud.

The thought of seeing him again makes her feel slightly ill. For most of her life she has believed that sex takes place at the end of a relationship, as a culmination, rather than at the outset. Given that she and Johnny have already slept together, she is confused and completely ignorant about what should happen next. Furthermore, she isn't even certain what she *wants* to happen. Fragments of that night float back to her: the tangled pale green bedding in the dim light of Johnny's room, the pile of dirty dishes stacked up in the sink, the circle of male faces reflected in the glow of the TV set. She does not think she can face these things again.

When she arrives at Adrian's house, it is empty. He has given her a key and permission to move in at her leisure. Adrian is at work and May has gone to a friend's house after school, so Lili has time to organise herself before their return. Still, she enters the hallway feeling as if she is trespassing, and at once wonders whether she has made a mistake. Will she ever feel at home here?

She pulls her bag into the hallway and takes off her coat. In the corridor are photos of Adrian's wife, Sian. Lili had not wanted to dwell on them the other evening, but now she bends down and peers at the woman in the photos. She is thin-faced and pale, with sandy brown hair and a longish nose. Attractive, decides Lili, but not beautiful. Her eyes, surrounded by a web of faint lines, look directly at the camera in an unnerving fashion. As if she is privy to some knowledge that Lili does not have. In the other photo she holds the baby May up next to her. May wears the startled look of an infant – her mouth an open circle, as if she is surprised to find herself in the arms of this pale stranger – while Sian's expression radiates a complex mixture of happiness and something else. Lili stares at the photo, trying to comprehend the other emotion in her eyes: is it relief, perhaps? Or fear?

The room upstairs is just as she remembered: small but cosy. A room she can definitely colonise. She sets about unpacking her things, storing her clothes in the chest of drawers and stowing her small collection of books upon the bedside table. She has brought few mementoes with her from home: a small framed photo of Wen and a beautifully bound volume of Chinese poetry he gave her on the occasion of their twenty-first birthday. She places the photo atop the chest of drawers, alongside Wen's book of poetry, just as she hears Adrian and May returning below.

Before she can go down to greet them, May comes rushing up the stairs breathlessly.

"You're here!" She stops short and surveys the room with wide eyes.

"Yes, I am here," Lili laughs.

"You don't have very much stuff, do you?" May wrinkles her nose.

"No, I didn't bring much from China," concedes Lili. "Too much trouble."

Just then Adrian appears in the doorway.

"Hello," he says. "All moved in?"

"Yes." Lili smiles at him, feels a slight sense of embarrassment as their eyes meet across the room.

"Who is this?" asks May. They both turn to see her standing by the chest of drawers pointing to the framed photo of Wen.

"This is my brother," says Lili.

"Oh," says May. "What's his name?"

"His name is Wen."

"Does he live in China?"

Lili pauses, her eyes flicking to Adrian and back to May.

"He used to," she says then. "But he died."

May's face falls. Lili has the sudden sense that unlike most children her age, May comprehends only too well the meaning of these words, and their terrible finality.

"Oh," says May uncomfortably, her eyes sliding towards her father.

"May, why don't you go take care of your homework before dinner?" says Adrian. May nods and slips quickly out of the room, her relief evident. Adrian turns to Lili.

"I'm sorry. She finds it difficult."

176

"Of course," says Lili. "I understand." *Who among us does not find it difficult?* she thinks. Adrian clears his throat a little awkwardly, but does not ask about Wen. Perhaps he too finds the subject difficult, she decides.

"I brought some pizza home for you and May. I was hoping you might be able to watch her for a few hours this evening. I'm afraid a meeting came up unexpectedly."

"Yes, of course," says Lili quickly.

"You don't mind? It's very short notice."

"No. It is fine." Lili smiles reassuringly. They have not really discussed how her responsibilities with May will work on a day-to-day basis. But she is prepared to be flexible.

"It'll give you a chance to get to know her a bit better. And anyway, I won't be late."

"Don't worry," says Lili. "May and I will be fine."

Later, after they have eaten pizza, she and May sit at the kitchen table writing Chinese characters. Lili shows her how to write the word for woman, and explains that the character derives from a figure holding a broom horizontally in the air. May frowns at the drawing.

"A broom? Really?"

Lili nods. May screws up her face.

"It's a bit... old-fashioned, isn't it? A broom?"

Lili laughs.

"Mandarin is an ancient language, May. Five thousand years old."

"Still," says May doubtfully. "Couldn't it have been a flower or something?"

"It could have been, but it wasn't," says Lili.

"Show me how to write *man*," May says.

Lili sketches out the character, first drawing a square, then adding a cross inside.

"The top half is a field divided into four squares," she explains. "The bottom bit is shaped like a tool used to dig the ground, and that part means *strong*. A man must be strong to work on the land, so together these two make up the character *nan*, which means *man*."

"I guess you don't have to be strong to sweep," says May. "But it still doesn't seem fair."

"No," agrees Lili. "Many things in life are not fair," she adds, thinking briefly of Wen. As if reading her mind, May lays down her pencil and looks at her.

"I'm sorry your brother died," she says solemnly. "Your mum and dad must have been sad."

"Well," Lili says. "They are dead too."

May's eyes grow round. "Are you an orphan?"

Lili hesitates. She does not think of herself as an orphan. But perhaps she should.

"You're just like me! I'm an orphan," adds May excitedly.

"But you have a father," reminds Lili.

"But I was an orphan. Before. With my first family. Adrian got me from an orphanage."

"Oh, yes. I see," says Lili uncertainly.

"Adrian says he'll take me there to visit one day. But I don't know when."

"To visit would be good," says Lili.

"But I'd like to go to China with *you*." May raises her eyes a little shyly, then picks up the pencil and begins to sketch a person carrying a broom. "I mean, you speak the language and all," she continues, not looking up. "Adrian would be pretty useless in China, wouldn't he?"

"Many people learn English now in China. You and Adrian would be fine."

"But people would talk to me in Chinese and expect me to understand," says May, her face knit with concern.

Lili ponders the likelihood of this. May does look Chinese. "But they would know from your clothes that you are a foreigner," she says finally.

May looks down at her school uniform and pulls a face. "How?"

"They just would," says Lili.

"Do they have school uniforms in China?"

"Yes, but different from yours. They are all the same colour: blue."

May frowns, chewing on the end of her pencil.

"I like blue," she says, as if colour is the only impediment.

Lili smiles. "Anyway, you will learn Chinese from me. So by the time you visit China, you will speak very well."

"I guess so. Do you like *Friends*?" she asks, abruptly changing the subject.

"Of course. Everyone likes friends."

"No, I mean the TV show. Adrian says I'm too young for it, but whenever he goes out and leaves me with a babysitter, we watch *Friends*. Adrian has the whole series on DVD."

"I have seen it in China."

"So? Can we watch some now?" asks May eagerly. She jumps off her chair, then pauses, eyeing Lili.

Lili is not a parent, and has no idea whether *Friends* is suitable for a child of May's age. But she does not wish to anger her, so she reluctantly agrees.

Some time later, they are curled up on the sofa in the middle of their third episode when Lili hears the key in the front door. She moves to switch off the TV but May stops her.

"Don't! It's nearly over!" cries May.

Adrian appears in the doorway with a smile.

"Hey, you two," he says. He looks pointedly at May. "Bit late for you, isn't it, young lady?"

At once Lili rises. "I'm sorry," she says.

"It's okay," says Adrian. "May knows full well what time she's meant to be in bed."

He casts a disapproving look at May, who fixes her gaze pointedly on the TV, ignoring him. Adrian raises his voice.

"Don't you, May?"

"Shhh," says May. "It's nearly over."

Adrian turns to Lili with a sigh. "Just so you know, bedtime is nine o'clock."

"Nine-thirty!" says May crossly, her eyes still trained on the TV. "And ten o'clock on weekends!" she adds defiantly.

"I will remember," says Lili.

"Besides, *you* said you wouldn't be late tonight," says May in an accusing tone.

Adrian shrugs. "Sorry. Dinner took longer than I expected," he admits.

"He had a date," says May, shooting a brief glance at Lili.

"May!" Adrian frowns at her. "It wasn't a date, just a… dinner," he says finally.

"With a woman! He told me!"

"A colleague," says Adrian. "A female colleague. That's all."

"*Wo shi nu ren*," says May in Mandarin. Adrian looks at Lili for an explanation.

"She says she is a female," explains Lili. "Today we start our lessons."

Adrian nods approvingly.

"Oh. Good. Quite right, May."

"*Ni shi nu ren*," says May, looking pointedly at Adrian.

Adrian looks again to Lili. Lili hesitates awkwardly, then turns to May.

"May, your father is a *nan ren*. Remember? A man."

May laughs and jumps up from the sofa, skipping out of the room. Adrian sighs and turns to Lili apologetically.

"As you can see, she knows how to wind me up," he says.

Lili frowns, uncertain of his meaning.

"I'm sorry," says Adrian. "She knows how to make me angry. To manipulate me."

"Oh. Yes. I understand. All children do this," she says, slightly embarrassed.

Adrian nods. "Suppose so," he says. "Anyway, I'm sure

you're tired. Thanks for looking after May. I'll put her to bed."

Lili nods and heads for the stairs leading to her room. The house feels suddenly smaller with the three of them. She can hear May in the bathroom brushing her teeth, then a scuffle at the bottom of the stairs, followed by a whispered command.

"Good night," calls May from down below.

"Good night," says Lili.

March 2004

Wen sits on a bench outside Morecambe train station. He feels conspicuous in the red hat, but dares not remove it. The hat has become part of him whenever he ventures out of Angie's house: without it he feels vulnerable. He is here to meet Jin's train from London. For the past fortnight he has exchanged a series of brief emails with her, and in the end she agreed to buy a cheap day return to Morecambe. He walked the four miles from Angie's house to the station, arriving half an hour early, only to learn that Jin's train was delayed by twenty minutes, so now he must wait. There are few people about at this time of day but still he feels uneasy. Sooner or later, he worries, someone is bound to recognise him.

It has been nearly six weeks since the accident, and the story of the drowned cocklers has all but disappeared from the news. But yesterday Angie showed him an article saying the local government was planning to post more warnings along the coastline to alert people to the dangers of rising tides. The new signs would be in English, of course – incomprehensible to the Chinese migrants who came here to eke out a living on the sands, not to mention those from other countries. There had also been talk of new laws, according to Angie, and greater regulation of the cockling industry. But he cannot see how this will benefit his people. Regulations will not affect the army of illegal workers that bolster the production of food in England, he thinks. Regulations will simply drive people like him further underground: force them into even more desperate working conditions with even more dismal wages.

When he first left London, he had taken a job picking apples in Norfolk. He stayed for five weeks, through most of the autumn season, being driven from farm to farm each day at dawn and working a twelve-hour shift until early evening. Like cockling, the work was piecemeal: four pounds per basket of apples picked. But it was impossible to fill a basket in an hour, no matter how quickly he worked. During that period, he had shared a grimy caravan with six others, sleeping on a sagging sofa in the tiny sitting room. He was making no more money than he had in London, but the weather had been fair, and he was happy to be working out of doors after a summer spent washing greasy pots in a badly ventilated Hammersmith kitchen where he rarely saw the light of day. He was relieved too, to be finally free of Jin's hostile embrace. Jin and he were like fire and water: they could not help each other, only hinder.

Life with Angie is completely different. For a start, he and she are not adversaries. If he is water, then Angie must be earth, he decides, for water feeds earth, enabling it to flourish. Since that first instance a few weeks ago, when he came home late to find Angie stricken with fear, their relationship has moved on. With difficulty, he explained how he had lost his way on the journey home that night, had become confused by the plethora of streets, disoriented by row upon row of dwellings which all looked the same. Angie had placed a finger on his lips to silence him, then rummaged in a cupboard, eventually pulling out an enormous folded map which she laid across the kitchen table. The map was unlike any he had ever seen before: it was incredibly detailed, showing every building, every street, every bend in the road. On it he could even locate where the others had perished that night – and the terrible snaking river that had severed them from shore as the tide rose. While he was studying the map, Angie placed a set of spare house keys on the table next to him, then took forty pounds of cash out of her purse and laid it next to the keys. He stared at the money, a lump rising in his throat. *Four bags of cockles' worth*, he had thought. *Or a life.*

"You're not a prisoner," she had said. "You're free to go. And to return. If you wish."

He frowned, staring down at the banknotes.

"Your money," he said. "I cannot."

"Why?" she asked.

Why indeed? he had thought. He had no trouble partaking of her warmth and of her flesh. But it was the lure of money that had brought his countrymen to England in the first place, and the promise of it that had killed them. And the threat of unpaid money hung over him still.

"Take it," she said finally. "It's only paper."

Reluctantly, he put the notes in his pocket. But in the days that followed he could not bring himself to spend them. The notes were there now, nestled tight against his thigh.

The sky had been pale blue when he set out this morning, but within a short time it has transformed into a thick paste of grey. When he first came to England, he had been amazed at the changeability of the weather. Even on a perfect day, he could never be sure that it would not rain, as if the weather were teasing him with its ability to reinvent itself. It was enough to drive a man mad, one of his fellow cockle pickers had complained one bitter January day. Zhou had come to England more than three years before. He had recently paid off his debts to the snakeheads, and had finally begun earning for himself. Every cockle he picked was another brick in the house he would one day build with his earnings, he'd told Wen. He had a wife and a young daughter: he was indeed fortunate in that respect. But he hated life in England. He missed his daughter terribly, and longed to taste his wife's soup again. Most of all he missed the change of seasons, for as far as he could tell England had no seasons. One could freeze in summer or sweat in winter – it was all the same. The weather and the food, Zhou had said, shaking his head and sucking in his teeth. These two things would surely kill him if he were forced to stay here for ever.

Wen glances at the clock inside the tiny station. The train is due in the next few minutes. He rises and makes his way out to the platform. A few other people have arrived to meet the train, so he chooses a spot a short distance away and leans back against the wall, keeping his face down. When the train appears, his stomach tightens, as if he is about to step off the edge of a cliff. The train pulls to a stop several metres away, and after a minute, a string of passengers alight. Jin is one of the last off the carriage and he watches as she steps hesitantly onto the platform. She turns and looks around her. She does not see him, until he picks himself up off the wall and walks towards her. But when she does she freezes, her face suddenly unreadable. She stands silently as the crowd disperses around her, waiting for him to reach her. He pauses just in front of her.

"So," she says, looking up at him.

"It's me," he answers.

"I wasn't sure."

"Thank you for coming."

She hesitates, eyeing him.

"I had to be certain." She reaches up a hand to his face, then thinks better of it. "Take off the hat."

Wen glances around, then removes the red hat.

Jin frowns. "Your hair is longer."

He puts the hat back on and takes her elbow.

"Let's get out of here."

"Wait." She reaches inside her coat to pull out a small sealed brown envelope, which she hands to him. "This is for you."

He takes the envelope; can tell from the feel of it what it contains.

"It's yours," she adds. "I thought you might need it."

He shoves the money deep into the pocket of his coat.

"Where shall we go?" he asks.

She looks into his eyes. "To the sea."

Out on the street, they walk along the pavement side by side.

"I had an email from your sister," Jin says.

"Lili? When?"

"Last week. She wants to come over."

Wen stops dead, turning to her. "Here? To England?"

Jin nods.

"To teach Mandarin in London. She wants me to get her work at the institute."

"When?"

"As soon as her visa comes through. Six months maybe. Autumn perhaps."

Wen stares at her, trying to make sense of this new information. His sister, here, in England. Would she be safe from the snakeheads? But it would be Old Fu back in China, not Little Dog, who would be looking for the schoolteacher Mei Ling. Perhaps it would not occur to either of them to look here.

"Why?" he asks finally. Jin shrugs.

"Money, I suppose. I don't know. Why does anyone come here?"

He shakes his head slowly.

"I no longer remember."

"You've changed," says Jin.

"I died," he replies evenly.

After a few minutes' walk, they reach the promenade that fronts the sea. Jin crosses the road and looks down towards the stone jetty that pushes out into the bay. Wen looks around self-consciously, but there are few people about this time of year.

"Is this where they dig for fish?" she asks.

"No."

"Where?"

"Further north. And out to sea." He gestures towards open water.

"Out there?"

He nods.

"But not now," she says.

"Only at low tide. And at certain times of year. It is terrible work," he adds quietly.

"You could have come back to London."

But I didn't, he thinks. *And now that time is past.*

"Did you know them? The ones who died?"

"Yes. Not well, as I hadn't been here that long and people come and go." His voice nearly breaks on this last word.

"You don't need to speak of it," Jin says quietly.

"It is impossible to put into words. What happened that night."

"Then do not try," she says.

"I should have died with them."

It feels good to say it out loud, this terrible thought that has been stalking him all these weeks. He could not bring himself to say it to Angie. Why, he wonders fleetingly, does he have the courage to say it to Jin?

Jin stops and turns to him, shaking her head emphatically. "It wasn't your fate."

"What did I do to deserve life? The others had families, children. That night on the sands, when we realised we were in danger: it was like we suddenly beat with one heart; we were like one giant living organism, with all our hopes and fears and disappointment. Life here was nothing like they imagined it to be. This country made fools of them. It robbed them of their dignity, then took away the only thing they had left."

Wen's chest heaves with emotion. Jin eyes him silently.

"Not everyone who comes here has this experience," she says finally.

"No," says Wen. "A few get lucky. Now I know that the life they were looking for here is real. I've seen this life. I've even grown accustomed to it. But it will never exist for them," he adds grimly.

A shadow flickers across Jin's face, but she says nothing. Wen can see her mind at work, his allusion to his present circumstances turning uneasily in her brain. He refused to answer her emails asking where he was living and with whom. Though somehow she has guessed that it is a woman, and that she is not Chinese. If this bothers Jin, her pride clearly prevents her from saying so.

They walk to the end of the jetty, where a small café sits to one side. Jin peers through the door. It is past two and only a few people are seated inside.

"Are you hungry?" asks Wen.

"I'm starving," says Jin, pushing open the door. Wen stiffens. He would not have entered a café right here on the jetty. But Jin is already inside, so he follows. Once seated, she scans the English menu quickly, while he glances around nervously at the other patrons.

"Take off your hat," she says without looking up from the menu. "It's rude in England to wear a hat inside."

Wen reluctantly removes the hat. Jin lays down the menu.

"Let's have fish and chips," she suggests.

He nods, admiring her confidence. He has lived in Britain all these months but has never eaten fish and chips. When the waitress arrives a moment later, he lets Jin do the talking for them both. Jin orders the food, then asks for two glasses of water, while Wen regards her intently. Her command of English is good, but this is not the only thing that sets her apart from other Chinese he has known here.

When the fish and chips arrive, he watches as Jin pours salt and vinegar onto her plate. The batter is heavy, almost like pastry, though when he cuts into it with a knife the fish seems fresh enough. He would have preferred it steamed with ginger and spring onion, but suspects such methods of cooking are too subtle for English tastes. The chips are golden brown and stumpy; dipped in vinegar they taste okay. He eats the entire plate, mostly out of habit, but at the end of the meal he feels greasy and uncomfortably full.

Jin has eaten all of her fish but only half of her chips. She pushes the plate to one side and lights a cigarette, offering him one from the pack. When he shakes his head she raises an eyebrow in surprise, a thin spiral of smoke curling up from the side of her mouth. He has not smoked since the accident, something else about him that has changed. Though Angie drinks, he has never seen her with a cigarette, and he wouldn't dare presume to smoke in her home.

The waitress clears their plates and places the bill face down between them. He insists on paying for them both, reminding her of the cash in his pocket. As he carefully pulls a twenty-pound note from the envelope, he tries not to think of what the money represents – or which gruelling job he did to earn it. When the waitress has taken the money, he leans forward intently.

"I need you to do me a favour," he says cautiously.

Jin raises an eyebrow. Wen looks around the room a little self-consciously.

"They can't understand you," she says with a snort of impatience.

"I need to get a new passport. On the black market."

"What happened to yours?"

"Gone," says Wen with a dismissive wave. "Along with the rest of my stuff. Besides, it would be no good to me now. It isn't really a new passport I need – it's a new identity."

Jin frowns. She takes a deep pull from the cigarette and blows a careful smoke ring into the air between them.

"So you're going to give it all up," she says, looking around the café. "Your name? Your family? Your history?"

Wen falters. He had not thought of it in this way. But she is right. He will have to give it all up. All except for Lili. He has not yet decided what to do about Lili.

"For the most part, yes," he admits. Jin tilts her head to one side and stares at him for a long moment, then reaches forward and taps ash into a dish.

"What about me? What were you planning to do about me?"

Once again Wen is silenced by her bluntness. He thought that Jin understood that he could not be with her; he thought that she was reconciled to this. Perhaps she wishes to punish him by making it explicit.

"I will always be indebted to you," he says quietly.

Jin's nostrils narrow slightly. She nods at the envelope.

"The passport will cost you most of that money."

He pulls it out and throws it back to her. It lands with a thump on the table, and Jin stares at it a moment, before picking it up. She thumbs through the cash and pulls out a small stack of twenty-pound notes and hands them back to him, then puts the rest of the cash in her bag.

"I'll start with this. If I need more, I'll let you know."

When they leave the café, the wind has begun to blow. Jin steers them towards a stone column with a statue of a seabird on top. "Here," she orders. "Stand right here." She positions him carefully by the statue, then pulls a small digital camera from her pocket.

"What are you doing?" he asks suspiciously.

Jin doesn't answer. An older couple are just walking towards the café and Jin hurries up to them.

"Excuse me," she says in English. "Could you take a photograph?"

The woman smiles and takes the camera from Jin's hand, while Jin crosses over to Wen and links her arm in his. Wen stands frozen, taken aback. He does not want his photo taken here – indeed, he is appalled by the idea, but he is silenced by Jin's boldness.

"Okay?" the woman calls from behind the viewfinder.

"Yes," says Jin.

Wen glances sideways in time to see Jin smile for the camera. He hears a ringing in his ears as the woman takes the shot. *This picture will be my undoing*, he thinks. When she is finished, the woman walks towards them, the camera extended in her hand. Jin thanks her, and when the couple are out of earshot, Wen turns to her in disbelief.

"Why did you do that?"

"Because I wanted proof."

"For whom?"

"For me," she says. "In case I wake up tomorrow and decide that you were nothing but a ghost." She turns on her heel and walks back to land.

October 2004

On Saturday, Lili offers to take May out for the afternoon so that Adrian can finish some work. They hop on a 94 bus to Piccadilly Circus, then walk up Shaftesbury Avenue and into Chinatown. May clutches Lili's hand tightly as they walk along the crowded pedestrian streets festooned with coloured lanterns. They wander in and out of several shops on Gerrard Street, then buy some rice noodles in a Chinese grocery. At one point, they pass an elderly Chinese woman in a light grey trouser suit who nods at them approvingly. Lili realises with a start that the picture they form is that of mother and child, and she has the sudden sense that she is masquerading. Almost without realising, she drops May's hand, but a moment later she feels May's small fingers seeking out her own.

"Do you like coming here?" asks May.

"Of course."

"Is it like home?"

"Not really. But it is more like home than other parts of London."

"Do you miss it?"

Lili considers this. She misses Wen. But does she miss home?

"Sometimes," she answers. "But not today." She is vaguely surprised by this truth.

"Sometimes I think I miss it," says May elliptically.

"But... you were only a tiny baby when you left."

"I know. But some days I wake up with a funny feeling. Like I should be somewhere else."

Lili glances down at May. If Wen's ghost is here with her on earth, then maybe the spirit of May's mother is here also, pulling the child back to her homeland. But it is impossible to know if May's Chinese mother is dead or living: the woman may well be mother to some other child by now. The thought makes her uneasy. May is too young to realise now, but the day will come when she will have to reconcile herself to this uncertainty.

She leads May over to a small Chinese restaurant and pauses in front of the window. Just inside is a counter with two enormous steaming vats of soup. A string of plump golden ducks hangs upside down in the window, their wings splayed open, their necks a dark pocket where the heads have been severed. Further inside Lili sees that the restaurant is crowded with mostly Chinese people sitting at square wooden tables. May stares at the window, her eyebrows knit together.

"Are you hungry?" asks Lili.

"I'm not sure," May says doubtfully.

"What's wrong?"

"The ducks. Why do they hang them in the window?"

"So we can see them. If you want to buy a duck dinner, then first you want to see it."

"But... they don't look nice."

"Maybe not to you. But to all those people inside they do."

"I guess so." May turns away from the window. "Can we go somewhere else?" she asks tentatively.

"Of course. But this is the most authentic restaurant in Chinatown. Like the real China."

"Could we go to McDonalds?" May asks.

They find a McDonalds on Shaftesbury Avenue and May orders a Happy Meal, delighting in the small plastic toy that comes out of the brightly packaged box. She tears open the wrapper and quickly assembles the toy: a small wind-up version of a cow from a recent Disney movie.

"See?" says May, holding up the cow. "I bet the duck restaurant doesn't have these!"

Lili glances at the writing on its base. The cheap plastic figure has been made in China, no doubt by someone who has never eaten a burger. She shows the writing to May.

"This came from China. Most toys come from China."

"Chinese kids are lucky," says May, biting into her hamburger.

May's remark silences Lili. She does not have the heart to point out that the vast majority of products made in China

197

are for export. Her stepmother's cousin spent several years working in a toy factory. She did eleven-hour shifts six days a week painting blue Caucasian eyes onto flimsy latex dolls. By the end of each day, the smell of latex fumes was so strong it made her throat and eyelids burn. Her mother's cousin eventually developed emphysema, and was forced to leave the factory and find work elsewhere as a cleaner.

"When I was a child, we did not have toys like this," Lili says.

"Did you have Happy Meals?"

"No."

"Too bad for you," says May, squeezing ketchup onto her fries.

"I guess so. But we had other things. Dumplings, and rice balls, and red bean cakes."

"Red bean cakes!" May pulls a face.

"They are very nice. We can buy one and take it home for your father."

"Okay," says May with a shrug. "But I bet he won't like it."

When they return home, Adrian is working on a set of drawings in his study. He swivels round in his chair as they enter. May rushes over to him excitedly and climbs onto his lap.

"We went to Chinatown!"

"Fantastic," says Adrian.

"And we ate lunch at McDonalds!"

"McDonalds?" Adrian raises his eyebrows and glances up at Lili.

"This is her choice," says Lili apologetically.

Adrian looks back to May. "You chose McDonalds over Chinese food?"

"I didn't like the ducks," says May disapprovingly.

"What ducks?"

"The ones without heads," says May. "In the window."

"Oh," says Adrian. "Those ducks." He nods apologet ically at Lili. "Anyway, I'm glad you had a good time."

"We did." May jumps off his lap and runs out the door.

"Today I fail in your daughter's education," says Lili sheepishly.

"Not at all," says Adrian with a smile. "I'm very grateful you took her out."

"Next time I will remember: no ducks."

"You couldn't have known."

"In China, it is custom to show people what they eat before cooking."

"Yes, of course," says Adrian. "Very sensible. But here people don't always like to be reminded that what they eat comes from something living. It's hypocritical really. Your way is much more honest."

"I understand this, too. When I was a child, I found a chicken. I hid it in a box on the roof of our building. I called it *mi-mi*, which means 'secret' in Chinese. But one day when I went to school, the chicken flew out of the box and fell onto the ground in front of my building. My stepmother found it. That night she prepared a special meal for us. But when I realise it is *mi-mi*, I cannot eat. My brother, he tried to help me. He asked to eat mine, but my stepmother then is very angry. She did not understand. The English way of thinking, it is very… emotional."

"Sentimental," says Adrian.

"You had a pet chicken?" says May.

Adrian and Lili turn to see her standing in the doorway.

"Yes," says Lili.

"Do you eat chicken now?" May asks, her eyes narrowing.

"May!" admonishes Adrian.

"It's okay," says Lili. "Yes, I like chicken now very much."

May tilts her head to one side, considering this.

"Well, I guess if you really like it," she says finally. "But I wouldn't eat a hamster," she adds, disappearing once again from view.

Lili retreats to her room, but before long her mobile rings and she sees Johnny's name light up on the tiny screen. It has been nearly a week since she slept with him and they've not yet spoken, although this is the third or fourth time he has rung. She stares at the receiver as it vibrates.

"*Wei?*"

"Lili. I thought I had the wrong number."

"I'm sorry."

"You've been avoiding me."

"No," she says quickly. "I've been busy."

"I forgive you. Can we meet? For dinner?"

An image flashes into her head: a row of male faces ranged across the flickering darkness of Johnny's sitting room.

"I have to work," she lies.

"Tomorrow then."

Lili hesitates. She realises she will have to see him.

"Okay," she says reluctantly, uncertain what she is agreeing to. Is it dinner or more?

She arranges to meet him at the same restaurant she took May to. She will feel safer in Chinatown, she decides, more in control.

•

The following night they sit at a small wooden table just behind the steaming vats of soup. She has deliberately placed her back to the plate glass window and its garland of headless ducks. When she entered the restaurant, she was surprised to feel a sudden shiver of aversion, as if she had somehow contracted May's disgust from the previous day. But she does not object when Johnny orders braised duck together with a pot of stewed tripe. Once the waiter has departed, Johnny fixes her with a look.

"So why so busy?"

"I've just moved."

Lili tells him about her arrangement in Notting Hill. Johnny leans back in his chair and crosses his arms.

"Just you and him and the daughter?"

"Yes. Like an au pair."

"Except he's a widower."

"Yes."

"So there's no wife."

"No."

"Do you trust him?"

"Of course. He's very kind. Definitely a gentleman."

"Still. You should watch out. He's probably lonely. And frustrated," Johnny adds pointedly.

"I don't think so. Besides, I think he has a girlfriend."

"Oh." Johnny relaxes a little.

It is only a small lie, Lili decides. Adrian must certainly have friends who are women, at any rate. And he doesn't seem frustrated to her, only somewhat overwhelmed by the task of parenting a young child on his own. She eats some tripe and picks at her rice, but when the duck arrives the look of it is enough to put her off. Johnny urges her to eat, but in the end he finishes most of the plate himself.

After the meal, they walk onto Gerrard Street together. Darkness has fallen, and there are fewer people about. As they round the corner, Johnny pulls her into the lee of a building and kisses her. She feels his lips on hers, but this time the clench that grips her insides is one of panic rather than desire. She eases apart from him, desperate to be away.

"Come back with me," he murmurs into her ear. "I've been thinking of you."

"I can't," she stammers. "I have to work early tomorrow." *Another lie*, she thinks, *this one even easier than the first.*

"Then when?"

"I'll call you."

He is standing there, eyeing her. The lies are multiplying now: one begets another. Lili takes a few steps backwards. *It is like the ducks,* she thinks. *Things change so quickly.*

The following day, Lili is in the small kitchenette in the language school making tea when she hears Jin's voice in the hallway just outside.

"Don't be stupid," hisses Jin urgently. "If you go back, they'll come after you!"

Lili freezes. Something about Jin's tone causes the hairs upon her arms to stand on end.

"Then you're a bigger fool than I thought," Jin says.

Lili hears the phone snap shut and just has time to turn away before Jin rounds the corner. Jin stops short when she sees her. The colour drains from her face. Their eyes meet for an instant, then Jin turns on her heel without a word and walks out of the room. Lili stands motionless in the tiny kitchen, her face suddenly hot. The last time she heard Jin call someone a fool, it was Wen. Somewhere downstairs a door slams. Lili glances out the window to see Jin dash across the road, her coat and bag hastily clutched in her arms. She watches as Jin disappears around the corner.

A moment later, Fay comes into the kitchen, a cigarette in the corner of her mouth. She turns the kettle on and takes the cigarette out, exhaling.

"What's wrong with Jin?" asks Lili.

Fay shrugs. "Maybe boyfriend trouble," she says.

"I didn't know Jin had a boyfriend."

"Who knows? Jin likes her secrets," says Fay, reaching into the cupboard for a teabag. She drops it in a mug and fills it with boiling water.

"Does she?" Lili's voice sounds odd, as if she is squeezing it out of her throat.

"I hear you've solved your housing problem," Fay says, changing the subject. "I guess you found a sugar daddy after all." Fay smiles, arching her eyebrows knowingly.

"No," Lili stammers. "It isn't like that."

"Don't be coy," Fays says in a no-nonsense tone of voice. "I'm flattered. You took my advice, after all. I thought Jin was the operator. But I can see I've underestimated you," she adds approvingly. She picks up her mug and walks out of the room.

April 2004

Three weeks after they meet up, Wen receives an email from Jin. Through contacts in Chinatown she has found someone who will sell her a black market passport, but he will need to send her a photo of himself. *Make sure it's a proper one*, she writes. *Not some snapshot from your friend's camera.* Wen reads the bitterness in this last line. He did not confess to sleeping with Angie, but somehow Jin had known.

He has seen an ad for passport photos in the window of a chemist in Morecambe, so the following afternoon he walks into town. It is early April and the weather has just begun to turn. The ocean breeze is brisk and clean; the sharpness of the sea air no longer suffocates him. As he walks along Marine Drive, it dawns on him that the unease he experienced on his previous visits to Morecambe has lifted. The shops have begun to look familiar, and for the first time he does not feel as if he is trespassing.

In spite of this, when he reaches the chemist, he is relieved to find it empty. He has rehearsed the words in his head several times, and now he utters them cautiously to one of the two middle-aged women behind the counter. Miraculously she understands him. She indicates that he should follow her to the back of the shop, where a tall stool sits in front of a charcoal backcloth. He sits on the stool and she positions him, lifting his chin slightly with her thumb, her hazel eyes looking straight into his own.

"You'll have to take that off," she says with a nod, turning away.

Wen suddenly remembers the woolly hat. It has become such a part of him whenever he goes out that he'd forgotten he was wearing it. He pulls it off with an embarrassed flush and she takes a few steps back from him, holding up the camera.

"Don't smile," she says. But before he can unravel her words, the flash goes. After a moment, she hands him the digital image for his approval. Wen stares down at the picture on the tiny screen. It is not the one he has kept in his head all these months. He tries to work out why, and eventually it strikes him that he has lost the haunted look he once had. The chemist clears her throat.

"All right then?" she says expectantly.

"Okay," he nods.

"It's four copies for six pounds," she explains, crossing over to the counter.

Wen needs only two copies but decides not to make a fuss. He takes out a twenty-pound note from his pocket.

Apart from the lunch he bought Jin, it is the first money he has spent since the accident. Now, as he hands the woman the note, he feels a kind of sinking dismay, as if he is re-entering a world that he was relieved to leave behind. Living without the burden of money has liberated him these past few months, has somehow made him more human. Though he would not have described his comrades who died that night in the water as motivated by greed, the need to earn money had obliterated everything else in their lives. It was money that had lured them across the ocean, tore them from the arms of their loved ones, forced them into subhuman living conditions, and set them against one another. Money corroded them somehow – and ultimately stole their lives.

Every illegal Chinese he'd ever met had a story to tell about being swindled out of cash by unscrupulous bosses, gangmasters and middlemen. Lin had found his first job in the UK through an agency in Chinatown. He'd been sent to a farm in the north-east where for eleven-hour shifts he worked harvesting leeks. The job was back-breaking, but Lin consoled himself that he would at least be earning good money. At the end of his first week, he was shocked to see that his pay packet contained only eighty-seven pounds. When he confronted the overseer, he was told that deductions for national insurance, rent and agency fees meant that this was all he was entitled to. He had not earned even two pounds an hour! On such paltry wages, it would take him more than seven years to clear his debt to the snakeheads. In his darkest moments, he later told Wen, he had never imagined that England would prove such a harsh and indifferent land.

The cashier turns back to Wen, handing him the change. "It'll be just a few minutes," she says, indicating the photographic printing machine at the back of the shop. Wen nods and retreats slightly to one side so she can serve another customer who has just entered. At that moment, a battered white van draws up outside and lurches to a halt. The rear door slides open and Wen catches a glimpse of Chinese faces inside: tired men and women hunched too closely on the seats, wearing a range of dark-coloured anoraks. *Cockle pickers*, he thinks. He freezes, and feels his heart begin to race inside his chest. A young man jumps out of the van from the back seat, one hand clutching the other with a bloody rag. His thick black hair is pushed over to one side and there is a smudge of dried grey mud on one cheek. Holding the injured hand out in front of him, he pushes open the door of the chemist with his shoulder and steps inside. Wen immediately shifts round to face the shelf in front of him, pretending to study the row of shampoo bottles and deodorants, though he continues to watch the Chinese man out of the corner of his eye. Once inside, the man hesitates, and for a moment looks as if he might change his mind. Wen has never seen the man before, and yet there is something about him that is utterly familiar: the hair, the clothes, the furtive glances over the shoulder, the fear and desperation in his eyes. Everything about this man he recognises. *This man could be my brother,* he thinks. *We are twins in all but name.*

Just then the chemist comes out from the back of the shop carrying his photos. She hands him a neatly folded piece of card containing them. Her colleague finishes serving the customer and glances over to the Chinese man, who steps towards the counter and holds up his hand. The woman frowns at the bloodied rag.

"You've done a job there," she remarks. "Let's have a look."

The Chinese man approaches the counter and peels back the rag gingerly. Wen sees an angry red gash down the side of his hand, long and deep, the blood now mostly congealed. The chemist shakes her head.

"You were lucky. No veins or arteries there. Only flesh. Still, it's a nasty one."

The Chinese man looks at her, his brow furrowed. Wen sees that he does not understand a word, though the chemist appears unaware. She turns back to the shelves behind her and hunts around for a few moments, before placing a box of dressings and a small bottle of blue liquid in front of him.

"You'll be wanting these," she says.

The Chinese man stares down at the items.

"How much?" he asks.

The chemist points to each of the items in turn.

"Two pounds nineteen for the bandage and three twenty-nine for the disinfectant."

The Chinese man reaches in his pocket with his good hand and pulls out a small roll of ten-pound notes, perhaps seventy or eighty pounds in all. The week's wages, thinks

Wen. The man holds out one note, then points to the box of bandages.

"This," he says.

"You'll be needing the disinfectant," she admonishes. "Otherwise the wound could get infected."

The Chinese man shakes his head. "No," he says, tapping the box. "This." The chemist shrugs and rings up the item, handing him the change.

"You should see a doctor for that. It may well need stitches," she says, now a little peeved. The Chinese man stares at her blankly. Wen resists the urge to explain to him what she is saying. "The hospital," she repeats a little too loudly. "Do you know where the hospital is?"

"No," says the Chinese man. He grabs the box and turns, leaving the shop quickly.

The chemist sighs and shakes her head at her colleague, who raises an eyebrow. Then both women shoot a glance at Wen. He colours, feeling as if he ought to explain the man's actions. It is obvious that his presence prevents them from censuring the wounded man openly, as they might have done. He moves to the front of the shop and watches through the window as the man jumps into the van and the other cocklers slide the door shut. The engine sputters a few times and the van pulls out into the traffic, disappearing eventually round a corner.

A part of him feels bereft, though he is not sure why. He does not know these people, and he certainly does not envy their circumstances, so why should he regret their leaving? He walks out onto the street, the image of the injured man burned into his mind. An illegal Chinese would have to be on the verge of death before he would dare to seek medical treatment in this country. Doctors and hospitals were a link in the chain of authority that led to police, government officials, immigration and deportation. They could lead to a fate that, for some, was worse than death.

Last summer, a friend of Wen's from the restaurant in London had the misfortune to be hit by a car while waiting for a bus. He was knocked unconscious and when he came to, he was in a hospital bed. When he failed to answer the social worker's questions, a supervisor was called. She in turn called the police, who then notified immigration. Before his injuries had even healed, he was back on a plane to China. Once home, he faced a stiff fine from the Chinese authorities and he was still seven thousand pounds in debt to the snakeheads. Now he must pay off his debts on a fifteenth of the salary he was making in England, a task that would take him a lifetime, with nothing to show for it. One night in January while Wen was on the drive back to Liverpool, he had received a despairing phone call from his friend: drunk and weeping, he lamented that he lacked the courage to take his own life. Such tales were legion in the Chinese community. Newcomers quickly learned the twin tenets of life here: caution and forbearance. If one suffered, one did so in silence. Never ask for help, treatment or protection of any kind. Because there were no entitlements.

Wen pulls the hat down low and heads in the opposite direction, away from the bay. He walks to a post office where he buys an envelope and stamp and posts the photos to Jin, together with a hastily scrawled note. *I am sorry to trouble you*, he writes. *I hope this will be the last time.*

When he returns home, he is full of restless energy. He washes up the dishes from breakfast and mops the kitchen floor, but even then does not feel anything like the bone-numbing tiredness he used to experience after a day of digging cockles on the beach. Seeing the van-load of his compatriots reminds him that he has not truly laboured since the accident. For the past several weeks he has done nothing but study English, cook and do housework. He is not built for such inactivity; he realises this now. Perhaps it is perverse, but suddenly he aches to feel that sort of tiredness again. He looks around at Angie's already tidy kitchen and his eyes alight on the back door to the garden. He tries the door and finds it locked; he has never seen Angie use the garden. He rummages through the kitchen drawers until he finds a clear plastic bag full of keys, which he tries one by one. After a few minutes, he succeeds in opening the door, and for the first time he steps out into the garden.

It is long and narrow and densely overgrown, so dense, in fact, that he cannot see the end. At one point there must have been lawn down the middle, but now it is knee-high weed, overlaid with shrubs from the borders that have flung themselves wildly across the centre. The garden has several trees, some of which he recognises: on the left is a mature elder that has spread unchecked in every direction, opposite what appears to be a very old and gnarled fruit tree that lists heavily to one side, perhaps an apple or plum. Further back, a pair of oddly shaped conifers sits on the right, and an enormous oak towers over the end of the garden, shrouding everything in gloomy darkness. Beneath the long weedy grass at his feet, he sees a winding path of mossy stone set into the earth. He steps from one to the next, trying to make sense of the layout.

The garden is thickly planted along the edges mostly with shrubs that are now so overgrown that they are unrecognisable. Winter is only just ending, yet many have already sprouted new leaves. Wen knows little about plants and flowers, though his stepmother kept a kitchen garden while he was growing up, and he often helped her with the heavier tasks, such as turning the soil and spreading the manure they exchanged for produce with a local farmer. His stepmother grew all kinds of vegetables: long beans, garlic, spring onions, radish and winter melon. Every inch of earth was cultivated, as the family depended on the proceeds.

Wen looks around at the profusion of unchecked growth around him: a plot of land of this size would be a great luxury in today's China, especially one that was not used to grow food. He pushes his way to the back of the garden until he comes up against a crumbling brick wall several feet higher than his head. On the right is an old wooden shed, its door hanging lop-sided on rusty metal hinges. He pulls open the door and finds an array of rusty tools covered in cobwebs: two long rakes, a large, slightly bent pitchfork, a pile of shovels and small-handled spades and a pair of shears. To one side sits a towering stack of empty plastic pots and several pairs of old canvas gloves, now cracked and mouldy with damp. He picks up a glove: too small for a man, he decides. It must have belonged to a woman, together with the tools. Someone planted and nurtured this garden, a long time ago. He wonders who? For it was certainly not Angie.

He goes to work at once, taking out the tools and testing them one by one. The shears are so rusty they will not close, but he cleans and oils them, then sharpens the blade by grinding it in circular motions against a flat paving stone. Soon the shears are sharp enough to cut again, and he starts at the back of the garden and works his way round, trimming back the trees and shrubs to some semblance of their original shape. After a brief time, he strips off his jumper, working only in a t-shirt and jeans, his face covered in sweat. He works solidly for the next few hours, his arms and back burning from the effort, the way they used to after a day hunched over the sands with a tamping board. The more tired he becomes, the more satisfied he feels, for it is a relief to labour once again.

The plants are different from those at home, but he has an instinctive feel for what is uninvited, can recognise those whose sole purpose is to impede and strangle the progress of others. These he rips out ruthlessly and systematically, making sure he gets the ends of the roots. By the time darkness begins to fall, he has worked his way through much of the garden, amassing an enormous pile of debris out of sight in a corner at the back, against the wall. He does not stop until his hands erupt in blisters from the wooden handles of the shears. Only then does he make a cup of tea and settle himself on the threshold of the back door to survey his efforts, his t-shirt now muddy and damp.

His stepmother used to say that a garden could not thrive without affection. Though she had only a tiny plot of land by the river, the care she lavished on it was extraordinary. The vegetables were laid out in neat rows with no space in between, as she considered even an inch of unplanted soil to be wasteful. She had enclosed the plot with walls of woven matting on three sides, leaving one end open towards the river, believing that the proximity and sight of running water was vital to the garden's *chi*. On summer evenings, after the weeding was done, she would light incense and sit for hours in the darkness watching the waters flowing past, listening to the tinkle of a tiny metal chime suspended in one corner. It was important always to hear the wind, she had told him. She taught him how to crush dried bones and eggshells between two rocks, and spread them carefully over the soil, as well as how to distinguish between those insects which were pests and those which were beneficial, and therefore to be spared. Her own father had been a farmer, and he wondered sometimes whether she missed life in the countryside, having married a factory worker and settled on the outskirts of a small city. But if so, she never said.

He does not hear Angie enter through the front door, so absorbed is he in the gathering dusk of his thoughts. When he does realise, she is standing just behind him in the open doorway, her eyes trained on the garden.

He jumps to his feet and turns to her expectantly. She stands frozen, staring out at the garden. Then she retreats inside without a word. Wen follows her into the kitchen and watches silently while she removes a tumbler from the cupboard, reaches for the bottle of whisky under the sink and pours herself a generous glass. She raises the glass to her lips and drinks, then lowers it to the counter.

"Angie?"

She turns to him, and he sees her chest rise and fall. She opens her mouth to speak, then decides against it and takes another drink of whisky.

"What is problem?"

"The garden," she says finally. She breaks off, motioning towards the outside. "You didn't tell me."

"It is gift. From me."

"You don't owe me anything, Wen," she replies with a sigh. "Especially not that." She nods towards the garden. She turns back to the counter and refills her glass, and at once he understands that it is not the fact of the giving, but the nature of the gift that has upset her.

"Why not garden?" he asks, taking a step forward.

Angie does not look at him, but instead focuses her eyes on the tumbler of amber liquid in her hand, turning the glass round and round in circles, watching the swirl of it.

"This house belonged to my mother. The garden was hers," she explains, almost swallowing the last word.

Wen waits for her to say more. They sit in silence in the darkness of the kitchen for what seems like an eternity.

"My mother was good with plants," she says finally. "She could grow just about anything. But she was rubbish with people."

"I am sorry."

216

Angie takes a deep breath and exhales, as if trying to purge herself of the past.

"My mother had her garden. And my father, by all accounts – because I never met him – my father had his whisky." She pauses and picks up the bottle, frowning at it.

"So I guess I take after him. Or maybe there's a little bit of both of them in me."

Wen has not recognised all of her words, but the tenor of her voice is enough to make him understand. It is the first time she has spoken of her family, and now he realises why. He steps forward and reaches for the glass. She releases it to him, and he sets it down on the counter, pulling her into his arms. She buries her face in his shoulder and inhales deeply.

"You smell like mud."

Her voice, muffled against his shirt, is already thick with alcohol. He pulls back and looks down at her, marvelling at her ability to confound him.

"What is mud?"

Later, after they have gone to bed, he strokes her hair in the darkness.

"I do not make garden," he says quietly.

"No," she protests, arching around to look at him. "Please. Make the garden. Make it anyway you like. It's your garden now."

She turns away and pulls him in close behind her, so that his body is wrapped entirely around hers. Wen buries his face in her hair. He feels her body start to unwind, feels the shiver of her muscles as they release, and within a minute hears her breathing settle into whisky-induced sleep.

Roses, he decides. That is what he will plant. English roses for an English garden.

October 2004

Lili doesn't see Jin for several days and wonders whether she is avoiding her. The weather has turned cold, and when she steps outside Adrian's house each morning, she can smell the crisp onset of winter. Overnight the trees that line the street have lost their leaves, and the afternoons are no longer punctuated by warm bursts of sun. Instead, a thick layer of pale grey cloud seems to have descended over London, and Lili wonders whether this will be the colour of the English winter. On impulse, and in defiance of what she knows would be Jin's scorn at the price, she buys an expensive black wool coat at a shop in Oxford Street. She desperately wants to look as if she belongs, and the belted red jacket she purchased from a department store in Tangshan just before she left now seems woefully out of place: it is the wrong cloth, the wrong cut, the wrong colour. She can see that now, even though she had thought it was the height of fashion at the time.

When she collects May from school wearing her new coat, May stops and surveys her approvingly. "Nice coat," she says. "Better than your old one," she adds, slipping her hand into Lili's. Lili feels a small flush of pride, as if she has passed some sort of test, even though May is only a child. At home she carefully folds the red coat and stows it in the bottom of her wardrobe; she knows she will never wear it, even after she returns to China. It strikes her that the coat marks a tiny shift in her persona: how many others have there been since coming to this country, and what will they add up to?

Over the next few weeks, Adrian works later in the evenings, several times phoning home and asking if she will put May to bed. It is as if Lili's presence has suddenly freed him from the burden of fatherhood. Lili doesn't mind; she is happy to be of use, though she finds herself wondering about his life outside the house. May seems pleased to have her there and Lili relishes being part of a family again, even if the family is not her own. She and May quickly settle into a pattern: homework, Chinese study, dinner, a few reruns of *Friends* and then bed. Sometimes they draw or play board games after dinner.

One night, May enlists Lili's help in making a Halloween costume for a fancy dress disco at school. May is busy cutting cat shapes out of black paper, while Lili sews a costume out of an old sheet May has persuaded Adrian to donate.

"What's the word for 'ghost' in Chinese?" May asks.

"*Gui ʐi*," says Lili. May repeats the word out loud a few times, careful to copy Lili's tone.

"I can't decide whether I want to be a ghost or a devil," she adds. "How do you say devil?"

"That is also *gui*. But this time we say *mo gui*. Like a ghost with evil power."

May looks at her askance. "But devils and ghosts aren't the same."

"No. But in Chinese, we use the same word. In fact, we used to call foreigners *gui ʐi*. A long time ago."

"Why?"

"Because when Western people first came to China, to us their skins look very pale. We think they are dead spirits who have come back to life. So we called them *yang gui ʐi*, which means 'ghosts from across the ocean' or actually, 'foreign devil'." Lili grins mischievously at May.

"So if I went to China, would I be a *yang gui ʐi*?"

"No, not you. You would be a *hua qiao*. An overseas Chinese."

"Would Daddy be a *yang gui ʐi*?"

"Yes. But people do not use this word so often now. It is not so... polite."

At once Lili regrets her frankness: the word stems from a dark corner of China's history and dishonours those it describes. But such things are beyond May's comprehension.

"So what do they call foreigners now?"

"They call them *wai guo ren*. That is like: outsiders. Because to us, that's what they are."

"Do you feel like an outsider here?"

"Sometimes. But not with you." Lili smiles reassuringly at May.

"We all feel like an outsider sometimes," says May with a shrug. "Do you have Halloween in China?"

"No. But in summer we have Ghost Festival, when we honour the spirits of the dead."

"Do you get sweets?"

"Not really. But we leave food for the ghosts."

May frowns. "Why?"

"Well, during that time, we say ghosts are free to wander the earth. And perhaps they are hungry."

May stops cutting. "You mean for *real*? People believe ghosts wander around and eat stuff?" She raises a sceptical eyebrow.

Lili shrugs. "Not everyone believes this."

"Do *you*?" May pinpoints her with her gaze.

Lili feels her pulse quicken.

"I believe that sometimes, the spirits of dead people are here with us," she says carefully.

"You mean like now?" May looks around the kitchen. "*Here*?"

"Maybe not now. But sometimes. I believe they are here to help us, to look after us." *Or perhaps we are here to look after them*, she thinks.

"So you're not afraid of ghosts?"

Lili's mind flies to Wen and his easy smile. How could she ever be afraid of Wen?

"No," she answers, her voice suddenly disappearing.

222

"What would you do if you saw one?"

Lili hesitates. If Wen came to her, she would ask him why he left. "I don't know," she says finally.

"I'm not afraid of ghosts either," says May, returning to her colouring.

Lili goes back to sewing. As children, she and Wen had been encouraged by their stepparents to make offerings to the memory of their real parents, killed in the earthquake. But in spite of the framed wedding photograph her step-mother kept on an altar table in a corner of their sitting room – a photo of a young couple with nervous smiles and unreadable dark eyes – Lili found it difficult to believe that they had ever been real. It was only recently, in the wake of Wen's death, that she had begun to respect such traditions, setting up a small shrine to him in her bedroom and burning joss sticks in his memory.

One evening in August, when Tangshan was stifling with heat and humidity, she had walked to a park not far from where she lived. It was the fifteenth day of the seventh lunar month, the day when the dead return to the earth. The park was beside a narrow river that had once been polluted, but in recent years the area had been rehabilitated by the authorities. Lili was not alone in her desire to mark the Ghost Festival. The park was full of people that evening. Some had come to escape the heat, but many, like her, had come to honour the spirits of the dead. She walked to the bank of the river and lit a candle, pushing it across the water in a tiny boat she had fashioned from newspaper. The act had seemed futile at the time: the water was low, and the night so still, that her boat had drifted only a few feet from shore. Soon it became mired in the shallows along with several others, forming a forlorn flotilla. Lili looked around at the crowds along the bank: elderly widows accompanied by filial sons, young couples, middle-aged sons and daughters, all making offerings to long-dead husbands, parents, siblings. But nowhere in the stagnant waters could she discern even a trace of Wen's presence.

He isn't here, she had thought with dismay. *Perhaps if I had travelled to the ocean.* But she could not afford the time for such a journey, nor the fare, when she was desperately saving for her trip to England. That night, she turned her back on the river and walked slowly home through the sweltering heat of the city. When she had almost reached her flat, she stopped to eat a bowl of noodle soup at a small canteen. The restaurant was crowded and she found a table to herself in a back corner. She became conscious of a raucous group of young people on the far side of the room. She would not have paid them much notice, had the persistent laughter of one of the young women not drawn her attention. The woman had her back to the wall so Lili could see her flushed face and animated expressions clearly. She wore a tight white tank top and a bright red chiffon scarf knotted at her throat, and her shoulder-length hair fell in permed rings about her face. She was pretty, in a coquettish sort of way, the kind of girl who had stalked Wen when they were young. Her lively comments were directed towards the man sitting opposite her, whom Lili could not see, though he was slimly built and wore a black t-shirt.

The young man remained mostly silent, she noticed, until something the young woman said caught his fancy and he laughed. Lili froze, for his laughter somehow recalled Wen's. As she stared at his back, she became suddenly, irrationally convinced that he *was* Wen. She sat rigidly for the next few minutes, willing him to turn around, until eventually her stares caught the attention of the woman, who glared at her. Lili felt herself flush. She looked down at the remains of her noodles, her heart racing. She sat indecisively for a moment longer, then gathered up her things and threaded her way through the tables towards the doorway, conscious that the young woman was still eyeing her.

It was only after she had stepped outside the restaurant that she allowed herself a glance backwards through the window at the young man sitting opposite. It was not Wen, of course; and at once she was flooded with relief. She stood watching them, feeling Wen's ghost presence ebb away from her in the darkness. But as she turned away she was overcome by a creeping sense of shame. Why had she not been disappointed rather than relieved?

•

Lili and May lose track of time, and when Adrian returns from work he is clearly dismayed. "Still up?" he says pointedly to May when he walks into the kitchen.

"I wanted to finish my costume. Besides," May counters a little defiantly, "Lili said it was okay."

Adrian shoots a quick glance at Lili, but says nothing. Lili feels her face colour. May drapes the sheet over her head and waves her arms.

"See? I'm a ghost!"

Adrian picks up a stack of post on the counter and flicks through it distractedly.

"Very scary. Now off to bed," he says tersely.

"Lili taught me a new word," says May, hopping around him in the ghost costume. "*Yang gui zi*. It means 'foreign devil' and you're one."

May waits for Adrian to respond. He glances at the last envelope and sighs, tossing it back onto the counter, before turning to her.

"What?"

"*Yang gui zi*. You're a foreign devil. But I'm not."

Adrian looks at her, his lips pressed tightly together, then turns away.

"Bedtime, May," he says in a voice so clipped that May dances out of the room and down the hall without another word of protest. Adrian opens the refrigerator and looks inside.

"I'm sorry," says Lili nervously. "We did not notice time."

"It doesn't matter," Adrian replies, pulling out a bottle of beer. "Is there any food left over?" Lili motions towards a wok on the stove.

"Yes. We save some for you." Adrian goes over to the pan and lifts the lid.

"What is it?"

"It is pork mixed with vegetables and rice."

"Did May eat this? She usually hates courgette."

"Yes. May likes it very much."

226

Adrian shrugs and dishes the remaining food onto a plate, then sits down at the table. Lili starts to retreat, then pauses in the doorway.

"I am sorry to teach her this word. I explain to her the Chinese belief about ghosts."

Adrian looks up at her uncomprehendingly. Lili realises that Chinese beliefs are the last thing on his mind.

"Sorry?"

"It doesn't matter. You are very tired."

"I'm under quite a lot of pressure at work at the moment," says Adrian.

"Oh. I am sorry. If I can help, please... just ask me."

"You're already doing enough. May seems happier than she's been in ages." Adrian takes a long pull of beer.

"I am glad. I like May very much."

"Well, she adores *you*. She isn't the kind of child who shows affection very easily, but trust me, she's much happier now, much more... settled."

Adrian rises then and fills a glass of water at the sink. Lili wonders what he thinks of her. It shouldn't matter, but suddenly it does. She would like to hear him say that her presence has brought harmony to this house, not just for May, but for him as well. But though she spends a few more minutes clearing up, he says nothing more. When he has finished eating, Adrian pushes his plate to one side and picks up the newspaper, scanning the headlines. Lili watches him: his sleeves are rolled up part way and his arms are covered in fine blond hair and freckles. His hands are long and thin, and there are ink stains on his fingers. Adrian looks up after a moment with a questioning glance, aware suddenly that she is watching him. Lili flushes and turns to go.

"Lili?"

"Yes?"

"Do you think you could watch May on Saturday night? It's just... I've got dinner plans."

"Of course."

"Thanks. Sorry to be out so much lately."

"It is no trouble."

Adrian looks back down at the newspaper, and Lili hesitates.

"Good night," she says.

"Good night," replies Adrian without looking up.

•

Once back in her room, Lili sits on the bed and ponders the round carpet. Adrian seems changed somehow; her being here has altered him. She thought that she was helping May, but in reality she is enabling Adrian to find a new life. The idea troubles her, but she is not sure why. Surely he is entitled to his own life? Her mind flies back in time to Chen. When she was in her last year of university, she took a class in American literature. Chen was in his early thirties, had only recently been appointed to the English department, and was unlike any teacher she'd ever had. He listened attentively to his students and seemed less interested in teaching than in guiding them towards their own insights, an approach she and the others found vaguely unsettling. He urged them to read everything they could lay their hands on, and kept a small library of foreign books that he made available to those who were interested.

Chen seemed unfazed by the strictures under which they all laboured. That spring the government had announced a campaign to crack down on serious crime. Officials all over the country were exhorted to "Strike Hard" against criminals. The campaign was aimed at crimes such as murder, but it extended to large-scale theft and corruption cases, and hundreds of those found guilty had been publicly executed, sometimes in open-air stadiums filled with jeering crowds. These campaigns always had a sobering effect on university life. Only seven years had passed since the student uprisings in Tian An Men Square. And though it was rarely mentioned, the memory of that time lay dormant within them all.

Chen seemed interested only in literature; his actions could never be construed as political. Lili had seen other students quietly returning books to him after class, so one day she plucked up her courage and stopped by his office. It was tiny, little bigger than a cupboard and there were books everywhere: piled on his desk, in towering stacks upon the floor, and on shelves double-filled along the wall. When she appeared in the doorway, he frowned at her through his glasses: he was small and thin, and not particularly handsome, but he had an air of quiet understanding that she found reassuring. When she asked whether she might borrow a book, his face opened at once, as if he was seeing her for the first time, and he welcomed her in warmly, directing her to one shelf in particular. Flushing, she scrutinised the shelf: many of the books she'd never heard of.

Others were fat volumes that she knew she'd struggle to finish.

She wondered briefly whether he might suggest one, but he was watching her intently, and she realised that the act of choosing held significance. She did not want to disappoint him. Her eyes raced down the line of unfamiliar titles, pausing at a slim volume whose author, at least, she had heard of: *The Old Man and the Sea.* She plucked the book from the shelf and he gave an interested nod, as if the choice said something about her, though she did not know what. She excused herself quickly and spent the next three evenings on her bunk labouring through the book. In truth, she found it hard going: the long descriptions of the struggle between the man and fish began to irritate her after a time, and so little happened in the course of the story. Later that week, she appeared in Chen's doorway, the book in her hand. He paused in his work and smiled up at her, pushing his chair back from the desk.

"What did you make of it?"

"I liked the descriptions of the sea," she said tentatively.

"And the fish? What did you make of the marlin?" He used the phonetic translation: *ma ri lin.*

She hesitated. Was he teasing her? The fish was a fish, of course. And it fought heroically but died, only to be eaten by the sharks. So its death was pointless.

"I did not understand why he needed to kill it. The old man came to regard the fish as his brother, and seemed more attached to it than anything else in his life," she answered.

"Ah," said Chen. "So in the end, was the fish his friend or his adversary?"

"I wasn't sure."

"Perhaps it was both," he suggested with a smile. "There is room in literature for ambiguity," he added.

Lili frowned. It was not the answer she'd expected. She wanted Chen to tell her outright, to *instruct* her; after all, he was her teacher. But he seemed reluctant to do so.

"The important thing was that they respected each other," continued Chen. "And each kept their dignity. In the end, the old man and the fish were equals."

"But the fish died."

"Yes, but the old man did not succeed in bringing it home. In death he did not better it – rather, it returned to the sea."

Lili paused. She had not thought of it this way. Chen smiled benignly.

"Shall I give you something else to read?" he asked, sensing her unease. She nodded, relieved. He pulled another battered paperback from his shelf and handed it to her. She looked down. It was a slim volume of poetry by Emily Dickinson.

"Try this," Chen said. "It is completely different. You might find that it appeals to you more than *Hai Ming Wei*."

The poems did appeal to her. Though many of the words were unfamiliar, she liked the crisp brevity of the writing, and the sureness of the poet's voice. When she finished she read the biography at the back of the volume. Emily Dickinson had been something of a recluse: she had lived in her family home all her life and never married. Lili wondered then whether Chen was suggesting something with the choice; perhaps he'd realised there was a side of her much like the poet. If so, Lili wasn't sure if she should be flattered or offended. But she was eager to discuss the poems with him the next day.

And so their friendship began. Each week he chose for her a new paperback, and at night when her room-mates had finished their studies, she lay on her bunk deciphering its contents. They would discuss the books when she returned them, and each time he coaxed her gently towards an interpretation, while still encouraging her to find her own truths in what she read. As the weeks went past, she found herself looking forward to these sessions more and more, even dressing with care and taking extra time with her hair and make-up. She felt silly doing so: Chen was a married man, she knew as much, with a wife and child living in another province. Moreover, his behaviour towards her had never once suggested even the barest hint of impropriety. But she found herself wondering what sort of woman he had married, and what kind of husband he was.

One day, after he'd returned from visiting his wife and daughter over the Spring Festival, she worked up the courage to ask him about his family. "My wife is an English teacher," he answered matter-of-factly.

Like me, thought Lili. He married someone like me.

"Her mother has been unwell these past few years, so she wishes to remain at home to look after her," Chen added.

"It must be difficult to be so far apart," Lili said.

"One grows accustomed to distance," he replied with a small smile. "Even if it is not what one would choose. And it makes our time together more precious."

Lili felt her mouth go dry. She wanted him to say that in fact the distance suited him; that his marriage was a loveless match that had long since run its course. But instead he fished in his desk for a photo and pulled it out, handing it to her. Lili took the photo with a trembling hand and stared down at the woman and child. His wife's looks were bookish and unassuming, but her smile was warm and there was a sparkle in her eye that filled Lili with envy. She held a young child in her arms who frowned sternly at the camera.

"That is Ran Ran, my daughter," said Chen proudly. "She is three now. And very stubborn."

"She's adorable," murmured Lili, wondering whether she should also remark upon his wife.

"Thank you. I am very fortunate."

Lili watched as Chen carefully returned the photo to his drawer. She had no interest whatsoever in her male classmates, yet this kind and gentle man aroused in her a complex set of feelings. She rose and made her excuses, stumbling from the room. It was only when she reached her dorm that she realised she'd forgotten to ask him for another book.

Later that spring, Chen announced to the class that he was launching a translation contest for anyone who was interested. The winner would receive a new edition of the *Oxford English Dictionary*. Lili worked hard on her entry: a passage from *Hard Times* by Charles Dickens. She also spent time in Chen's office helping him to catalogue the submissions, as the response had been overwhelming. While she sorted and organised a filing system, he sat at his desk reading through them. Occasionally he would chuckle aloud, or shake his head at an error, which he would mark carefully. When he particularly liked something, he would sit forward excitedly, and his eyes would shine with favour. Each time Lili would crane her neck to see whose writing had brought on this response, and each time she would feel a small pang of jealousy that it wasn't hers.

One evening, he cleared his throat deliberately and waved a sheaf of paper at her. "I've come to yours," he said.

"Oh." Lili waited uncertainly.

"Perhaps you should go now," he suggested gently.

She rose, flushing, and gathered up her things. "Yes, of course. Excuse me."

"I look forward to reading your submission," he said kindly.

The next day in class he gave no clue to his response, though she searched his face for some indication. Afterwards, she lingered briefly, but when another teacher entered to speak to him, she left quickly. Two days later, there was an announcement of the winners posted on the main bulletin board in the English building. Lili stood in front of the board, stunned. Her entry had not even been placed among the top three. A popular male student from the year below had won with a translation of Walt Whitman, and the second and third prize had gone to girls in her year. One was even in her dorm: a quiet, round-faced girl with hair that fell nearly to her waist, whom Lili had never given a second thought. Though she had not expected to win, she had thought that her status as his unofficial assistant would count for more. But of course it had not, she reflected sullenly as she walked to her next class. Chen was unswervingly fair in his treatment of his students. His conduct was unimpeachable. Was that not why she admired him?

When she got home that evening, there were raised eyebrows from her room-mates. She realised she'd made one too many references to the contest and its possible outcome, even laughing over some of the entries. One student, she had told them a few evenings before, had translated the word *aromatic* as *romantic*. For the next few weeks, she could not bring herself to visit Chen in his office. She came and went quickly from class and took care never to meet his gaze. One day, only a week before they were due to break for the summer holiday, he asked her to stay behind after class. When the others had gone, he leaned back upon his desk and crossed his arms.

"You've not come to see me lately," he said.

"I've been busy with exams," she replied evasively.

"I see." Chen gave a small nod. "I thought perhaps you were disappointed by the outcome of the contest."

"Not at all. I'm sure the winners were far more deserving."

"Your entry was very good, very capable."

"But not outstanding," she said.

"Perhaps not," he admitted.

"I should have worked harder."

A pained expression crossed Chen's face.

"You have a genuine talent for English, Lili. But translation isn't just a question of rendering a book's meaning, it's about capturing the author's intentions. You must interpret not just the words, but the essence of the work." Chen paused then.

Lili saw that his shirt was missing a button, and there was a small stain to one side of his collar. *I could fix these*, she thought fleetingly.

"At any rate," Chen added gently, "I think you will make a fine teacher one day."

"But not a translator," she said.

"I'm sure you can succeed at that too, if you put your mind to it."

She looked up at him. *But I cannot succeed in capturing you*, she thought.

"Thank you," she said instead, rising to go.

"By the way," Chen said as she was leaving. Lili paused in the doorway. "My wife and daughter will move here in September. Her mother has recovered from her illness."

Lili felt a lump rise in the back of her throat. Did he think this news would make her happy?

"Congratulations," she murmured.

"Thank you. It's been a long time in coming. You'll be gone by then, won't you? It's a pity. She would have liked to meet you."

Lili stared at him, unable to speak. The thought of meeting his wife face to face, of making small talk, filled her with dread. How could their minds run in such different directions? Perhaps she had fooled herself about Chen; perhaps he was not her kindred spirit after all.

That was the last time she had spoken to him, though several months later, when she was passing by the campus, she caught a glimpse of him queuing at a bus stop with his wife and child. He looked older somehow, and more harried. He held tightly to his daughter's hand, and when the crowd surged around them, he quickly swept the child into his arms. Lili watched from the window of her bus until they'd disappeared from view.

•

Now, sitting on her bed in Adrian's house, the familiar emptiness has returned. Once again, she has succumbed to the lure of a false future, this time without realising. Until now she had thought of Adrian as something of a tragic figure – single, lonely, bereft – a man struggling to raise a child that was not his own. Now she sees that he is something far different, a man in control of his destiny. Lili looks over at the framed photo of Wen. He too had taken charge of his fate, had gone in search of something that lay beyond her understanding. *Had he found it?* she wondered. *And had it been worth the price?*

June 2004

As spring turns to summer, Wen's days fall into a routine. Mornings are devoted to studying English and afternoons to housekeeping, cooking and gardening. Angie's garden has thrived under his care: the rangy lawn, once full of weeds, is now lush and green. He has pruned the trees and shrubs back to their intended shape, and restored order to the flower beds, which have begun to bloom in a profusion of colour. He found a mass of old bricks at the back of the garden and spent several days laying a paved area at the top of the garden by the back door. He laid the bricks in the shape of a lotus: a symbol of purity and compassion in his culture, but he struggled to explain its significance to Angie. She seemed surprised that he had taken the trouble to lay the bricks in a pattern, and this in turn surprised him, as he would not have undertaken such a labour without doing so. At such times he realises how deeply his culture is embedded in him.

Most of the time, though, he feels his country receding. The longer he is away from it, the more he senses its complexity, as if he is a passenger in a tiny rowing boat watching an enormous ship from afar. For the first time he can see the ship in its entirety, but he will never understand its inner workings, what propels the ship forward through the waves. And he no longer understands the place he once occupied within its rigid frame. Perhaps he never did, for a part of him has felt this distance, this uncertainty, all his life.

As soon as he was old enough, he had begun to question the unlikely circumstances of his birth, and the cataclysmic act of nature that tore apart his family. But it was not until he was sixteen, when his stepmother lay dying with cancer, that he summoned the courage to ask her about the earthquake that had killed his parents. She'd spoken of it before, but only in the vaguest terms, and largely as a means of marking time, as in: *after the quake, we did not see the swallows for many years*. But this time, she fixed her tired gaze on him and gave a frown of such sadness that he instantly regretted asking. Then she turned her head away and spoke very slowly, her eyes clouding with memory.

"That was an extraordinary summer," she said. "It was too hot. As if the earth was trying to burn us all out of our homes. In the weeks leading up to the quake, many people had dragged their mats outside at night to sleep in the open air. They were the lucky ones, when the time came. That morning, the water rose in the well. As I stood there, it rose and fell three times. I remember wondering why I'd never seen such a thing before. I turned away without drawing water – something made me turn away – as if I should not see. That was the first sign. Later that night, the lights started. Beautiful coloured lights strung out across the sky. Silver blues and greens, like the shimmering scales of a fish. I suppose we should have known, after all we'd been through, not to trust such beauty."

She paused then, for a moment overcome. He thought perhaps this was all that she would say, and decided maybe this was for the best. But then she began to speak again. "Afterwards, no one cried. There was too much sorrow. Anyway, we were too numb to mourn. It was days before the army came to rescue us. We did what we could in the meantime, but we had no tools, no machinery, no food or clean water. And then the rain came. It fell in torrents, for days on end, to wash away all the death. But of course it only made things worse. There were piles of corpses everywhere, lining the roads, clogging the alleys. Piles as high as a house, rotting in the rain, waiting for a proper burial. And as soon as the rain stopped, the flies. Great black clouds of them, so thick that you could hardly breathe.

"We were lucky to find you in all the chaos. We knew they'd rescued newborn twins from the hospital wreckage – who didn't? The story was broadcast for days on the radio. But when we came forward to claim you, at first the local authorities refused to see us. They didn't believe we were blood relations. They thought we were childless gold diggers. They'd planned to send you to a special orphanage with all the others. The orders had come straight from Beijing: none of the children orphaned by the earthquake were to be given to local families. They were to be raised by the state as model citizens, loyal to the party. We fought hard to get you; and in the end we bribed the hospital superintendent with all our savings. It was the only way.

"Life was bitterly hard. We slept outside in tents for months, all through that long cold winter. I kept you both inside my quilt, right next to my skin; it was a miracle we didn't freeze. We'd lived through so much already – first the Japanese occupation, then the famine years, and afterwards, the terrible upheaval of the Cultural Revolution. But this was different, because we bore it alone. We did not share it with the rest of the nation. Afterwards, they tried to call us the Brave City. But we weren't brave. Not really. We had no choice.

"I nearly left your stepfather more than once during that time. In those first few years, there were many hasty marriages, men and women who'd lost their spouses and quickly recoupled, so it would not have attracted much attention. But I had twins to raise. You and your sister. Two precious gifts. And I couldn't do that on my own. So I stayed."

"Thank you," he murmured.

She took his hand then, and pressed it to her chest.

"You've been a good son. Not of my own flesh perhaps, but of my own heart. That is what matters most. I've often wondered why I found so much fortune out of circumstances that caused such misery for others. I'll never know."

Wen had asked himself the same question: why had he and Lili been spared, when so many others had perished? Growing up, the fact of their shared fortune had led them in different directions. Lili was grateful and determined to make the most out of life. Wen was more philosophical: his parents' tragedy was also his own. He would carry it with him always, like a birthmark. It wasn't that he made little of life's opportunities. It was that he was painfully aware of how fleeting they were.

•

One Saturday, after he has finished laying the patio, Angie drives him to a large garden centre where they buy a round painted wrought-iron table and two chairs. The set is half-price and costs ninety-nine pounds: a small fortune at home, but perhaps not so much here, he now realises. A thin-faced older salesman hovers behind them while they look over the furniture. The man directs all of his comments to Angie. She asks a few questions, then turns to Wen.

"Well? What do you think?"

Wen looks at the salesman. "What if rain?"

It is the first time he has spoken and the salesman's eyebrows shoot up in surprise.

"It has a rustproof coating," the man replies after a moment's hesitation. "And a five-year guarantee."

"Five years," says Angie, staring down at the table. She runs a hand along its surface.

Five years, thinks Wen. Angie turns to him and their eyes meet.

"Five years is good enough for me," she says.

A few days later, Wen goes for a walk along the coast, heading south of the promenade at Morecambe Bay. The weather is unsettled, and perhaps because of this, he too is restless. He passes an old church and a graveyard, then climbs a flight of stone steps up to the top of a bluff looking out over Half Moon Bay. Here he finds the ruins of an ancient building, another church perhaps, and a scattering of ancient graves hewn into stone. Wen pauses at the site: the six graves have been laid out in a grim line, their corpse shapes etched deep into solid rock. One is disconcertingly smaller than the rest: it must have contained the body of a child. The stone cavities are half filled with rainwater, and the sight unnerves him, for death and water are linked too closely for him now.

Straight out to sea a line of dark clouds rolls along the horizon. As he stands gazing out across the water, he realises that he has been summoned here by the storm, that the spirits of those he worked alongside now reside here, trapped for ever in its fury. He freezes, the bone-aching cold of that night rushing back through him, together with the terrifying darkness of the sea. If he closes his eyes, he could be with them. He feels slightly faint, as if his legs are no longer beneath him. He turns and stumbles back down the ancient stone steps, leaving the sea and its ghosts behind.

On the way home he turns inland, seeking refuge in a maze of streets lined with old cottages. He walks without purpose or direction, staring at each house as he passes. The neighbourhood is obviously prosperous: two years ago a road such as this one, with its freshly tarred surface, neatly manicured lawns and immaculately restored old cottages, would not have been conceivable to him. Now it forms part of his reality. The idea still confounds him: the distance he has travelled, the changes he has known, the life he has endured. He comes to the end of a long, winding road, where a large, slightly run-down house is set well back from the street. The lawn is thick and green and overgrown, though he can tell it has been lavished with care in the past. A tall hedge obscures much of the garden from view, but when he peers through the rusty iron gate, he sees a profusion of flowers blooming all along its borders. Roses, he realises – the most beautiful roses he has ever seen.

He hears the methodic sound of clippers. Someone is working in the front corner of the garden over to his right, just out of view. Wen pauses, knowing he should carry on, but wanting to see more. After a minute the clipping stops. He hears a slight shuffling of steps and in another moment an old woman comes into view: small, a curved back, her head bent low, silver-grey hair piled in a dishevelled manner atop her head. She wears faded cotton trousers and a pale blue apron tied about her waist, and slung over one arm is a basket filled with pale pink roses. She does not notice him at first. He watches her walk slowly across the lawn, can hear the laboured whistle of her breath and see the slight tremor of her head as she concentrates on every step. When she is almost in front of him, she pauses, her head slowly rising towards him like that of a giant tortoise. She blinks through her spectacles, and draws a breath. They stare at each other for a moment, before he bows to her apologetically.

"I am sorry," he says.

"No need," she replies matter-of-factly.

Her words confuse him. Perhaps she thinks he is selling something?

"Your garden. Very beautiful."

He smiles and indicates the garden with a wave of his arm. She turns and surveys the garden, nodding in agreement.

"Thank you. The world needs beauty." She turns back to him. "Do you like to garden?" she asks politely.

He hesitates, did not realise the word could be used as a verb rather than a noun.

"Yes, I like garden very much. Your roses." He breaks off, his English failing him.

"You may come in and see them if you like."

She beckons him in, through the metal gate, and he enters the garden, crossing over towards the bed she was working on. She turns and follows. He points to the rosebush: it is thick with deep red flowers, each blossom extravagantly splayed open by layers of perfectly formed petals. He bends closer to finger one. It smells faintly of peach.

"Difficult, this rose?"

"Difficult? To grow? Not particularly. Just temperamental. Roses are like children. They need time and attention, yet in fact they will tolerate a great deal." She pauses for a moment and reaches up to snap off a dead-head. "I suppose these roses are my children," she muses.

"You have no children?" he asks pityingly. She turns to him with a smile.

"I have two children. Grown now. With families of their own."

"Oh," he says, relieved. "They live here?"

She tilts her head to one side, regarding him.

"No. They live a long way away. But I have my garden to keep me busy. And my roses."

Wen wonders fleetingly about her children, whether they visit with their families, whether they take time to admire her garden.

"These roses come from China, in fact," she says.

He looks at her with surprise.

"I am from China," he says.

She smiles. "I thought as much. The Chinese grew roses for centuries before they were brought to Europe. We owe them a great deal."

"I do not know," he murmurs.

"China roses are very hardy. They root easily and are very adaptable."

"Hard?"

"They're strong. And they can survive in many different places."

Wen nods. *Survive*. A word he has come to understand only too well.

"But what I like best is their colour," she says. She reaches over and snips a stem at its base with her shears. She holds the blossom out to him, and after a moment's surprise, he takes it. "You see?" she says. "The reddest of reds.

Tinged with the faintest hint of blue."

Wen studies the delicate arrangement of petals, as if someone had fanned out a deck of cards at perfect intervals.

"It's called Crimson China. The colour never fades, but gets darker with age. So it grows more and more beautiful each day. To my mind, these roses try harder than all the others," the old woman adds with a smile.

He hands the rose back to her, but she shakes her head in protest.

"Please. Keep it. A small gift."

"Thank you," he says, a little embarrassed.

"Would you like some cuttings?"

He stares at her uncertainly. The word is new to him: a type of drink perhaps?

"No, thank you," he murmurs, rather awkwardly.

"I have some in my greenhouse, ready for replanting."

Wen struggles to decipher her meaning.

"If you come again tomorrow, at teatime, I'll have them ready for you." She turns and starts to shuffle away.

"I am sorry?"

She stops and turns around.

"Tomorrow. Shall we say four o'clock? I will have the roses ready for you then," she says slowly, careful to enunciate each word. Wen is not certain he has understood, but nods in agreement.

"Thank you," he ventures.

"You can thank me tomorrow," she says with a wave of her hand.

He watches her step carefully across the long grass, and disappear around the corner of the house.

•

That night he does not tell Angie of his encounter with the old woman, but writes down the name of her road, which he has carefully memorised. He wonders whether he will be able to find her house upon his return, or whether he has imagined the entire episode, so unlikely does it seem. But the following afternoon, when he retraces his steps down the winding lane, the house is there behind the old rusty gate, with its tangled lawn and spectacular roses. Wen pushes open the gate, walks up to the house and rings the doorbell. He waits politely for a few minutes before trying it a second time. At length he hears the shuffle of her step and she appears along the side of the house, once again wearing the faded cotton trousers and pale blue apron. Today she also wears a large floppy straw hat.

"There you are," she says when she sees him. "I thought perhaps you'd forgotten. I've got them repotted. Come round the side, will you?"

She turns and disappears around the side of the house and he follows her down a stony path until they reach an old greenhouse covered in cobwebs. Some of the glass is missing or broken and the inside is a mass of pots and containers with plants in varying stages of growth. He sees a large open bag of potting soil on the floor and a row of freshly planted plastic pots, each containing a single plant.

"Have you brought something to carry them in?" she asks.

He hesitates, and she gives a wave. "No matter, I've got some old carrier bags here somewhere."

She fumbles around in the corner of the greenhouse and eventually produces two white plastic bags. She takes the pots and sets them in the bags carefully, before handing them to him.

"There you are," she says with satisfaction. "Six in all. Mind, don't plant them too closely. Roses need plenty of space. And this variety loves the sun, so make sure it's not overlooked. There is a rose for every type of garden. With a bit of luck and trial and error, you'll find one that's suited to yours."

She pauses then and scrutinises him.

"You *do* have a garden?"

"Yes," he says, nodding.

"Good, I was worried for a moment you might wish to sell them. You wouldn't, would you?"

"I buy the roses?" he asks tentatively.

"Heavens no, I don't want your money. The roses are a gift," she says pointedly. "From me to you."

"Thank you," he says, for a moment overcome by her kindness.

He follows her back down the gravel path and across the lawn. As she shuffles through the grass ahead of him, she suddenly stumbles on a patch of weed, pitching sideways. He rushes forward to catch her elbow, steadying her.

"Oh my, thank you!" she says with a breathless laugh. "I used to have a boy who cut the grass, but he disappeared.

I'm afraid it's got rather shaggy."

"You want I cut grass?" he offers.

She turns to him. "Would you?" she asks, eyes widening.

"Yes."

"That would be marvellous. I would pay you, of course," she adds hastily.

"No," he says quickly. "No pay. This pay," he says, lifting the two carrier bags with a smile.

She raises a bemused eyebrow.

"You'll work for flowers?"

He nods. After all, he thinks, flowers are what he wants right now; flowers are what he needs. Though after months of hard labour for terrible wages, the irony of this is not lost on him. She smiles.

"How lovely."

That night he tells Angie of his encounter with the old woman, and shows her the six rose pots, which for the moment he has set out on the wrought-iron table. Angie looks at him askance.

"She just *gave* them to you?"

"Yes."

"Why?"

"I don't know."

Wen shrugs. The old woman is no doubt lonely, but something prevents him from saying this to Angie. Certainly, she seems isolated, in a way that few people in his country ever are. In China, people live atop one another: if you do not live with other family members, then most likely you are surrounded by those in your work unit or housing block. The state plays far too big a role in organising and supervising daily life for individuals to lead such solitary lives. But Angie, too, is a loner. Wen knows that now, even if he didn't at first, and the fact of his presence hasn't altered this. He wonders if Britain is filled with such people, and whether they choose solitude, or whether it is thrust upon them. Perhaps it is a stage his own country may one day reach, though it is difficult to conceive of.

•

The following afternoon, he returns to mow the old woman's lawn, which takes him almost three hours, as he must pause every few minutes to empty the clippings into an enormous heap of compost at the rear of the house. When he is finished, she insists on serving him tea and biscuits in the garden, on an old slatted table that wobbles precariously when she sets the tray upon it. She pours milk in his tea without asking, then pauses over the sugar, to which he shakes his head quickly. He can stomach milk in his tea, but not sugar.

When he eventually rises to take his leave, she gives him a large bag full of compost she has prepared earlier.

"For the roses," she explains. "They need feeding."

Then she removes a carefully folded twenty-pound note from her apron and stuffs it into the breast pocket of his shirt with her long mottled fingers. Embarrassed, he tries to return the note, but she flaps her hands at him in a no-nonsense motion.

"If you do not take the money, then I shall feel guilty

asking you to return," she says pointedly. "And the hedges need trimming almost as badly as the grass."

She gives a vague wave towards the hedge. Wen smiles. Without even trying, he has found himself back in employment.

•

That night when he returns home, Angie is sitting at the kitchen table with a heavy-set man he doesn't recognise. It's the first time he has seen anyone else enter her home, and at once he is disconcerted.

The man is in his early forties and wears jeans and a plaid shirt. His face is pale and slightly puffy, as if it has been injected with air, and his thick brown hair has turned grey at the edges. A creased black leather jacket is slung over the chair behind him. As Wen comes through the front door, laden with the bag of compost, they both turn to him, faces unexpecting. Wen has the sudden sense that he is stepping into another universe.

"Wen, this is Ray," says Angie.

Wen nods a little uncertainly at the heavy-set man. "Hello."

Ray tilts his head to one side and raises five fingers in a fleeting wave. Wen's mind flies to the black tracksuit Angie gave him that first night. He'd never asked who owned it. Ray raises an eyebrow at Angie.

"You're a dark horse," he says, ignoring Wen's presence.

"Shut up, Ray." Angie's tone is so casual that Wen thinks he has misheard.

He carries the compost past them out to the garden, where he sets it down beside the table. When he comes back inside, Ray is pulling a pack of cigarettes out of his jacket pocket. He puts one in his mouth and takes out some matches, pausing just before he strikes one. He looks up, eyes darting quickly to them both.

"Mind if I smoke?"

"Would it matter?" says Angie.

"It's *your* house," Ray counters.

They stare at each other for a moment, then he strikes the match and lights the cigarette. Angie waits until he exhales, then holds out her hand. Ray passes the cigarette to her and she inhales deeply, blowing the smoke up into the air. At once the tiny kitchen fills with the smell of nicotine, and the sensation of it almost causes Wen to faint.

He has not smoked since the accident, and now images from his former life come wafting back to him. At the end of each day's cockling, their fingers stiff with cold, he and Lin permitted themselves the luxury of a hand-rolled cigarette out on the sands. Lin would gaze across the endless expanse of sea, wondering what was happening on the far side of the world, whether his son would be doing home-work, or outside in the street playing football with his friends, whether his wife would be making dumplings, or gossiping with her sister on the phone.

Angie takes another long drag then passes the cigarette back to Ray. "Ray's my brother," she says to Wen, exhaling out of the side of her mouth. "Just in case you were wonder-ing," she adds.

Once again Wen nods. He did not know she had a brother, had never pictured her with any family at all. Though of course she must have family. Wen waits, uncertain whether he should sit down with them or remove himself to the garden, where the roses are waiting to be planted.

"Nice job with the garden," says Ray, indicating the outside with a nod.

"Thank you," says Wen. For an instant he wonders whether Ray is making fun of him.

"Actually, Ray was just leaving," announces Angie, rising to her feet.

"I suppose I was."

Ray pushes the large white envelope across to her side of the table, then stands up, shrugging on his leather jacket. He turns to Wen.

"See you again maybe," he remarks, a note of challenge in his voice.

"Yes," Wen replies.

Angie follows Ray to the front door. Ray leaves without another word, but not before he and Angie exchange a knowing glance. Wen recognises the look of intense familiarity that passes between them: only lovers or siblings exchange such glances. His mind flies at once to Lili. Where is she now?

Angie closes the door and leans back against it with a sigh.

"I need a drink." She crosses over to the sink and takes out the whisky from beneath the counter, pouring herself a large tumbler.

"You did not tell me you have brother."

"No," she says taking a swallow. "I did not."

"Why?"

"We aren't exactly close."

Close. He knows the word, but her meaning eludes him.

"Ray's a bit of a bastard," she says then.

Wen understands this word only too well, having been called it several times by angry fishermen. He nods towards the envelope on the table.

"What is this?"

Angie raises an eyebrow. "*That* is my mother. Or what's left of her."

Wen waits. Angie is being deliberately difficult, he feels, though he does not understand why.

"The papers she left behind when she died," says Angie with a sigh. "They've been tied up for more than a year. But it's finished now. Her life is well and truly over."

Wen frowns. It is only the second time she has spoken of her mother, and the bitterness with which she speaks makes him uneasy.

"My mother left me this house when she died," explains Angie, casting a glance around the room. "And everything in it. It's like living in her tomb. I should have sold it straight away. But there were legal problems, and I couldn't. And now it's like... she's taken me prisoner." Angie pauses to refill her glass.

"Ray got the money. And I got the house. He bought some property, and now he's a landlord in Liverpool. If you can call it that. Those houses you lived in when you were cockling? They could've been Ray's. They probably were Ray's." She snorts and takes another drink.

"That would be something, wouldn't it? Me, you and Ray. With my mother the one thing that ties us all together." Angie pauses and looks straight at him. "She was out there that night. The night I found you. My mother was out there on the sands."

Wen shifts uneasily.

"But what I don't understand is: why she gave me you."

Angie's eyes cloud over. She sways slightly. The whisky has affected her quickly tonight. She must have been drinking earlier.

"You should have died," Angie continues. "But you didn't. And now I have my mother to thank."

She drains the glass and thumps it down on the table.

Wen turns and walks out the door to the garden, leaving her behind him. He does not like her tone, even if her words are not entirely comprehensible to him. It is as if the sudden presence of her family has thrown up a wall between them. He grabs a shovel and the carrier bags of pots and makes his way down the garden to the spot that he has already chosen in his mind: a south-facing bed where the roses will have plenty of sun and space. He lays the pots on the grass behind him and begins to dig intently, throwing each shovelful of earth off to one side. Within a few minutes he has dug a hole deep enough for a mature tree, let alone a rose.

"Hey."

He turns and sees Angie behind him in the grass.

"I'm sorry," she says.

He nods, bending to pick up one of the pots. He gently pulls the plug of dirt from the pot and places it in the hole, scooping earth in from the sides and pressing it down too hard with his hands. Once it is planted, Wen steps back to look at it: the spindly stalk appears forlorn by itself against the wall, fragile and fleeting, as if someone had plucked it from its rightful home and placed it there with no rhyme or reason. He thinks of the old woman's garden, of its beautifully tended beds and their fragrant abundance. He cannot imagine her roses flourishing here against this wall. Perhaps he was wrong to move them.

November 2004

May sits at the dining table colouring a picture, while Lili chops onions for a pasta sauce she is making.

"What do you think?" says May, chewing on the end of the marker. She points to the picture of a vase filled with flowers.

"It is very nice. Purple is my favourite colour."

"It's for my mother. Tomorrow is her birthday," remarks May casually.

She picks up a green marker and begins to draw some leaves on the flowers. Lili stops cutting. May's head is bent over the table concentrating on the picture. Lili sees that she has folded the sheet of paper in half to make a card.

"My English mother," adds May, almost as an afterthought. "The one who died."

It takes Lili a moment to find her voice.

"Oh," she says. "I'm sorry."

258

"It's okay. We used to bake a cake or something, but last year we just went out for dinner. Adrian didn't want to stay at home." May often calls Adrian by name when he is not around, a habit that Lili finds disconcerting.

"I see. What will you do tomorrow?"

"Dunno. We haven't talked about it yet. Hey! Maybe we can all go out!"

"I do not think so," says Lili uncertainly.

"Why not? You live here now. You're like part of the family."

Lili does not know how to reply. She turns back to the onions instead, and scoops them into a frying pan, adding oil. A few moments later they hear the front door open. May jumps up, grabbing the card, and rushes down the hallway.

"Daddy, look what I did for Mummy!" she shouts.

Lili pauses cooking, trying to make out Adrian's response. A moment later she hears them approach.

"Hello," says Adrian. She sees with relief that he is in a good mood this evening.

"Daddy, can we go out for dinner tomorrow?"

"Sure," says Adrian.

"Can Lili come?"

Adrian looks over at Lili.

"Does Lili *want* to come?"

Lili feels her heart stop.

"Of course she does!" says May.

"Well, all right then," says Adrian. He turns and walks out of the kitchen.

The following evening Adrian suggests they go for

Chinese food, so Lili takes them to Wen's hotpot restaurant, promising May there will not be a duck in sight. She has not been back since the day she spoke to the owner, though she has desperately wanted to return. She would not dare go alone, however, and reckons that Adrian and May will provide the perfect buffer. Perhaps she will not even be recognised by the owner. But even as she steps inside the front door, Lili realises she has erred. Everything is just as she remembered: the row of dark red booths along the far wall, the cloying smell of oil in the air, the mottled brown linoleum floor. As she enters she sees the hostess she spoke to that day, wearing the same tight-fitting black dress, though today her long black hair has been swept back in a chignon. The hostess looks up as they enter and Lili sees the flash of recognition in her eyes, coupled with surprise. She picks up a stack of menus and walks over to them.

"Good evening," she says carefully, her eyes flicking briefly to Lili's.

"Could we have a table for three?" says Adrian.

"A booth!" says May, clutching Adrian's sleeve.

"Yes, of course," says the hostess. She leads them across the room to the far wall and shows them to a booth. Adrian and May slide in on one side, but before Lili can take her seat, the hostess turns to her and speaks in Mandarin, lowering her voice.

"We didn't expect to see you again," she says nervously.

"Is there a problem?"

"Some men came. The other day. They were asking about your brother."

Lili freezes. "Why?"

"I don't know. They were rough types. From Fujien. They wanted to know if he'd been back here. Or if we'd seen him."

Lili stares in surprise at the woman.

"I don't understand," she says.

"I told them he was dead, of course! They asked me how I knew. So I said we'd spoken to you." The hostess steals a glance towards the kitchen. "He *was* your brother, wasn't he?"

"Yes."

"They didn't seem to know about you," she says uneasily. "They asked me if I knew where you worked, but I told them I had no idea." The hostess pauses, awaiting her response.

"Thank you," murmurs Lili.

"Your brother. Is he dead or isn't he?" asks the hostess.

Lili's eyes drift to Adrian and May. May is playing with a pair of disposable wooden chopsticks, trying to pick up the corner of her napkin, but Adrian is watching them, the menu open in front of him. She looks back at the hostess and nods, a lump rising in her throat. "Yes."

"Then I don't know what they were on about!" The hostess tosses her head angrily. "They kept asking questions, so in the end I told them to look up his old girl-friend at the language school in Shepherd's Bush." She pauses and lowers her voice. "Was your brother in some kind of trouble?"

Lili hesitates, thinking of Jin. "I don't know," she says.

The words come out in English, though she hadn't meant them to. The hostess shakes her head slightly. Just then, the owner steps into the dining room from the kitchen, calling her. He does not seem to recognise Lili at first, but then his eyes alight on her and he frowns. He gestures to the hostess and she scurries off to him. Lili slides into the booth opposite Adrian.

"Is everything okay?" he asks.

"Yes."

"What was all that about?"

"Nothing. I know this woman a little."

Adrian stares at her expectantly. Lili feels as if he is looking straight into her past.

"My brother, he used to work here," she explains.

"Oh," says Adrian, his face paling. "I'm sorry. Perhaps we shouldn't have come."

"No," she says quickly. "It's okay. I wanted to come."

"Do they have fortune cookies here?" asks May, oblivious to their conversation.

"Sorry?" Lili asks.

"Fortune cookies. You know, little cookies with paper fortunes inside?"

"I don't know," she answers. Truly she knows nothing at the moment: the facts of her life keep shifting beneath her. Each time she reaches a place of equilibrium, something happens to upset it. She tries to concentrate on the menu and the prospect of hotpot, one of her favourite dishes at home.

"Is hotpot spicy?" asks May.

"I hope so," says Adrian.

"But I don't like spicy!"

"Yes, you do," says Adrian. "You just think you don't."

"No, I don't! I've told you a thousand times!"

Their conversation filters through to Lili. She looks over at May. How can the child be Chinese and not like spicy? Are not such things hard-wired into her genes? A waiter arrives to take their order, and perhaps it is Lili's imagination, but he seems to glance in her direction one too many times while they are ordering, as if he is expecting her to disclose something startling at any moment. Adrian asks her advice about several dishes, then orders hotpot for the two of them and a dish of stir-fried beef with rice for May.

The hotpot arrives a few minutes later: a large black cauldron filled with steaming soup of a milky colour. May gives a little shriek. They turn to her with alarm. She is pointing at the hotpot. "Look!" she cries.

A dried black seahorse floats disconcertingly on the top of the soup, its tiny eyes and nostrils perfectly visible.

"This is dried," says Lili quickly. "It gives special flavour to the soup."

"Daddy!" May pulls a face.

Adrian picks up a spoon and fishes the seahorse out, wrapping it in a napkin and putting it out of sight.

"There," he says. "All gone."

"You're going to *eat* that now?" asks May.

"May," he admonishes.

Lili looks over to see the restaurant owner staring at her from the kitchen door. As soon as their eyes meet, he turns and disappears inside. For the rest of the meal, she feels vaguely uneasy, as if her presence is unwanted. They should not have come to Wen's place of work. What was she thinking? She tries to enjoy the hotpot but it is different from those she has eaten at home: the broth not spicy enough, the meat lacking in flavour. She is relieved when May yawns with tiredness and Adrian calls for the bill. As they rise to go, she sees the owner watching her again, this time from near the door. She walks towards him a little apprehensively, stalling slightly so that the others go ahead of her, and when she is just in front of him he steps forward.

"Forgive me," he says in Mandarin. "But we don't want any trouble here." His tone is grimly apologetic, but when she meets his gaze he shakes his head slowly from side to side. She stares at him for a moment, her face growing hot, remembering his praise for Wen.

"I understand," she replies. She turns to go and sees that Adrian has stopped to wait for her in the doorway, his face creased with concern.

"Is everything all right?"

"Everything is fine." Her voice wavers oddly.

When they return home, Adrian goes to put May to bed. Once in her room, Lili tries ringing Jin on her mobile, but there is no answer. She contemplates getting a bus to Hounslow, but it is already late and the evening's events have exhausted her. She turns to the photo of Wen on her dresser, wishing for the hundredth time that it could speak. Perhaps he was in trouble before he died. Perhaps this is what Jin has been hiding from her. She resolves to find Jin tomorrow and confront her over Wen's death. Lili goes downstairs for a cup of tea, and while she is waiting for the kettle to boil, Adrian comes into the kitchen.

"May's asleep," he says. He turns to the cupboard and takes out a bottle of whisky and a glass.

"I need a drink." He holds up the bottle. "Whisky?" Lili feels her insides dip. She does not know whether she should have a whisky with Adrian.

"Yes, please."

Adrian pours two half-tumblers of whisky and hands one to her. Lili takes a swallow, feels the heat in the back of her throat.

"So what happened tonight?" Adrian asks, leaning back against the counter.

"I'm sorry?"

"At the restaurant. You looked upset."

Lili's stomach tightens with apprehension. She is not prepared to answer questions about Wen.

"My brother…" She falters, uncertain how to continue.

"The one who died?"

"Yes. He was twin with me."

"Oh. I didn't realise. I'm sorry. How did he die?"

"He drowned," she says.

Lili takes another swallow of whisky. She feels a hot tear well, did not realise she was close to crying. She turns away quickly and wipes at the tear with the back of her hand.

"When did it happen?"

"In February."

"Not long then," says Adrian.

265

"It feels like... much longer."

"Grief takes time. I'm afraid I'm a bit of an expert."

Lili wants to ask about his wife, but doesn't know how.

"The first six months were the hardest," Adrian continues. "I used to dread this time of day. The evenings, after
May was asleep. I guess it was the silence I hated. And the
solitude." Adrian is staring down into the amber liquid,
his tone softened by memory. "She was gone, but I felt her
presence everywhere."

"Yes," Lili murmurs. "I feel this too."

"In the end I had to change things. The food we ate. The
clothes we wore. The colour of the walls. Even the sheets
we slept on. I changed it all. I guess that's how I put her to
rest." Adrian's voice fades slightly on this last word, and he
turns abruptly and reaches for the whisky bottle, refilling his
glass.

"But I felt disloyal," he says with a shrug.

Lili realises she has stopped breathing. His candour has
taken her by surprise. But she wishes he would continue.
Adrian suddenly shakes his head, remembering himself. He
runs a hand through his hair.

"Sorry," he says awkwardly.

"Please. No."

"It was a long time ago." He gives a small smile. She feels
a pang of jealousy for his wife. To be the cause of a grief
that envelops him even now, after all these years.

"I'm sorry about your brother," he says. "It must be very
difficult when you're so far from home."

Lili nods. It is difficult, but not for the reasons he

assumes. She realises that her grief for Wen is completely different from his own: that as much as she misses Wen, his absence has not greatly altered the circumstances of her life. For though he was her twin, Wen was not her partner: they had not built a life together. As much as anything, she relied on the idea of him; on the knowledge that he was there. Now the fact of this makes her feel very much alone. Adrian drains his glass and puts it into the dishwasher. She watches as he fills the machine with detergent and turns it on. She sees the muscles of his shoulders move beneath his shirt, and for the first time wonders what his lips would feel like on hers. When he has finished, Adrian straightens and turns to her.

"We should get to bed," he says.

Lili cannot speak. She does not want him to leave. He senses her reluctance, and she sees a shadow of uncertainty pass across his face. Can he tell what she is thinking?

"Good night," she says finally, releasing him. He nods to her a little uneasily and turns to go. She stands there for a long time after, listening to the hum of the dishwasher.

July 2004

It is not until Wen's third visit that the old woman finally tells him her name. He had wanted to ask more than once but hadn't known how. But on this day, after he has pruned her hedges, she serves him lemonade at the wooden table in her garden, and sits down opposite him with a sigh.

"My name is Miriam," she says with a smile.

Wen repeats it twice, but cannot master the second syllable. She frowns.

"Why don't you call me Mim? My late husband was fond of this name."

"Mim," says Wen.

"Exactly."

"I am Wen," he says, patting his chest with his hand.

"Wen," she repeats. "A little unusual. But easy to remember. And at my age that counts for everything." She smiles at him.

In truth he would be happier to call her Auntie, or Old Wife, terms of respect reserved for elders in his culture. It feels strange to him, this use of her given name, as if they had been classmates.

"Do you have family, Wen?" she asks.

"Yes. I have sister. She is twin."

"How remarkable," she says. "I too was a twin. But my sister died just after birth. I was the strong twin, you see. The one who survived. But as a child, I always felt that she was there, watching over me."

"I am sorry," he says.

She gives a dismissive wave.

"Oh it was a very long time ago. I haven't thought of her in ages. What of your parents? Are they back in China?"

"My parents are dead. When I am... small baby," he adds, holding up his hands close together.

"How dreadful! Was it an accident?"

Wen hesitates, his English failing him. He clutches the edge of the old wooden table and wobbles it to and fro.

"The ground... like this," he says.

Her eyes grow round.

"An earthquake?"

"Yes," he says. *Earthquake*. It is a word he must remember, for it forms so much a part of his history.

"What happened to you and your sister?"

"We live with new family. So okay."

"I see. And where is she now?"

Wen feels a knot form in the pit of his stomach. He has not even told Angie of his sister, so he does not know why he has chosen to disclose Lili's existence now.

"She is in China," he says.

Though in truth, he is not entirely certain of her whereabouts. He has not been in touch with Jin for two months, not since she emailed him to say that she had managed to obtain his new passport, and asking for an address she should post it to. He had been reluctant to send the address at first, but in the end was forced to. The new passport arrived two days later in a plain brown envelope. He was startled to see that it was Korean. Inside was his photo, together with the name and details of a complete stranger. His new name was Soong. He felt a pang of guilt stealing the name of another man, and wondered how this man Soong came to lose himself, and whether he was dead or alive. But given the circumstances he could not afford to be sentimental.

Over the following weeks, Wen takes to visiting Miriam most afternoons for an hour or two. There is always something for him to do, a broken shelf or a wobbly railing that needs mending, or a tree that needs pruning. She enjoys his company – he can see this – and his visits punctuate both their days, lending them structure and purpose. She continues to pay him small amounts of money at odd moments, usually when he least expects it. One day while he is working in her garden, he hears her call his name. She has spent the morning cleaning out an old shed at the back of the property, and now the ground around the shed is littered with rusty tools, dirty rags and stacks of old plant pots. As he approaches the shed, he hears her call to him from inside.

"I found something you might like," she says. In the next instant she appears in the doorway, clutching the handlebars of an old bicycle. He smiles and his heart leaps a little. He has not ridden a bicycle since he left China. He walks forward and takes the bicycle from her, carrying it onto the grass. It is badly rusted and one of the tires is punctured, but with a bit of work he could certainly get it moving once again.

"Thank you," he says, smiling.

"My pleasure," she replies, brushing the dirt from her hands. "I'd quite forgotten it was there."

•

One Sunday in late August Angie is sitting in the garden with a newspaper while Wen is crouched on all fours weeding a flower bed nearby. He hears her exclaim suddenly. He looks up and sees her face drain of colour.

"What's wrong?"

"Last night... on the bay," she says.

She hesitates and he can tell from her tone that something is not right. He rises and walks over to where she sits.

"Chinese cocklers... they rescued more than a hundred this time."

Wen feels his mouth go dry. He tries to read the article but the letters swim before his eyes. Angie quietly lays a hand upon his forearm.

"It's all right. No one died."

Wen nods, a lump rising in his throat, and turns back to the flower bed.

He had seen them only a few days before. He had been

cycling home along the coastal road from a garden centre just north of town when he passed an enormous trailer loaded with Chinese cocklers. He stopped as the tractor dragged the trailer out onto the sands, watching as they receded in the distance. He had wanted to shout something, to wave his arms and warn them away. But he did nothing, realising it would be pointless to try. There was little he could say to dissuade them from earning a livelihood. These people were surely aware of the dangers – news travels fast, and they would certainly have heard of the tragedy in February. But they wanted an honest day's work and were prepared to face enormous risks to get it. As he stood watching them, he had wondered whether they were frightened at that moment. Whether they were thinking of loved ones at home, or of the dangers that awaited them out on the sands. It was impossible to know.

Wen rocks backwards on his heels. He calls over to where Angie is sitting. "What is day today?"

"The twenty-ninth. Why?"

He does a rapid calculation in his head. It is the fifteenth day of the seventh lunar month in the Chinese calendar. The day when the spirits of the dead are free to roam the earth and visit the living.

"We must go to sea," he says.

She raises an eyebrow, then nods. "Okay."

They wait until nightfall, and walk to the shore nearest Angie's house. He would prefer to go to Hest Bank, to the scene of the accident, but he cannot risk being recognised, especially after the events of last night. For all he knows, there will be teams of Chinese cocklers out again tonight. When they reach the shore, he walks out on the sand and lights a long taper of newspaper. He falls to his knees, facing the ocean, and bows three times, resting his forehead against the cool sand each time, until the flame has nearly reached his fingers. Eventually he drops the taper in the sand. He sits back on his haunches and stares out at the ocean, wondering where the ghosts of his comrades now reside: with their loved ones at home? Or here, hovering over the waters of Morecambe Bay?

Angie shifts behind him in the darkness.

"Are you all right?"

She lays a hand upon his shoulder. He nods, unable to speak. He thinks of Lin's widow and his son, at home lighting incense in his memory. Perhaps one day he will return to China and find them, reassure them that Lin remained a devoted father and husband to the end. But surely they would ask the obvious: why had Lin died, when he himself had survived? He could not face them with the answer, for he had not been strong enough to save the others, only himself. Wen rises to his feet, overcome with emotion, and turns his back on the sea.

On the way home he is quiet, his thoughts still turning to Lin. He remembers the month they spent picking apples in the countryside. Though he'd not realised it at the time, they had been happy during those few weeks. Their life had been simple; unmarred by tragedy. At night, when the day's work was done, they would lie on their backs in the grass smoking cigarettes and staring up into the sky. Lin dreamed aloud of the house he would build upon his return, plotted out the dimensions of each room and the colours he would paint them. Wen too thought about home, though more often than not his thoughts ran to memories. He and Lin were different in that respect: Lin's life was built almost entirely on anticipation, while Wen tended to dwell in the past. Neither gave much thought to the present, but now he sees the error in this. For one should never ignore the moment.

•

The weeks pass and Wen wakes one morning to realise that summer is gone. His English has improved steadily. He no longer studies in the mornings, having exhausted the language CDs some time ago, but continues to do odd jobs for Miriam, and gradually begins to help several of her neighbours as well. Soon he is trimming hedges for a small group of elderly people in the area, fixing broken guttering, scraping chipped paint from worn window sills and digging out tree stumps from their gardens. Miriam acts as a sort of benevolent gangmaster, introducing him to each of them in turn and quietly advising them on how much to compensate him. They pay him by the job or by the hour, according to her suggestions, and Wen gratefully accepts their folded banknotes. By late October, he is working almost full-time.

One afternoon he cycles into town to collect a prescription for Miriam at the chemist. He leaves the bicycle leaning against the front of the shop, and when he emerges, a dark-haired man is standing next to it smoking. The man turns to him and in a flash Wen recognises one of Little Dog's men.

He freezes. The man has evidently been waiting for him. He drops the cigarette to the ground and stubs it out with his shoe, then exhales.

"Back from the dead?"

Wen stares at him, for a moment unable to think or even move. His eyes slide briefly to the bicycle and back to the man's face. Then he turns on his heels and runs. From somewhere behind him he hears a car start and gun its engine after him. He turns down the first street he comes to, pitching straight into a woman with a toddler in a pushchair. The woman screams and Wen leaps to one side, falling sideways.

Out of the corner of his eye he sees a small blue hatchback pull round the corner, coming to a halt not ten feet ahead of him with a screech of its tyres. At once the driver's door opens and Little Dog steps out. Wen turns and nearly collides with the man from outside the chemist, who has come up just behind the woman with the pushchair. The man throws a punch that clips Wen on the right side of his head and the woman screams again, dragging the pushchair backwards into the road in an effort to get out of the way.

Just then a burly Englishman wearing an apron emerges from the door of a butcher's shop beside them. He shouts at them to stop and for a moment, all of them do: Little Dog, the man from the chemist and Wen all freeze and stare at each other, their chests heaving. In that instant Wen sees a police car drive slowly up the street he has just come from. All three men turn and watch as the car approaches. The woman with the pushchair waves urgently at the police car, calling out for it to stop. Wen sees Little Dog weighing up his chances. Little Dog nods to the other man to get into the car and he drives off just as the police car pulls over and a policeman gets out to speak to the woman. Wen doesn't wait for the outcome, but turns and sprints back towards the chemist, jumps on the bicycle and pedals as hard as he can.

Miraculously, Miriam's medication is still in his pocket when he reaches her house several minutes later. As he steps off the bike, he realises that he is drenched in sweat and that his legs are trembling. He tries to compose himself for a moment, crouching down on his haunches. One side of his face throbs from the blow he received, but apart from that he is fine. Alive and well, he thinks grimly, and back from the dead. How long did he imagine this life could last? Miriam comes around the side of the house and her eyes widen with alarm.

"What happened?"

"I fall from bike, it is nothing," he says, rising.

She raises a hand to his face, frowning.

"Looks like you've been in the wars," she remarks. "Come inside and get cleaned up."

Later, he cycles home slowly under cover of darkness, pondering what to do next. When he arrives, he is relieved to see that Angie is not yet back from work. He shuts himself in the bathroom and soaks in the bath for a long time, the way he did that first night all those months ago. He cannot stay in Morecambe Bay; that much is obvious. Now that they know he is alive, they will do their utmost to find him. *Our organisation is like the long tail of a dragon*, Old Fu had said. *Wherever you go we will find you.* He will have to go to London. And from there, on to somewhere else. He has the Korean passport and enough money saved to buy a plane ticket. To France perhaps. Or America, where at least he can speak the language. He looks around the tiny bathroom, at the familiar cracks in the ceiling and the array of plastic bottles lined up by the sink. He has memorised them all by now: their shape and colour and scent. He will miss this life, he thinks with regret.

That night he lies to Angie for the first time, and when he utters the words they sound strange to him, like a false language he has just invented. When she asks about his injured face, he tells her that a car narrowly missed him and he lost his balance and fell onto the kerb. She leans forward and touches the spot lightly, then turns and pours him a measure of whisky. He hesitates before he accepts it; she has not stopped drinking, though she drinks far less now than when he first arrived. He should have made her stop, he thinks. Should have asked this one small thing of her. He takes the glass and she pours herself one, settling down beside him on the sofa.

"I must go to London," he says abruptly, his voice hollow.

He cannot look at her. But out of the corner of his eye, he sees her frown slightly.

"Why?"

"I have business... I need do."

"Business," she repeats.

He nods. Neither of them speak for a minute. He can see

her weighing up his words. She has never pressed him for details of his past, has almost deliberately avoided seeking knowledge that might prove destructive of the life they have created together.

"Will you come back?"

"Yes."

"When?"

"Soon."

His voice fades, as if swallowed by the truth. He takes a drink of whisky to mask his discomfort. But instead of the familiar burn, all he tastes is bitterness.

He leaves her in heavy slumber before dawn the next morning, stealing silently from her bedroom. He has already stowed a few things in a rucksack: some spare clothes, the passport, the money earned from Miriam and her neighbours. At the last moment he adds the English-Chinese dictionary Angie bought him, the key to the life they have created together. He lets himself quietly into the garden one last time: it is a cold autumn night and the ground is wet with heavy dew. He wanders around in the darkness, lamenting the fact that he will not see it through an entire year of growth. A few minutes later, he pulls the front door closed behind him and cycles to the train station, where he is forced to abandon Miriam's bicycle against an old iron railing. He dares not consider what she would think of him now. For he is running away, saving himself, just as he did the last time.

November 2004

The morning after they go for hotpot, Lili goes to the language school in search of Jin, determined to confront her once and for all. She knows that Jin is teaching all morning, so she arrives at the school just before noon and lingers in the tiny kitchen. When Jin eventually comes in, she raises an eyebrow in surprise.

"Are you teaching today?"

"No," says Lili. Jin looks at her oddly, then steps round her to fill the kettle with water. "I came to see you." Lili pauses, uncertain how to continue. Just then Jin's phone rings. She glances at it quickly, then opens it and turns away, speaking quietly.

"*Wei?* I can't talk now," she says quietly. "I'll ring you later." She snaps the phone shut and turns back to Lili.

"What's up?"

"It's about Wen."

"What about him?"

"Last night I went to the hotpot restaurant. They told me that some men came looking for him a few days ago."

"And?"

"Why would anyone come looking for him nine months after his death?"

"How would I know?" Jin shrugs and reaches for a mug from the shelf.

"I saw the photos in your room," says Lili. "You went to see him. At Morecambe Bay."

Jin glances sideways at her. "Maybe I did."

"But you told me you didn't."

"What does it matter?"

"It matters if he isn't dead," says Lili flatly.

Jin stops and looks at her a long moment. "You're chasing ghosts," she says, and walks past her out the door.

•

Lili returns home later than usual that evening. When she enters, she can hear Adrian and May eating dinner in the kitchen, together with someone whose voice she does not recognise. She goes to the doorway. Adrian, May and an attractive blonde woman are seated at the table with empty plates in front of them. At once they stop talking and look up at her. Lili flushes and starts to turn away.

"I'm sorry," she says.

Adrian jumps to his feet. "Not at all. Come in. We're just finishing. There's a bit left over if you're hungry."

"No, thank you. I ate before," says Lili quickly. Though in truth she has not.

"Okay," says Adrian. "This is Eliza, by the way. She's a... colleague of mine at work."

"It is nice to meet you," says Lili awkwardly.

"And you," says Eliza. She throws a bemused look at Adrian.

"Eliza's from Botswana," interjects May.

"Oh," says Lili, a little confused. The woman does not look African.

"She's seen lions! Loads of them," adds May. "And giraffes!"

"I see."

"Would you like a glass of wine?" asks Adrian.

They stare at her, and for an instant all she hears is the clock ticking on the stove.

"No, thank you. I am very tired. I will go to bed."

"Well, good night then," Adrian says, sitting down.

He seems relieved she did not accept his offer. Lili hurries upstairs to her room and closes the door. Later, she hears the sound of Adrian putting May to bed. She listens closely for the noise of the front door, but hears nothing. She would like a cup of tea, but is reluctant to go downstairs, in case Eliza and Adrian are alone together. So instead she goes to bed earlier than usual, her stomach rumbling beneath the bedcovers.

Later, in the middle of the night, she is woken by the sound of May wailing. Lili sits up at once, listening intently. Lili can hear Adrian trying to placate her in measured tones. She rises and hastily puts on her dressing gown, thinking that perhaps she should help. But when she starts down the stairs, the sound of Eliza's voice in the hallway stops her dead. Quickly, she retreats back up to her room. After a few minutes, she hears Eliza and Adrian speaking in hushed tones in the hallway, followed by the whispered closing of the front door. She listens until the house is silent once again, but the atmosphere seems strangely altered, and she has trouble returning to sleep.

•

The next morning, she rises early and is making toast when May appears in her school uniform, looking tired.

"Good morning," says Lili cautiously.

"Morning," says May dully. She takes a bowl out of the cupboard and fills it with cereal, then crosses to the refrigerator for milk. Adrian comes in and when he sees Lili, his jaw tightens slightly.

"Hey, Lili," he murmurs, turning to the kettle.

The three of them eat in silence. May refuses to take her eyes off the bowl in front of her, as if she has been hypnotised, and Adrian stares resolutely at the newspaper headlines. When May finishes, she leaves the room abruptly. Lili rises and clears her own plate into the dishwasher, together with May's bowl, before turning to Adrian.

"Is everything all right?" she asks tentatively.

"Everything's fine," says Adrian without looking up. He turns to another section of the newspaper. "May's just tired, that's all," he adds.

That evening when Lili returns home, she hopes to slip upstairs unnoticed, but Adrian comes into the hallway just as she rounds the corner. She hesitates.

"Hello," he says with a nod. He approaches May's bedroom door and knocks lightly. "May?"

Lili crosses to the stairs when she hears May's muffled voice from behind the door.

"I'm not hungry."

Lili pauses. She hears Adrian sigh.

"Come on, May," he pleads in an exasperated voice.

"I *said* I'm not hungry!"

Lili turns back to face him. Adrian shakes his head.

"Maybe *you* should try," he says. "I'm not having much luck."

He jerks his thumb in the direction of May's door and raises an eyebrow.

"I don't know," she says.

"Just see if she'll come out for dinner, will you?"

He turns and walks back to the kitchen. Lili approaches May's door and knocks gently.

"May? It's me. Lili."

She hears a shuffling inside the room, and after a few moments, the door opens a little. May stands in her oversized school uniform, unsmiling. In her arm she clutches two stuffed rabbits with long pink ears.

"What is it?"

"May I come in?"

She shrugs in response and steps to one side, allowing Lili to enter. May closes the door behind her and crosses back to her bed, where a wide circle of toy animals has been laid out.

"What game do you play?"

"It's not a game. It's school."

"Oh."

May clambers onto her bed and begins repositioning the animals.

"Are you the teacher?"

May nods, lining the animals up in three rows in front of her. She positions the two rabbits at the front.

"May, are you angry?"

"Why would I be angry?" says May stubbornly.

"I don't know. Did something happen last night?"

May sucks in air, then climbs off the bed, going over to a large round basket that holds more animals. She reaches in and pulls out several more, crossing back to the bed.

"She's not his wife," says May, placing the animals behind the others.

"Who?"

"Eliza."

"Of course not."

"And she's not my mother either," May adds under her breath. "Even if she *has* seen elephants."

"No, of course not," Lili stammers.

May looks up at her fiercely.

"I don't want another mother. Two is enough."

"Yes, I understand. But your father. Perhaps he needs someone?"

"Why? He's got us, hasn't he?"

"But, it's not the same. You understand this, don't you?"

May shakes her head.

"He was okay before."

"But… people change."

"Well, I don't want them to," says May stubbornly. She climbs off her bed and gathers up all the soft toys in her arms, dumping them back into the basket.

"I need to do my homework," she says, brushing past Lili.

Later, after an awkward meal during which May refuses to speak, Lili finds herself alone in the kitchen with Adrian. She wipes a pan with a tea towel.

"I'm sorry. I do not think May is happy to talk with me," she says.

"It's okay. I appreciate your trying. It wasn't really fair of me to ask."

Adrian pours himself a glass of wine from an open bottle on the counter, then sits down at the table with a sigh.

"After Sian died, I waited a long time before I began to see other people. Other women," he adds with a shrug. "I knew it would be difficult."

"May is still young. Perhaps… when she is older?"

"I guess so," Adrian says. "I thought that she was old enough. And I thought that having *you* here would some-how make it easier. Sort of… introduce a woman to the house again. But I was wrong. Ironically, I think it's made it worse. May thinks of us as one big happy family now."

Adrian shakes his head, unaware of the effect of his words. Lili freezes, her face growing hot. She has under-stood the meaning but not the implication of what he says. Is he asking her to leave?

"I'm sorry. If you wish, I can go."

He looks up at her with surprise.

"No. No, I'm sorry – that's not what I meant. Honestly, I don't want you to go, Lili. May *adores* you. She'd be devastated if you left."

Adrian stops short. They stare at each other for a moment. Lili silently wills him to continue. But he reaches for the wine bottle instead and refills his glass.

"Okay," she murmurs, turning back to the dishes.

•

The following day, Lili finishes teaching at six. When she comes out of the school, it is dark and a light mist has begun to fall. As she heads towards the bus stop, two Chinese men step in front of her, blocking the pavement. She has never set eyes on them before. One is short and well groomed, his clothes and shoes expensive-looking. The other is medium height, with a small scar on one cheek and hair that is combed straight back. It is the short one who commands her attention, stepping forward slightly and raising his chin. Lili can smell the faint musky odour of after-shave. She sees a tiny cut on the side of his cheek.

"Zhang Lili?"

"Yes."

"Zhang Wen's sister?"

Lili feels a flash of apprehension. "Who are you?"

The man steps closer, until they are almost eye to eye.

"We're associates of your brother's."

"Associates? My brother is dead!"

"Then by rights, his debt should fall to you."

"I don't know what you're talking about."

"Your brother knows."

"I told you Wen is dead!"

The short man studies her for a long moment. He glances over at the other man.

"So he lied to you too. Along with everyone else."

"Wen never lied to anyone," Lili says fervently. And for a moment, she almost believes that this is true.

"Your loyalty is touching. But it is not deserved. When we find him, you can tell him so."

She looks from one to the other, then pushes past them and hurries along the pavement. She glances back over her shoulder, where they remain standing in the darkness. She sees a brief flame as the short man lights a cigarette. She crosses the road and glances back one last time. The taller one has turned away and is walking in the opposite direction, but the short one is staring after her, holding the cigarette in his hand.

When she arrives at the bus stop, she is out of breath and trembling. Her phone rings.

"*Wei?*"

"Lili, it's me."

It takes her a moment to recognise Adrian's voice.

"Sorry to bother you, but something's come up this evening. Do you think you could watch May?"

Lili hesitates. Right now she needs to find Jin.

"I am sorry," she says. "I must go to meet a friend."

"Oh." His voice deflates slightly.

"Perhaps later."

"Okay," he says hopefully. "How long?"

"Maybe one hour?" she says.

"Thanks. I really appreciate it."

She boards a 237 bus to Hounslow, vowing to herself that this time she will not be bullied or misled. She needs to know once and for all whether Wen is truly dead. When she arrives outside Jin's building, she realises that she still has the key to the bedsit in her handbag. She races up the flight of stairs to Jin's room, pausing just outside, where she can hear movement within. Lili knocks and waits for a response, but there is only hushed silence. *How could Jin know it is me?* she wonders angrily. She fumbles in her bag for the key and unlocks the door, pushing it open. And there, not like a ghost at all, sits her long-dead brother, Wen.

November 2004

Wen stares in horror at Lili's face. She remains frozen in the doorway, her eyes fixed on him. He watches as shock turns to joy. Then, for the briefest instant, he sees the angry shadow of betrayal. The enormity of his deceit surges over him. In the next instant she stumbles forward and throws her arms around him, her breath coming in sobs. He pulls her down next to him.

"Lili," he says, brushing a lock of hair from her eyes. "I don't deserve to be here."

"I knew you were alive," she whispers. "I felt you with me, from the moment I arrived."

"I'm sorry."

They hold each other, saying nothing. Wen has the sudden notion that they are back in their mother's womb, their bodies entwined, their limbs indistinguishable, while the world outside rages.

At length, she pulls back from him, wiping her eyes. "Where have you been all these months?"

"In Morecambe Bay."

"Alone?"

He shakes his head. She waits for more, but he offers no explanation.

"Why didn't you let me know?"

Why indeed? he thinks. *Fear. Cowardice. Guilt. Shame. A demon with many heads.* He takes her by the shoulders and looks into her face.

"I have wronged you in so many ways. You must forgive me."

She nods obediently. Wen wipes the tears from her cheek with the flat of his thumb, feels a tremor run right through her. He has always been able to dictate the terms of their relationship.

"You're alive and you're safe. That's what matters most," she whispers, resting her forehead against his.

"Yes."

Just then they hear a key in the door and Jin enters, stopping short when she sees Lili. In her hand she carries a bag of shopping.

Wen sees her eyes darken. *What is it Jin feels in this moment?* he wonders. *Anger? Jealousy?*

"So," she says, nodding at Lili. "Now you know." She closes the door behind her and moves to the counter, unpacking the bag of eggs, tomatoes, onions and rice. When she has finished, she turns back to them.

Lili pulls back slightly from Wen. "Why did you lie?"

"Because he told me to," says Jin flatly. "So if you want to blame someone, blame him."

Jin jerks her head at Wen and Lili turns back to him.

"I don't understand."

"It's complicated," says Wen. "One day I will explain."

Lili frowns. Just then her phone rings. She pulls it from her bag, stares at it a moment, then turns it off.

"I have to go. Someone is waiting for me."

Wen nods and kisses her forehead.

"But when will I see you?" she asks worriedly.

"Soon."

"Tomorrow?"

"I'll let you know," he replies.

Reluctantly, Lili picks up her coat and bag and moves to the door, where she pauses, turning back to face them. Lili locks eyes with Wen for an instant and smiles, then slips out the door. When she has gone, Jin turns to him with a raised eyebrow.

"One lie begets another."

"Did you get it?" he asks, ignoring her comment.

"Yes."

He rises and crosses over to her. She takes a pale brown envelope out of her handbag and hands it to him. He looks inside it briefly, flicking through the notes.

"Thank you." He looks up at her.

She shrugs. "What am I here for?" she replies curtly.

•

The following morning, he hops on an 18 bus for Chinatown. London feels oddly familiar to him now: perhaps the act of returning confers this upon a place, he decides. As the bus lurches through the crowded streets towards the West End, he realises that so much more of life here is open to him now. He comprehends much more: the questions of fellow passengers as they board the bus, the street signs outside, even the look in people's eyes carries with it a new sense of clarity. He feels, for the first time, almost at home. The thought pains him; for just when he has grown accustomed to life in England, he must leave.

Once in Chinatown, he heads straight to the travel shop Jin has told him about. It specialises in dealing with people like him. They will not look too closely at your passport, she had said. Nor ask too many questions. They're used to dealing with illegals. He locates the shop down a small side street after a few minutes; in the window is a list of destinations followed by ticket prices. He stands outside and lets his eyes roam the list: Beijing, Hong Kong, Taibei, Seoul, New York, Sydney. Places he has only heard of, for the most part, but never expected to see. He feels in his pocket for the passport and the envelope of cash. He has memorised the details of his new identity and practised saying them, though when he speaks his new name aloud, his voice still sounds strangely artificial. When he enters the shop, a Chinese woman is seated behind a desk, speaking in Cantonese on the phone. She looks up at him and hastily ends her call.

"Can I help you?"

Wen does not speak Cantonese and is uncertain whether to use English or Mandarin. But then he remembers he is meant to be Korean.

"I want to buy a ticket," he says in English. "For airplane," he adds hastily.

"Where to?" she asks.

Wen swallows. Until now, his mind had not been made.

"New York," he ventures.

"Do you have a visa?" she asks.

Wen shakes his head. He removes the passport from his pocket and hands it to her.

"I am Korean," he says. "Do I need visa?"

She raises an eyebrow. "Everyone needs a visa for America," she says with a slightly bored expression.

Wen colours. His heart flails inside his chest; he is certain the woman must be able to see it. "Where can I go with no visa? Which country?"

She frowns, then turns to her computer, tapping on the keys. "On a Korean passport?" She studies the screen for a few moments, then turns back to him.

"Canada," she says. "You don't need a visa for Canada."

Wen thinks of trees and snow: he doesn't know why. He knows virtually nothing about Canada. But he is fairly certain they speak English there. "Which city?" he asks.

She shrugs.

"Toronto, Vancouver, Montreal."

The names mean little to him. "Which one is best?"

The woman laughs. "You want *me* to choose?"

He smiles. "Please."

"Vancouver's meant to be nice," she says. "It has mountains and is right beside the sea."

Wen feels a sudden wash of panic.

"Not sea," he says quickly.

"Okay. Then Toronto's the place for you. Big Chinatown there, Mr..." She looks down at the name in his passport. "Soong," she adds, arching an eyebrow.

"How much is ticket?"

"Just you?"

He nods.

"One way or return?"

"One way."

A lump rises in the back of his throat.

"I can get you a fare for two eighty-five. Cash payment only. When do you want to travel?" It takes him a moment to calculate the numbers in his head. He has nearly stopped converting figures into wages in recent months, a habit he thought would stay with him for life.

"Soon," he says.

She taps at the screen, frowning.

"How soon? Tomorrow?"

Wen nods. He removes the cash from his pocket and peels off a series of twenty-pound notes, handing them to the woman. He waits while she processes his ticket, contemplating what kind of life awaits him in this city whose name he can barely pronounce. As she hands him the paperwork, his mind runs to Lili and the dazed look upon her face as she left. Did she know, even then, that he was running away?

When he comes out of the shop, he walks back to Lisle Street and wanders up and down for a time. It has been so long since he has been surrounded by his own people that it feels strange to him now. He pauses outside a large restaurant filled with customers: the staff are all Chinese but the place is mainly full of white people. Wen studies a menu hanging in the window: the dishes are overpriced and cater to Western tastes. Just inside the window, a waiter is clearing dirty plates from a large table. He is tall and thin with slightly rounded shoulders, and there are permanent dark moons beneath his eyes, as if he has not had a proper night's sleep in months. Wen watches him for a moment, piling the dregs of a meal into a large plastic container. What did this meal cost? he wonders. And what trifling wage will this man take home at the end of the day?

At length, the waiter raises his eyes and looks straight at him. He stops, his movements frozen, and Wen wonders briefly whether they have met: perhaps they worked together somewhere along the way? Or do they simply recognise each other's condition? Suddenly, an older Chinese man in a crumpled pin-striped suit is standing beside the waiter, berating him angrily. The waiter nods repeatedly and hurriedly finishes clearing the table, before lifting the box and turning away. The manager raises his eyes to Wen, takes in his dress and appearance and knows at once that he is not a potential customer. He scowls and gives a flick of his hand, indicating that Wen should move on.

Wen finds a bakery and buys some steamed buns filled with barbecued pork. He wonders what currency he will have to use in Canada, dollars or pounds, or something else altogether, and what his money will be worth. As he leaves the shop, he bites into one of the buns: the sweet pork filling fills his mouth. But as he does he senses a presence just behind him, like the tip of a wave. All at once, Little Dog's voice is in his ear, and he feels the point of something sharp jutting into his kidney from behind. Two men appear at his sides: one he recognises from outside the chemist, the other he has never seen before.

"Keep walking," says Little Dog quietly. "Or this time you'll die for good."

November 2004

The following day Lili sleeps late. Adrian and May are gone when she rises, and she is relieved to have the house to herself. She contemplates getting a bus to Hounslow, but something prevents her. She knows she will have to wait for Wen to contact her, but how long? A day? A week? A year? Now that the initial shock has passed, she must stifle the slow swell of anger that is building within her. If Wen deceived her, he must have had good reason, she tells herself repeatedly. She is due to teach at the language school this afternoon, but she remembers with dismay that it is Jin's day off. For now she has no choice but to carry on.

That evening when she finishes teaching, it is cold and dark as she leaves the school. The first person she sees when she steps out the door is Jin. She is standing on the pavement just outside smoking a cigarette, a scarf wrapped several times around her neck to keep out the chill. Jin steps forward as soon as Lili emerges, and Lili realises with a start that Jin is waiting for her. Her heart skips a beat.

"What's wrong?"

"They've taken him."

"Wen?"

Jin nods.

"Who?"

"The snakeheads."

"How do you know?"

"They rang. A few hours ago."

"You spoke to him?"

Jin purses her lips. She says nothing for a moment.

"I heard him," she says finally, her voice dropping to barely more than a whisper.

"What do you mean?" Lili asks unsteadily.

"I heard him scream. In the background."

Lili feels suddenly ill. She turns around and bends over, overcome with nausea. She retches onto the pavement, then coughs several times. She feels Jin lay a hand upon her shoulder.

"Are you okay?"

"I'm all right."

At length she straightens up again, sucking in deep breaths of air. She wipes her mouth with the back of her hand.

"What do they want?" she asks.

"They want their money."

"Does he have it?"

"No. He has some, but not enough."

"What will they do to him?"

"Whatever they want. In the eyes of the world, he is already dead."

"How much does he owe?"

"Nearly twenty thousand dollars."

"So much!" Lili says, astonished. She did not realise Wen's debts ran so high. Jin nods grimly.

"Who has that kind of money?" asks Lili.

"Who knows? Not Wen. And not me either."

"What about Fay?"

"No," says Jin dismissively.

"But her husband's a businessman!"

"Who spends money like water! And is swimming in debt."

"There must be someone else," says Lili.

Jin takes in a deep breath and exhales heavily.

"Wen was living with someone," she says slowly. "In Morecambe Bay."

"What do you mean?"

"He was living with an English woman."

Lili stares at her. So Wen had secrets from them both.

"Who was she?"

"I don't know. He never told me her name."

"So we have no way of finding her."

"No."

"What can we do?"

"Nothing. We can wait. And hope that he can make some sort of deal with them."

"We could go to the police," suggests Lili desperately.

"Are you insane? Even if they found him, they'd put him on the first plane back to Beijing. He'd wind up in prison! I'd rather be in the hands of the snakeheads."

"Perhaps he can still work off his debt," says Lili.

"Maybe. Look, I'll let you know if I hear anything. Go home now. You look terrible."

Lili has no choice but to return home and wait for news. When she enters the house, she can hear Adrian cooking supper. She walks into the kitchen and sees him at the stove stirring something in a pot.

"Hello," he says, looking up at her.

"Where is May?"

"In her room. Are you hungry? I've made a stew."

Lili looks at the pot and shakes her head.

"I am not feeling well," she says. She starts to turn away.

"Are you okay?"

Lili hesitates. She would like to tell him. But the words are stuck somewhere deep inside.

Adrian stops stirring and turns to her. Lili freezes. Adrian is staring at her, his face creased with concern. She can smell the stew: a sharp meaty smell that clings to her nostrils and makes her feel slightly faint. Panic rises within her. Perhaps nothing in this world can be trusted.

Adrian stands there, the wooden spoon outstretched like an offering. "Some days are harder than others," he says.

May appears like a silent apparition in the doorway. When she sees the look on Lili's face, she turns to Adrian. "Daddy? What's wrong?"

"It's okay, May. Give us a minute, will you?" He nods to her to leave.

May swallows. "I think the dinner's burning," she says then.

They all three turn towards the stove, where the pot has begun to smoke. The smell quickly wafts through the room.

"Damn!" Adrian mutters. He grabs the pan and pulls it off the flame, then crosses to the back door and opens it, allowing the cold night air into the room.

"Lili? Are you okay?" asks May, stepping forward.

"I'm fine," says Lili, turning away.

Once inside her bedroom, she closes the door and leans back against it. Her eyes drift to the small shrine she has made for Wen, with the photo of him laughing in the centre. She crosses over and kneels down in front of it, lighting the row of candles she has arranged along the front of the table. When she has done this, she takes out a packet of joss sticks and lights one, clutching it in her hand as she bows three times towards Wen's photo, praying to the spirits of their dead parents to keep him safe.

Behind her she hears a soft tapping on the door. She remains motionless, and a moment later she hears it open softly. Lili looks over to see May standing in the doorway. May comes forward and picks up another joss stick, lighting it from one of the candles. Then she kneels down beside Lili, holding the joss stick in her hand. Lili frowns. May is staring earnestly at the photo of Wen, as if she'd known him all her life, as if they are all part of the same family. Lili feels a surge of gratitude then. She bows again towards Wen's photo, and May does the same. Together they bow again twice more.

A moment later they hear Adrian's voice from the doorway.

"May?" he says quietly.

They both turn to look at him, and for a split second Lili feels a pang of anger that Adrian has interrupted them. But then she remembers that this is his house, and May is his child. She rocks backwards and rises to her feet. After a moment, May does the same.

"Time to eat," he says.

November 2004

They take him to the blue hatchback, waiting down a side street. One of the men walks behind him with the knife pressed into his back, the other at his side. The pork bun he was eating has lodged halfway down his gullet. He is still clutching the sack with the other in his hand. As they approach the car, a uniformed parking attendant has just placed a ticket on the windscreen, and is turning away. Little Dog curses him in Mandarin and snatches the ticket, tossing it to the ground. He jumps into the driver's seat, while one of the other men opens the back door and shoves Wen onto the seat, then climbs in beside him. The third man gets into the passenger seat, and Little Dog starts the engine and drives off. The man next to him pushes him down sideways onto the seat and binds his wrists tightly with a rope, pulling it hard enough to make him wince. Then he pulls a pillowcase over his head. Wen drops the sack of buns onto the floor of the car.

They drive for hours, at first slowly, stopping and starting through London traffic, then eventually much faster. At some point it starts to rain. Wen can hear the steady drizzle on the roof of the car, together with the swishing windscreen wipers. At length he dozes off, and when he wakes the car has stopped. He hears Little Dog get out of the driver's seat and close the door; the other two men remain behind with him. The one next to him sighs heavily. Wen hears him stretch his legs.

"Fucking rain," he says in Mandarin.

"It's the dark that gets to me," says the other. "It's like living in a cave."

Wen stirs slightly. He needs the toilet but dares not ask. They sit in silence and a minute later he hears Little Dog return.

"Here," he says to one of the others as he gets into the car. "It's all they had."

Wen hears them passing round drinks and food. He hears the man next to him take a sip of something, then swear.

"Tastes like piss!"

"Give it to *him* if you don't want it," says the other.

Little Dog snorts. "Haven't you heard?" he says. "Dead men don't drink."

Now Wen is wide awake, Little Dog's words echoing in his brain. They carry on driving, and after another hour the traffic slows again. Little Dog swears several times. At length the car comes to a halt and Little Dog shuts off the engine. The man next to him orders Wen to sit up. He can tell that it is already dark outside, perhaps early evening. They take him from the car and propel him forward into a building, pushing him up a set of stairs and into a room where they shove him into a wooden chair. Wen feels them binding him to the chair with rope, his hands still tied in front of him.

"Shut the blinds," says Little Dog.

Someone turns on a light, he hears the scrape of a chair, and in the next instant, one of them has pulled off the pillowcase. Wen blinks in the glare of the light. Little Dog sits in front of him in a straight-backed chair, beside a small round wooden table. The other two men hover nearby: the one he recognises from before, the smaller of the two, leans back against the edge of the table, his arms folded over his chest. The other man is clearly the muscle: though not tall, he is heavy set, with thick arms and meaty hands. He stands beside Little Dog, his body twitching slightly. Wen glances quickly around the room. The door to the stairs is now shut. The walls are covered with a dingy pale green paint, and a bare bulb hangs from a cracked ceiling rose. Against the rear wall is a battered sofa. In front of it is an old television set on an overturned wooden crate. There is only one window, now covered by a set of broken venetian blinds, their slats slightly askew.

"So," says Little Dog, eyeing him up and down. "You must be a good swimmer."

"I was lucky," replies Wen cautiously.

"Not any more," says Little Dog. He nods to the heavy-set man, and the latter steps forward, raising one arm. Wen is slow to realise what is happening: he shuts his eyes at the last instant, feels the force of the blow against his right cheek and chin. The man's fist is like a mallet. He feels the skin split slightly; the pain is like a sharp pulse. He opens his eyes and Little Dog cocks his head to one side.

"We want our money," says Little Dog.

The man hits Wen again, this time from the other side. This punch is harder and it snaps his head backwards. He takes a deep breath, just as he tastes blood inside his mouth.

"I can get your money," he gasps.

"Really?" says Little Dog, leaning forward. "When?"

"Soon."

"Tomorrow?"

"A few days," says Wen. His head is a halo of pain. He squints through the haze at Little Dog and sees him shake his head slowly from side to side.

"Not good enough," he says, nodding to the other man.

Wen closes his eyes again: this time the punch is to his gut, and he feels a small amount of vomit rise up in his throat. He leans forward, gasping, nearly choking. Black spots dance in front of his eyes.

"Get his phone," he hears Little Dog say curtly.

The other man leaps up and he feels hands searching his pockets. They remove his wallet and phone and his passport and ticket. The man hands the ticket to Little Dog, who looks at it and raises an eyebrow.

"Going on holiday?" he says to Wen. He leans forward, newly angry. "You little shit! You think you can *hide* from us?"

"No," murmurs Wen.

He watches as Little Dog tears the ticket in half, then halves it again, and then once more. He throws the scraps into the air and Wen watches them drift to the floor. Little Dog nods to the big man again, who steps forward and hits him again in the gut. This time the vomit comes more easily, all over his knees, his feet and the floor.

"Shit," says Little Dog, irritated. "Go get some towels."

Later, Little Dog stands at the window, peering through the broken blinds. He holds Wen's phone, scrolling through the contact list. After a moment, he dials one and speaks tersely into the phone.

"*Wei?* Who is this?"

Little Dog listens for a moment. "There's someone here who wishes to speak to you," he says into the phone.

He turns and holds the phone out towards Wen, nodding at the thick-set man. For a moment, Wen thinks that they will put the phone up to his ear, but then he sees the lighter in the burly man's hand. It is small and sleek and made of stainless steel. The man steps closer and holds the lighter up towards his face. Wen pulls backwards with alarm, his guts starting to churn. He watches him flick the lighter with his thumb and the flame flares. The man flicks it once again and brings the flame closer to his face. Wen cranes his neck back as far as he can, his eyes glued to the flame. The burly man smiles and brings the flame right beneath his chin. It takes an instant for the pain to reach him; he smells his own flesh searing even before he feels it, but when he does he screams in agony. The burly man snaps the lighter shut and nods to

Little Dog, who turns away, finishing the call.

Afterwards, they untie him from the chair and handcuff his wrist to the base of a radiator by the window. Wen lies with his face against the floorboard, one eye sealed shut from the force of their blows, the taste of blood in his mouth. The burnt skin on his neck still feels as if it is on fire. At some point he has wet himself; he is not sure when, but he is relieved there is no longer pressure on his bladder. The men leave him lying in the darkness and go out. He hears them start the engine and pull away. Once they are gone, the pain seems to worsen. He could not move even if he wanted to: does not have the will nor the energy to escape.

His thoughts drift to Angie. What happened when she woke to find him gone? Did she understand at once the depth of his deceit? Some part of him crumples then; anguish seeps through him like a stain, more painful than the blows he has endured. Perhaps, he thinks ruefully, his fate has always been to betray.

At length he dozes off, waking only when they return some hours later. The stocky one opens the door, glances in to make certain he hasn't moved and closes it again. He hears them moving about for the next hour or so, then the small house falls quiet. He sleeps again, and dreams that he is walking on the beach with Angie by his side. He looks out across the water and sees Lili wading towards him, her face stricken. He steps towards her but his feet sink into the sand beneath him, and when he looks up she is gone. He continues sinking until the sand is up to his chest. Angie has carried on walking and does not see, and though he tries to shout, no words come. The dream ends abruptly, just as he is sucked beneath the surface.

In the morning when he wakes, the pain in his head has turned to a dull ache. His cheek and ribs hurt, and one arm is sore, but apart from that he is okay. He sits up slowly and leans back against the radiator. The house is silent; he has no idea whether Little Dog and his men are asleep or out. He is thirsty and his stomach growls noisily. There is something almost reassuring about the body's need for food during times of adversity, he decides. When he made the journey overland from China, he lived on nothing but pot noodles for months on end, often raw. At the time he grew to hate them, but each day his hunger outweighed his aversion, and at mealtimes he ate his portion as enthusiastically as the rest.

He has not thought of them in many months, not since before the accident. They had been nine in all: seven men and two women. The oldest was forty-seven, the youngest was just nineteen, and for four months they were his constant companions. Together with a minder, they were given false passports and flown from Beijing to Bulgaria. None of them had ever boarded a plane before, much less been abroad. Some had never even been to Beijing. Once in Bulgaria, they were taken in a van to a safe house in the countryside, where they were forced to remain in a large attic room for nearly three weeks. At first there was an air of camaraderie and joviality among them; but after several days this changed to boredom, restlessness and irritability.

Over the course of those three weeks, he came to know

each of them: their likes and dislikes, weaknesses and strengths, what marked them out as individuals. Old Wang was the eldest and assumed a sort of paternal role among them, bargaining with their minders for better food or more blankets when the weather outside turned cold. He told Wen that two years before he had been laid off his factory job in Shanxi Province, after nearly twenty years' service. Since then he had been unable to find steady work, drifting from one casual job to the next, trying his hand at any number of unsuccessful ventures. His first wife had died many years before; he had one son, now grown, who had recently married and was keen to start a family of his own. Five years earlier, Old Wang had remarried. His new wife was much younger than himself, and was blind, he told Wen, which explained why she had agreed to the marriage. At the time he had felt very fortunate to find a second wife in a country where young men outnumbered women by far.

But what he had not been prepared for was her shrewish manner. Blind or not, the woman was impossible to satisfy. One year after they were married, she gave birth to a daughter, much to Old Wang's delight. But his wife had set her heart on a son, and so had badgered him at length for a second child, though having one would incur severe financial penalties that he could ill afford. A year later, a second daughter was born, for which his young wife berated him ceaselessly, having heard an item on the radio about male chromosomes determining gender. Because of her blindness, she was unable to work, having turned up her nose at an opportunity to train as a masseuse, one of the only forms of employment open to blind people. Neither could she care properly for their two children, so he was forced to hire an *aiyi*, a witless girl from the countryside to help out. It was the combination of all these things – the loss of his job, a disabled wife, the need for hired help, and the prospect of educating two young children – that had driven him to go abroad. He missed his two young daughters terribly, but had been happy enough to leave the shrill demands of their mother behind. One day, he intended to build a house big enough for him and his wife to live at opposite ends, he told Wen with a grin. Maybe I will take a mistress, he added with a chuckle. If the house is big enough, my wife need never know.

The youngest member of the group was called Wang, though the others quickly dubbed him Little Professor. He was nineteen, soft-spoken, wore wire-rimmed spectacles and had brought with him a thick, well-thumbed volume of ancient poetry, which he read constantly. Wen remembers the silence that enveloped the room the day Wang first told them he had dropped out of university to go abroad: to forfeit a place at university was almost unthinkable. Wang explained in his quiet way that his father was very ill and required constant care, thus making it impossible for his mother to work. His treatment and medicine were very expensive, so Wang had little choice but to go abroad. Perhaps one day I will resume my studies in England, he ventured. Maybe I will even go to *Niuqiao*, he added with a grin, the phrase used by mainland Chinese to refer to Oxbridge. The others laughed, but at the time they had also thought *why not?* This young man was surely clever enough for any university.

The two women, though uneducated, both seemed fiercely capable – as if the fact of their sex made them all the more determined to succeed. Both were single parents who had left a child behind with relatives; one was divorced, the other widowed. Little Red explained that her husband had died in an industrial accident three years before when a large crane had malfunctioned. The circumstances had all pointed towards negligence on the part of the company, but in spite of her repeated complaints, no compensation had been offered. Instead, she had received a small wreath of chrysanthemums, together with a note saying that her husband's outstanding debts in the staff canteen would be cancelled under the circumstances. Since then she had struggled to make ends meet, but was determined that her only son would not suffer as a consequence of his father's death. He would go to the best schools, she told them, her voice trembling with emotion, and lack for nothing. The boy was brave, Little Red added proudly, and would weather the separation. One day, no doubt, he would thank her.

With the exception of Wen, they had been drawn together by desperation and necessity. He was the only one among them who had no dependants, and the others seemed surprised when they learned of this. Old Wang had leaned forward, his eyebrows knit together.

"So you do not *need* to be here?" he asked doubtfully.

"No," Wen had admitted. "I suppose not."

"You came because...?" Old Wang's voice trailed off.

The others listened with interest. Wen felt his mouth go dry. How could he explain? Despite coming from the largest country on earth, he felt crowded by his life and by his circumstances. Some mornings when he woke, he found he could not breathe, as if the life was being squeezed from him little by little each day. He had tried without success to explain this feeling to Lili. That day in the safe house, he had looked around at the bewildered faces of Old Wang and the others, and had decided to lie.

"I gambled badly on a business investment," he said finally. "And lost. So here I am."

Old Wang nodded several times, clearly relieved.

"For every millionaire in New China," he said, "there are a thousand paupers just behind."

After three weeks of pot noodles and no fresh air or exercise, Wen had begun to feel as dense and slack as a sack of grain. When they were finally told they would be moved, there was a brief bout of exhilaration, quickly followed by dismay. They were taken in the early dawn to three trucks transporting livestock and produce across the border. The trucks travelled in convoy and each day Wen and his compatriots were allocated to a lorry and instructed to hide in sealed compartments behind the driver, where they were forced to sit curled like foetuses in the dark for up to eight hours at a time, while a wooden lid was screwed shut over their heads. Wen thought the first day was bad, but on the second he was moved to a lorry carrying pigs, and the stench of faeces and urine was almost unbearable. At night they slept in barns, bedding down in hay lofts, relieved to stretch their cramped muscles.

On the fourth day, he and Little Red were told to climb into a box together. As she squatted down next to him she grinned.

"Don't worry," she said. "It's like the pain of childbirth. The further we get from it, the smaller it will seem. And one day, when we are back with our families living in a fine house built from our earnings, this journey will be nothing more than a pinprick in our memory."

Now, lying with his swollen face against the floorboard, Wen wonders what became of Little Red. He knew she was destined for an electronics factory in the north where a distant cousin of hers was already working. He hopes that her experience has been less fraught with peril than his own. But then the door opens and Little Dog enters, banishing the past in an instant.

"Time for a chat," he says.

November 2004

Lili spends the next few days almost feverish with apprehension. On the third morning, she rushes into school early to find Jin, but before she even has a chance to ask, the latter shakes her head.

"Nothing," Jin says. "I've tried ringing several times but his phone is off."

"If they let him go, he would contact us," mumbles Lili worriedly.

"I don't know."

"I wish we knew more about the woman," says Lili. "The one he was living with in Morecambe Bay."

Jin frowns. "Actually," she says, "I have an address."

The following morning Jin persuades Fay to let them have the day off. They take a train from King's Cross, changing once in Birmingham. Lili has never travelled on a train in England before, though it is much like a soft seat at home, she remarks to Jin.

"The toilets are cleaner here," says Jin. "But the food is worse."

For much of the journey, Lili gazes out the window at endless fields of winter stubble. The sky is overcast and the countryside looks bleak and inhospitable. At one point, she looks across at Jin.

"Did you take the train before? When you went to see him?"

Jin nods.

"And when you got there?"

"He met me at the station."

Lili turns back to the window, endeavouring to quash the small pang of jealousy she feels whenever Jin relates a detail of her life with Wen.

It is lunchtime when they arrive at Morecambe. Two taxis wait outside the station. They climb in the first and Jin hands the driver a small scrap of paper with an address. The driver looks at it and nods, handing it back to Jin. They drive along the coast road briefly, and Lili scans the bay, wondering whether Wen will be waiting for them when they arrive. After a few minutes, the taxi leaves the coast and winds through a series of residential streets, eventually pulling up in front of a small detached house. The driver turns back to them.

"This is it," he says.

Lili feels suddenly nervous and must force herself to climb out of the car. She watches as Jin pays the driver. When he has gone, Jin turns to her and takes a deep breath.

Lili realises they are both apprehensive. *But it is too late now*, she thinks resolutely. So she turns and leads the way up to the door.

She rings twice. They can hear a stirring from within, and at length a dishevelled woman opens the door wearing a blue dressing gown, hastily tied up. She appears to be in her mid-thirties, with shoulder-length wavy brown hair and eyes ringed with dark circles. To Lili, she looks pale and vulnerable.

"Yes?"

"Good afternoon," says Lili nervously. "We are sorry to trouble you."

The woman frowns. Lili glances at Jin, her nerve faltering.

"We've come about Wen," says Jin quickly.

The woman's eyes widen. "Who are you?"

Lili takes a deep breath. "I am his sister."

The woman looks at her intently for a moment, then steps back, opening the door wider. "You'd better come in."

They follow her inside. An empty bottle of whisky lies on the floor by the sofa, with another half-drunk bottle on the coffee table. Next to it is an array of glasses and a plate of half-eaten, day-old pasta.

"Sorry about the mess," she says.

Lili and Jin watch as she moves quickly around the room, hastily gathering up dishes and bottles. She carries them into the kitchen, piling them into the sink with a clatter. Then she fills the kettle with water, before coming back to them.

"Wen never told me he had a sister," she says. "Do you know where he is?"

Lili and Jin exchange a glance. Jin's eyebrows shoot up.

"We hope that you know," says Lili.

The woman shakes her head. "He told me he had business in London. That was four days ago."

Lili and Jin both hesitate.

"Is he gone?" asks the woman a little defiantly.

"Not gone," says Jin.

"What then?"

"The snakeheads have him," says Jin.

The woman looks from one to the other, swallowing.

"I think you'd better start from the beginning."

•

Later, when there is nothing more to say, Angie drives them to the train station. As Lili gets out of the car, Angie stops her with a hand upon her arm.

"Please. Let me know. Whatever you hear."

Lili nods, a lump rising in her throat. The two women stare at each other for a moment. *She is terrified*, thinks Lili.

The train home is more crowded. They sit by side rather than across a table. Jin says little, staring out the window.

"What did you make of her?" asks Lili.

"She's a drunk," says Jin flatly.

"She's frightened."

"So are we."

"Yes, but..."

Lili's voice trails off. Jin turns to look at her.

"But what?"

"It's not the same. For her."

Jin stares at Lili, her chest rising and falling with anger. Finally she turns away.

"Maybe not," she says.

For the remainder of the journey, Lili cannot banish thoughts of Angie from her mind. She'd expected to be repelled, but instead she'd been drawn to her. The woman was not like other English people she had met. There was something unsettling about her, as if she did not fit so easily within her skin. Clearly she drank too much. But she was more complex than that: brittle and hard, yet still easily torn, like the shell of a chestnut. It was this curious mix of strength and vulnerability that had impressed her. Like a woman who has once been broken, but has mended herself, and will do so again if necessary.

November 2004

The second beating is worse than the first. This time they use their feet instead of their fists. Wen remains on the floor, one arm handcuffed to the radiator, while Little Dog's henchman kicks him repeatedly, pausing for an agonising moment in between each blow. It is the anticipation of what will come that makes it unbearable, he thinks through a dirty haze of pain. This is the last thought he has before the toe of the boot clips him squarely on the back of the head, and he loses consciousness.

When he wakes again, the room is dark and deadly still. He is lying on his stomach, and with considerable effort, manages to roll over onto his back. For several minutes he lies staring up at the ceiling. Over time, the light in the room shifts almost imperceptibly as the first glimmer of dawn comes through the blinds. He tries to take stock of his injuries, though the pain he now feels is so great that it radiates through his entire body. His front tooth is chipped; he can feel the sharp edge of it with his tongue. A pity, he thinks, as he has always had good teeth. His right eye is swollen nearly shut. And though he needs to urinate, he senses that to do so might be agony, for there is a throbbing in his back near his kidney.

With his free arm, he pulls himself up to a sitting position, sending a lightning flash of pain down his right side. Something is wrong there too, he thinks. No doubt he has broken some ribs, though he hopes this is the extent of it. Black spots dance in front of his good eye, and he breathes in and out several times, hoping to disperse them. He has not eaten in two days, and can't remember when he last drank anything. He manages to pull himself up so he can peer through the slats of the blind. He can see a narrow side street, and a row of small, stucco houses opposite. He sits back down again, contemplating his options; they appear to be few.

He thinks again of Angie. Has she come to hate him yet? If so, then it is no less than he deserves. For by now he would have been in Canada, walking the streets of an unfamiliar Chinatown. He has been a coward and a fool. If he dies here, chained to this radiator, it will be a fitting punishment for all those he has abandoned in this life: Angie, Lili, Jin, Miriam. And perhaps most of all, Lin.

He hears a stirring outside the room and braces himself. After a minute, a mobile phone rings, followed by Little Dog's voice in the hallway. Little Dog speaks in low urgent tones at first, but after a minute, he raises his voice, swearing into the phone. Wen hears footsteps, then Little Dog shouting at the others, rousing them urgently. After a brief interval, one of them opens the door, checks to make certain he is there, then pulls it shut again with a slam. He hears the men descend the stairs and leave the house, and he pulls himself up to watch as all three climb into the car and speed off. Only when he can no longer see the car does he ease himself back down to a sitting position, breathing more easily. For now at least, Little Dog has bigger prey than him.

He looks at the handcuff on his wrist. His hands are small for a man, but not small enough. The radiator is the old-fashioned type, made of heavy cast iron. They have chained him to the base of it, the thin pipe that runs up from the floorboards. He knows nothing about plumbing, but realises that without proper tools there is no way he can unscrew the pipe from the radiator. He pokes his index finger into the hole where the pipe comes out of the floor. The hole has been sloppily made, cut wider than necessary, and the floorboard itself is old and slightly warped. Perhaps if he can get some leverage he could loosen it and see where the pipe leads. He looks around the room. They have been careful to leave nothing within his reach. The only object within his grasp are the blinds, made of flimsy grey plastic slats. But then his eyes alight on the cord: it is made of stout nylon, and at its base is a hard rubber bulb. He grabs hold of it and gives a sharp yank. Unexpectedly, the entire blind comes down on top of him with a clatter and a shower of plaster dust.

He takes the hard rubber bulb and tries to force it through the hole in the floorboard, but the bulb is just slightly bigger than the hole. He lies down and with his foot puts as much pressure as he can on the pipe from the side, moving it fractionally towards the wall until the bulb slips through the hole. He sits back up and pulls on the cord: as he'd hoped, the bulb has lodged on the other side of the board. Now he slips the cord around the far top corner of the radiator for leverage, then wraps it around his free hand several times, positioning himself as best he can. He leans back, pulling as hard as he can on the cord, watching his hand turn purple with the pressure. The nylon cord bites into his flesh, but as it does he hears the floorboard creak under the strain. He redoubles his effort, giving several rapid jerks on the cord, until suddenly the board gives way with a sharp crack, and the bulb flies up at his face.

He slips his hand into the crevice and pulls at one side. The board splinters and breaks, and in a second he is looking down into the floor cavity. The pipe is joined to another that runs along the side of a joist. He grabs hold of this new pipe and gives a sharp tug upwards, putting pressure on the adjoining boards. In this way, he manages to loosen and remove the next three boards. At length, after pulling on the pipe and surrounding boards for half an hour, he manages to break the far end of it. He bends it upwards to where it joins the other pipe just under the radiator and twists it round and round until it comes free. For a moment, he cannot believe he has succeeded. He sits staring at the jagged end of old lead pipe. Then he hears a passing car and quickly slides the handcuff downwards over the broken joint.

He jumps to his feet, forgetting his injuries, and nearly faints. He sways, leaning hard against the window sill, breathing in and out, trying to subdue the pain. After a minute he straightens, then walks out of the room and down the stairs. He pauses in the kitchen to drink some water, then crosses to the front door, peering out of a window. The street outside is empty. He tries the front door; to his surprise it is unlocked. Little Dog and his men were in too great a hurry when they left. He pushes the handcuff as far as it will go up his arm, grateful for the long-sleeved shirt he is wearing, and slips out of the house and down the street, heading instinctively in the opposite direction. He does not know where he is but he can smell the sea. He should be hungry but he isn't. It's as if his body cannot take too much at once. It is enough to be outside, unshackled, in the cool autumn air.

He reaches a main road and turns right, following the smell of the sea. After a few minutes, he passes a large hospital complex. It is early morning and the street is full of medical staff hurrying to work. He realises he must look dreadful, though in the rush no one seems to notice. For an instant, he fantasises about the hospital: the idea of a clean white bed with crisp sheets is tantalising. And he could use a painkiller or two. But he knows this is not an option, so he continues past the hospital down a long street of shops, and across more residential roads. He carries on walking for an hour – perhaps more – trying to put as much distance as

possible between himself and Little Dog, all the while looking around him constantly for fear he will be spotted. They
have taken his papers, his money and his phone: he should
have searched the house before he left, but the time to do so
might have cost him his life, so perhaps it is better that he
didn't. He crosses several busy roads and reaches a series of
vast warehouses. Beyond them he can see docks and a grey
line of water. For the first time he recognises the area: he is
back in Liverpool, just as he suspected. He turns south and
follows the shoreline for perhaps another hour. By now the
docklands are behind him and he has entered a more prosperous residential neighbourhood. He walks down a long
winding road that hugs the river.

Finally he reaches a park with gardens and benches. It is
an attractive place, the sort that he and Angie might visit on
the weekend, but at mid-week in late autumn, few people are
about. He pauses at a wooden bench in an out-of-the-way
spot, the tiredness overwhelming him. Fortunately the day is
sunny and relatively warm for this time of year. He reckons
he has walked for most of the morning. Perhaps he has come
eight or nine miles, though it is difficult to gauge the
distance. He is still terrified that Little Dog and his men will
appear from nowhere. He takes a deep breath and forces
himself to consider his situation. Little Dog would be
unlikely to find him here: he would expect him to flee
towards the city centre, to a bus or train station, not to a park
on the outskirts of town.

He looks around again nervously, and without warning,
a wave of longing washes over him. He misses Angie. The

feeling takes him by surprise, for he had not expected it. He feels strangely hollow, as if someone had scooped out his insides and thrown them on the ground.

In the last hour, the pain in his side has begun to worsen, and coupled with the longing, he feels very low indeed. He needs rest and sleep for his body to recover; he does not know what will help his soul.

And then an idea comes to him. He will walk to Angie. He will walk to Morecambe Bay, just as soon as he gets his strength. He closes his eyes briefly. The sun is warm upon his face and the temptation to sleep is overwhelming. He stretches out on the bench, shielding his battered face with his unshackled arm, and sleep takes him almost instantly. He dreams that he is back in Morecambe Bay, cycling along the coastal path. It is low tide: the sands reach as far as he can see. He climbs off his bike and begins to walk across the marshy beach, but soon he feels a hand upon his leg, pulling at him from beneath the sands. He looks down and sees a hand clutch at him desperately. Though he cannot see the face, he knows with certainty that the hand belongs to Lin. He tries to pull free but cannot: the grip of the hand is too strong. He wakes suddenly, the winter air freezing, and realises that someone is shaking his leg repeatedly.

"Sir? Sir? Time to wake up."

Wen stirs, lifts his arm and squints into the sunlight. Two dark shapes stand over him. He sits up, wincing with the effort, and tries at once to stand. But the blood rushes to his feet and he topples sideways.

"Steady on, mate," says one of the men, grabbing his

arm and easing him back down into a sitting position on the bench.

"Thank you," says Wen.

He looks up at them. They wear dark uniforms and their jackets are laden with badges and equipment. Police. A year ago he would have run from them, but now he can only stare. With his free hand he eases the handcuff further up his sleeve, wondering whether they will notice its bulk.

"Do you speak English?" one of them asks.

"Yes."

"There's no sleeping here. This is a public park."

"Sorry."

The two men exchange a glance. They are both white, English and dark-haired, though one is stouter than the other. Wen reckons they are a few years younger than he is. The smaller man purses his lips.

"Looks like you've had a rough night. Have you been drinking?"

"Drinking?"

"Alcohol."

"No. No drinking."

"What happened to your eye?"

"It... no problem."

"Walked into a lamp-post, eh?"

"Sorry?"

"Were you in a fight?"

"No. No fight. Just..."

Wen's voice trails off. Just what, he thinks? Drowning? Kidnap? Torture? How could he possibly explain what has happened to him? And where would the story begin? In Morecambe Bay? Or back home, in China?

"Are you injured, sir? Do you need a doctor?"

"No. No doctor. Please. I am fine."

The smaller policeman is frowning at him now; he seems genuinely concerned. For the first time, it strikes Wen that these men might not be his adversaries. They may even be prepared to help him.

"You don't look fine," says the heavy-set policeman. "Do you have somewhere to go?"

Both men stare at him now, awaiting his response.

"Yes. I have friend." Wen pauses, trying to organise the sequence of English words in his head. "My friend has house," he says then.

"Does your friend live nearby?"

"No. Not near I think."

The two men exchange another glance, and the heavy-set one sighs, running a hand through his hair. The thinner one rummages in his pocket and pulls out a mobile phone.

"Here," he says, handing Wen the phone. "Call your friend."

Wen takes the phone and dials Angie's number without hesitating. He imagines her moving towards the phone, and when he finally hears her voice he feels a small surge of joy.

"Angie?"

"Wen! Is that you?" Her voice is urgent, shot through with fear.

"Yes. Is me."

"Are you okay?"

"Yes."

"Bastard! Where *are* you?"

Wen cannot help but smile in response. *Bastard*. A term of endearment among the English. Where would he be without this word?

"Wen?" she says again.

Wen turns to the two policemen, who stand politely to one side.

"Excuse me. Where is here?"

The heavy-set policeman rolls his eyes.

"You're in Merseyside, mate. Riverside Drive. Near Promenade Gardens."

"Angie?" says Wen.

"Did they say *Merseyside*?" Her voice is incredulous.

"Yes. I am in park. By river. Near... garden."

"I heard. Stay there. I'm on my way."

He hands the phone back to the smaller of the two men.

"She is come," he says with a smile.

They look at him sceptically.

"Okay," says the heavy-set policeman. "You're going to wait for her? Right?"

"Yes," says Wen nodding. "Thank you," he adds.

The small policeman nods back. "Stay out of trouble," he says pointedly.

"Yes," says Wen, nodding. *I will try*, he thinks.

November 2004

Lili stares at the white plastic stick trembling in her fingers. The stick has two tiny windows, one round, one square. After a minute, a blue line appears in the left window, and in another few seconds a pale apparition appears on the right. Lili watches, her stomach tightening, as the two lines darken until their colour nearly bleeds into the white surround. She picks up the instructions on the floor. She has read them a dozen times, struggling to decipher the words she doesn't recognise: *urinate, immerse, hormone*. But whatever else she doesn't understand, one thing is clear: two lines means she is pregnant. She shoves the stick deep into the bottom of her handbag and slumps down onto the seat of the loo. How could this happen?

Her mind works back and forth, combing through the recent past. Her period must be three weeks late. She had been too distracted by Wen's disappearance to notice, but with a dizzy, sickening sense of the inevitable, she knows that Johnny is the father. They had used no protection that night. She had been utterly unprepared, had not anticipated the course of events, and he had volunteered nothing at the time. Doubtless, she would have been far too embarrassed to bring up the subject of contraception – a subject she knows nothing about. And so here she is with two blue lines. *What would Wen say?* The thought makes her feel almost breathless with humiliation.

Someone knocks on the door. She is in the toilet at work. Unable to stand the nausea any longer, she had run to the high street on her break and bought the test. It had taken her several minutes to find it in the chemist, and the price had made her balk, but she'd had little alternative.

"Lili. Are you in there?"

She freezes at the sound of Jin's voice.

"Just a minute."

She stands up, straightens her clothes and splashes water on her face before glancing in the mirror. *She will know*, thinks Lili. *How could she not?* Already she looks different: her face bloated, her eyes haggard, her expression fearful. She opens the door, preparing for the worst. But in an instant she sees that Jin is not concerned with her appearance.

"He's free," says Jin in urgent low tones.

"Wen? How do you know?"

"He rang. Just now."

"They let him go?"

Jin shakes her head. "He escaped."

"Where is he?"

"Back with her." Jin's tone turns slightly brittle at this last.

"What will he do?"

Jin shrugs.

"Pay them. He has no choice."

Lili rushes home after the next class. It is early evening and she lets herself in as quietly as possible, hoping not to draw attention to her presence. As she eases the front door shut, she can hear May chattering to Adrian down the hall in the kitchen, and the clatter of saucepans as he prepares supper. She tiptoes up the stairs to her room and crosses quickly to the dresser, where she keeps her money stashed in a sock in the bottom drawer. She takes out the sock and sits down on the bed to count her savings, making neat piles of twenty-pound notes. In all she has saved more than eight hundred pounds since she arrived, though laid out on the bed it does not look like much. Suddenly she regrets the few purchases she has made, glancing ruefully at her coat. She should have saved every penny.

A noise startles her. May stands in the doorway, staring at the money on the bed.

"What are you doing?"

"Nothing. Just... " Lili breaks off and looks down at the money.

May takes a few steps into the room, her curiosity roused.

"Is that all yours?"

"Yes."

"What are you going to buy with it?"

"It is for a friend," says Lili carefully.

"Oh. All of it?"

"Yes."

"Who?"

Lili hesitates. Just then Adrian appears in the doorway behind May.

"Hello. I didn't know you were home," he remarks.

"Lili's giving her money to a friend," says May.

Adrian nods, a little perplexed. "Go wash you hands for dinner."

May skips out of the room. They both listen to the sound of her retreating feet on the stairs. Adrian looks at her, and Lili has the sudden sense of being trapped in a beam of light.

"Is everything all right?"

"Yes."

"You're not in any… trouble, are you?"

Lili thinks of Wen and the snakeheads, and the pea-sized foetus in her womb.

"No. There is no trouble."

"Sorry. It's none of my business really." Adrian shrugs, embarrassed.

Lili glances at her watch. "I'm sorry. I have to go now."

"Oh. Yes, of course."

He watches as she stuffs the money into her handbag, then pulls on her coat.

"You're coming back, aren't you? I mean here. To *us*?"

She stops and turns to him. He is staring at her with his

foreigner's eyes, his voice full of apprehension, as if he is seeing her for the first time. She falters. If she ever wanted to be free of him – of this house, and of the burden of his child, then now is the time. For an instant, she fears that it will all come pouring out of her: the nausea and the shame and the fear that she is harbouring.

"Yes," she says, uncertain whether it is true.

November 2004

"You were leaving," says Angie. It is not a question, but still she waits for his reply. They are in bed, Angie curled on her side facing him, Wen on his back staring up at the ceiling.

"I'm sorry," he says. He turns to face her, sees something flash across her face. She lifts her chin a little defiantly.

"Why?"

Wen pauses. He does not know the English word for coward. "I was afraid," he says finally. But even as he speaks, he knows that this is not the truth. The truth has managed to elude him somehow. He cannot articulate, even in his own language, the emptiness he feels inside.

"Of what? The snakeheads?"

Wen shakes his head. He cannot lie any longer. But neither can he find the words to explain. It is not just them, he thinks. After all, he has been through the worst with them and survived. But the hollowness remains; the sense that he is lost within himself.

Angie raises herself up on one elbow. "What happened that night," she says slowly. "On the bay. It wasn't your fault."

Wen looks up at her, his chest frozen. She knows, even without him saying. How is it that she understands? She does not speak his language, and has never travelled to his country. Yet still she finds her way into his mind.

"Survival's not a crime," she says. "Even if you want it to be."

"I should be dead."

"Maybe. But you're not. You have to live within your life, Wen. You have to try."

He nods. She is right. His life is here. With her. And with the others, the ones who died.

"I must pay Little Dog," he says then.

"I don't have the money. But I know where we can get it."

•

Later, when she is speaking to Ray on the phone, Wen hears her raise her voice slightly. "This isn't a joke, Ray. You know me better than that."

Wen hears a muffled outburst from Ray, but cannot make out the words.

"You owe me." Angie enunciates each word separately. Perhaps he is mistaken, but her tone sounds slightly threatening. She listens for a moment.

"It's half past three. If you go now, there's plenty of

time. And Ray," she adds, "bring a set of keys. He's still in handcuffs."

After she hangs up, she turns to him and he raises an eyebrow.

"He'll get the money. Don't worry."

She comes and sits down by him on the sofa, staring up at the ceiling.

"Ray got into trouble a few years back. That's why he quit the police. He nearly got sent down." Angie looks over at him.

"To prison," she explains slowly. "Ray nearly went to prison. Except for me," she adds. "I helped him. That's how I know he'll pay."

Ray turns up much later, long after dark, clutching an old leather satchel. He sits down at the kitchen table with a sigh, and takes out a packet of cigarettes. This time he lights up without asking, drawing the smoke deep into his lungs before exhaling. He tosses the pack of matches onto the table and leans back, eyeing them both.

"So. We pay these geezers off – and then what? Who's to say they won't come back for more?" Ray looks at Angie pointedly.

"They not want more," Wen says quickly.

"How do you know?" Ray points at him.

Wen hesitates. How can he explain, with his few words of English, that this is a simple business deal gone awry, and that he is as much to blame as anyone?

"They want only money," he says. "This money. No more."

Ray snorts and shakes his head. He raises an eyebrow at Angie.

"Everyone wants more," he says. "It's the law of nature."

"Listen to him, Ray," says Angie, her voice slightly menacing.

Ray takes another drag, never once taking his eyes from Angie.

"After this, we're clear? Understood?"

"Clear as ice," she replies.

•

Later, when Ray has gone, Wen telephones his own mobile number. After three rings, Little Dog answers.

"*Wei*?"

"It's me," says Wen.

"I've been waiting for your call. You're not as stupid as I thought."

"I have the money."

"I thought you would."

"If I bring you the money, then that's the end of it. Agreed?"

There is a long pause on the line.

"You bring me the money, and our business is complete," says Little Dog slowly.

"I never want to see you again."

"Why don't we make it easy for you? Why don't we come get it?" says Little Dog.

Now it is Wen's turn to be silent, for he does not wish to reveal his whereabouts. Before he can think of a suitable location, Little Dog speaks again, his voice slightly incredulous.

"You're back in Morecambe Bay, aren't you? You just can't get enough of that place."

"I'll meet you outside the train station," says Wen tersely. "Tonight. At ten o'clock. I'll wait in the car park."

"Don't be late," says Little Dog.

November 2004

Lili manages to catch the last train out of Euston Station with a connection through to Morecambe. It is two and a half hours to Lancaster, and as she sits in the crowded carriage staring out at the darkness, she tries not to think of the baby rooted inside her. She is twenty-eight years old — old enough to pretend that she was almost past the age of child-bearing. Old enough to believe that soon it would no longer be a problem for her: the thinly veiled suggestions and raised eyebrows of those who knew her. For children had not been part of her plan, any more than men had. And she is certain that if she were still living in China, her plan would be intact. How had coming to this country altered it so completely?

She dozes off, the tiredness of early pregnancy overwhelming her, and when she wakes it is because the train has come to a halt. Amid the murmurs of the other passengers, she hears an announcement that the train has been delayed due to a signal failure. An hour later, when the train finally pulls into Lancaster Station, she realises with dismay that she has missed her connection to Morecambe. It is nearly half past ten. She stands uncertainly on the empty platform. A conductor walks past and she stops him.

"Please, is there another train to Morecambe?"

"Not tonight, miss, next train's at 5:07 in the morning."

"Oh."

"There's a taxi rank just outside, though. It's only seven or eight miles. Shouldn't cost you more than twenty quid."

"Thank you," she says, turning away. Twenty pounds less to give Wen, she thinks with dismay. But she has no alternative.

When the taxi pulls up outside, Angie's cottage sits hunched in darkness. She pays the driver and watches as he disappears round the corner before approaching the front door. She did not ring to warn them she was coming, afraid that Wen would try to put her off. She desperately needs to see him: to hear his voice and look into his eyes and know that he is real. But after she presses the front bell, the long silence draws her in. It had not occurred to her that they would not be here.

She feels a fool. She pulls out her mobile and punches in the landline number Angie gave her. Inside the house, she hears the muffled sound of the phone ringing. She listens to it for a full minute before she shuts it off. Angie had not given her a mobile number, and she had not thought to ask. Perhaps they have just gone out for food?

She sits down on the front step to wait. It is colder here than in London, and she pulls the black woollen coat as tightly as she can around her, huddling her arms about her knees. She cannot stay here all night: she knows that much. But she will wait as long as she can bear to, and hope that he returns. She dozes off again briefly, her face buried in the folds of her coat, and when she wakes she sees that it is just past midnight. She rises stiffly to her feet and, glancing one last time at Angie's house, heads in the direction of town. She walks for half an hour before she reaches a high street lined with darkened shops, restaurants and hotels closed up for the night. She had vaguely hoped there might be a café open, but sees at once that the street is ominously silent. Instead, she follows the signs for the train station. Perhaps there will be some sort of waiting room.

It does not take long to reach the station. She sees from a distance that it too is dark, though a police car is parked just outside, its silent lights flashing eerily. A line of yellow tape has been strung across an empty section of the car park, and a uniformed policeman stands to one side, making notes on a small pad of paper. He does not notice her approach, so engrossed is he in his task. It is only when she tries the heavy locked door of the station that he glances up at her. He is in his early fifties, with silvered hair cut short, and a long, thin face. His expression is weary, as if he has spent too much time in empty car parks in the dead of night.

"The station's closed, miss. It won't be open until dawn."

"Oh." Lili turns to him uncertainly.

He squints at her in the darkness.

"Excuse me, you're not a relative, are you?" He takes a step forward.

"A relative?"

"Have you come about the incident?" He motions with one hand towards the ticker tape.

"No."

"I'm sorry," he explains. "An incident occurred here earlier this evening. We're still gathering evidence. This is a crime scene. You may wish to come back in the morning when the station opens." He nods to her and looks back down at his pad.

"Yes, of course," Lili murmurs. But she has nowhere to go. She starts to turn away and hesitates. After a moment the policeman looks up at her again.

"Are you all right?"

"I have been walking a long time," she says rigidly. The cold has enveloped her now. She wonders whether the baby feels its icy grip. The policeman frowns.

"You look frozen. Why don't you go sit in my car for a few minutes and warm up. I'm nearly finished here. I can give you a lift. You won't find a taxi at this hour." He waves with the pad towards the waiting police car.

"Thank you," says Lili.

She walks over to the patrol car and climbs into the passenger seat, shutting the door. The car is much warmer than outside, and at once she closes her eyes, leaning her head back. From time to time a police radio gives a muffled sound on the dashboard. A few minutes later, the policeman climbs in next to her. She watches as he starts the engine and backs the car up.

"What happened here?" She motions towards the taped-off area.

"An assault."

"I'm sorry. I don't understand."

"A man was stabbed."

"Oh. Did he die?"

"He was badly injured. They took him to hospital."

"Why was he stabbed?"

The policeman shakes his head. "We don't know. He wasn't a local." He glances over. "Actually, he was Chinese," he says. "That's why I asked if you were a relative."

"A Chinese man?" she asks thinly.

"Yes," he says, pulling onto the main road.

"Where did they take him?" Her voice has dropped to barely more than a whisper.

"The victim? He's at the Royal Lancaster."

"Please. Could you take me there? To that place?"

At once the policeman slows the car and looks over at her uncertainly.

"You want to go to the hospital?"

She nods. "Please. I have money. If it is long way I can pay you," she offers.

The policeman takes a deep breath and lets it out, before turning the car around and heading in the opposite direction.

"That won't be necessary," he replies with a shake of his head.

November 2004

Wen and Angie arrive ten minutes early at the station. Angie pulls in and parks the car, shutting off the engine, before turning to him.

"Are you sure?"

"Yes."

She peers around. "I don't like the look of this."

"Is okay. They want money. Not me."

"I hope you're right," she murmurs.

They sit for a minute, the car's clock ticking loudly. The area around the station is eerily silent, deserted at this time of night. Finally, after what seems like an eternity, a small blue hatchback pulls in, parking twenty feet away from them. Angie strains to see inside the car.

"It's them, isn't it?"

"Yes." Wen can see that she is frightened, but he himself feels oddly calm.

She turns to him with alarm. "There are three of them! You didn't tell me there'd be three of them!"

"Stay here," he says.

He picks up the satchel at his feet and gets out of the car, walking round behind it until he is just beside the hatchback. Little Dog climbs out of the driver's side and walks round to face him. For an instant, Little Dog's eyes drift over to Angie, then back to Wen.

"Sampling the local fare?" he says with a raised eyebrow.

"I have the money," says Wen, ignoring his comment. He holds the bag out to Little Dog, who opens it briefly and glances inside. "It's all there."

"It better be." Little Dog steps backwards and knocks on the window of the hatchback. A moment later, the window slides down. He tosses the bag into the car. "Count it," he says tersely, before turning back to Wen.

"So that's the end of it," says Wen.

Little Dog does not answer. Instead, he takes a pack of cigarettes out of his pocket and puts one in his mouth. He offers the pack to Wen, who refuses, then lights the cigarette, taking a deep drag.

"What's your hurry?"

"I want to live in peace."

"In peace?" Little Dog snorts. "With her?" He makes a show of bending down so he can peer at Angie. Then he straightens. "She's a bit old for you, isn't she?"

Wen feels himself stiffen. "My debt is paid," he says.

"You think so?" Little Dog takes a step forward.

"You've got your money. Now leave me alone." Wen turns away from him.

"Hey, dead man."

Wen turns back to face Little Dog. He watches Little Dog drop his cigarette on the ground and crush it under his shoe, before reaching inside his jacket pocket. Little Dog steps forward, closing the distance between them, just as Wen sees the flash of metal in his hand. Wen freezes, his eyes locked onto the blade. He feels his mouth go dry, feels the rush of his heart, but he does not run, nor does he try to protect himself. A part of him has been waiting for this moment: as if the last nine months have been pushing him steadily towards this one encounter. Behind him, he hears the car door open. Angie calls to him tentatively.

"Wen? Are you okay?"

He turns and his eyes lock onto hers. At the same time, he is dimly aware of movement, of Little Dog coming towards him, and of the terrible glint of the knife. As he turns back towards Little Dog, he is surprised to feel not fear, but relief.

"Wen!" Angie screams just as the blade pierces his belly. It sears and tears, the pain far beyond anything he has known. He looks down, sees the knife buried in the folds of his clothes, feels a sickening jerk as Little Dog pulls it out again. Little Dog's face is only inches from his own, and Wen stares into the depths of his pupils as the pain runs through him like a current.

"Did you really think you could swim away from all this?" says Little Dog quietly. "From all of us?"

Little Dog's voice is barely audible, so low does he speak, as if his words are meant for Wen's ears only. Wen shakes his head slowly from side to side, his hands moving instinctively to his belly. Against his bare fingers he feels his insides seep and burn. Perhaps he was not hollow after all. Little Dog takes a few steps backwards. Wen watches as he pulls a tissue from his pocket and methodically wipes the blade, before folding the knife and returning it to the inside pocket of his jacket. His task finished, Little Dog looks up at him.

"Your debt is paid," he says then.

He turns and walks round to the far side of the car and climbs into the driver's seat, just as Angie rushes forward. Wen feels his legs start to give, feels his body collapsing on itself. Angie catches him as he sinks to the ground.

"Wen! Oh God. Are you all right?"

Wen turns his face up to hers.

"Is okay," he murmurs.

"You're bleeding! We need an ambulance."

"*Suan le*," he says in Mandarin.

But Angie has not heard. She is busy speaking urgently into her mobile in words he cannot understand. Wen closes his eyes. *It is finished*, he thinks, as he slips past the edge of consciousness. His debt is paid.

November 2004

When they arrive at the hospital, the policeman parks the car and escorts Lili inside. He asks her to wait while he enquires at reception. After a moment, he returns to her.

"The victim's in surgery. They're only just doing the paperwork, so I don't have a name. But the woman who brought him in is in the waiting room."

He motions towards a second room and Lili walks slowly to the doorway. Across the room she sees Angie sitting on a chair, and in that instant she feels a sickening twist in her gut, as if it is she who has been knifed rather than Wen. Angie looks up and their eyes meet across the room. She jumps to her feet and rushes over.

"Lili!"

"Is he all right?"

"I don't know yet."

Angie's eyes drift over to the policeman, who is standing

a few paces behind Lili, regarding them both intently. He steps forward, taking out his pad.

"Would you mind if I asked you both some questions?"

Angie and Lili exchange a brief glance, then Angie nods.

"Yes, of course," she murmurs.

"There appears to be a discrepancy about his name?"

"His name is Wen," says Angie.

"Is that it? Just... Wen?"

"His surname is Zhang," says Lili quietly.

The policeman turns to her briefly, then writes the name in his notebook, drawing a line underneath. He looks again at Angie.

"And you are?"

"His girlfriend."

"Your name?"

Angie hesitates. The policeman looks up from his notebook.

"Smith," she says. "Angelica Smith."

Lili sees the policeman's eye twitch slightly, but he writes down the name.

"His age?"

Angie darts a glance at Lili.

"Twenty-eight," says Lili.

Again the policeman looks at her.

"And you are?"

"His sister."

"Where is your brother from?"

"Hebei Province. In China," murmurs Lili.

"And his occupation?"

Both women are speechless. The policeman looks from one to the other with a raised eyebrow.

"He's a gardener," says Angie quickly.

"A gardener," the policeman repeats, making a note. "And you were with him at the scene of the assault?"

"I was in the car. I didn't see the attack."

"What were you doing at the train station?"

Again Angie hesitates, swallowing.

"He was meeting some friends. He owed them some money, and he was paying it back. But it was nothing illegal," she adds hastily.

"Stabbing isn't legal, Miss Smith."

"No, of course not. I only meant... he wasn't at fault."

"No, miss. He was the victim here. We understand that. Do you know the names of the people he was meeting?"

"He didn't say." Angie keeps her eyes lowered to the pad.

"They were his friends?"

"They were associates, not friends."

"Did you get a look at them?"

"Not really. I saw their car pull up. But it was dark."

"What kind of car?"

"Small. Sort of... a hatchback."

"Colour?"

"Dark. Maybe blue or black."

"Right. Small dark hatchback." He sighs. "How many people were in the car?"

"Three."

"All men?"

"I believe so."

"What race?" The policeman looks up at her.

"Chinese," she says. "Like him."

"Did you see them stab him?"

"No. He came back towards the car. Then he staggered and fell. That's when I realised he was bleeding. By then they'd gone."

"I see," says the policeman, closing the pad. He looks at both women. "Is there any other information that might be relevant here? Something you may have forgotten?" he asks pointedly.

Angie shakes her head slowly from side to side.

"No."

"Thank you for your time," he says wearily. He nods and turns away.

Once he has gone, Lili turns to Angie, her eyes beseeching.

"It was them, wasn't it? Why didn't you tell him?" she asks.

"Because he wouldn't want me to," says Angie. Her tone is quietly forceful. Lili looks around the room desperately. *But he may die*, she thinks. Though in her heart she knows that Angie is right.

There is nothing now to do but wait. They sit side by side. A white-haired man wheels a cart by and gives them cups of milky tea. Lili sits holding hers between her hands without taking a sip. The warmth is comforting, even if the smell makes her nauseous. After half an hour, a young doctor comes through the door wearing green scrubs and a surgical mask that dangles below his chin. He has dark curly hair and a rough shadow of beard. He glances quickly around the waiting room, and when his gaze alights on Lili, he approaches them.

"Are you friends of Mr. Wen?" he asks.

"Yes," says Angie rising to her feet.

Lili looks at the doctor: he cannot be more than her age. Yet he has the eyes of someone far older.

"He's out of surgery and his condition is stable. He's lost some blood, and the wound was fairly deep, but it just missed the wall of his stomach cavity. So he was lucky. With a bit of rest, he should be fine."

"Thank you so much," says Angie.

"Not at all." The young surgeon gives a weak smile.

"May we see him?" asks Lili quickly.

"He's in the recovery room at the moment. He'll be transferred up to one of the wards in a few minutes' time. You can see him then."

Once again they sit and wait, until a plump nurse in her early fifties motions them to follow. They take a lift to the second floor, where she leads them through two sets of double doors.

"It's after hours," she says quietly. "So you can't stay. But you can see him briefly."

She leads them down a long dimly lit corridor flanked by darkened wards on each side. Each room has half a dozen beds, some empty, some screened off by curtains. The nurse walks ahead of them, her soft white shoes squeaking lightly on the polished floor. Finally she turns into a room on the right and moves to a bed in the corner, drawing back the curtain slightly. Wen lies asleep, his head tilted to one side, his face pale but otherwise peaceful. An IV tube runs from the back of his hand to a half-empty bag of dark fluid hanging from a metal stand beside the bed. Lili feels a surge of relief.

"He's asleep," says the nurse quietly. "Best not to wake him. You can come again in the morning during visiting hours."

She draws the curtain closed once more and turns away. Lili stares at the curtain: each time she sees Wen it is more fleeting than the last. As if he is still just a figment of her imagination.

"Lili?" Angie lays a hand gently on her arm. "You look shattered," she says. "Let's go home."

November 2004

When he wakes, the first thing Wen sees is the washed-out light of dawn. He is in a narrow bed made with crisp white sheets, surrounded on four sides by pale yellow curtains. The room is eerily quiet: perhaps this is an English version of heaven? He closes his eyes and takes a deep breath, causing the pain in his abdomen to spike sharply. After a moment he hears soft footsteps approaching, and in another second a middle-aged nurse with tight blond curls is pulling back his curtains.

"Good morning, Mr. Wen," she says, moving to check his IV unit. He smiles weakly. He has never been addressed in this way, and is unused to such politeness. He wonders fleetingly what Angie has told them. He shifts slightly in the bed and draws a sharp breath.

"Are you in pain this morning?" she asks. "I'll just find out what I'm allowed to give you." Without waiting for an answer, she turns and heads off down the hallway.

Wen looks around. There are three empty beds and two that are occupied in the room, their curtains drawn. A machine beeps loudly on the far side of the room, and for the first time, he hears the laboured breaths of the person opposite him. He swallows. His throat is sore, his lips badly parched. He had not thought to ask the nurse for a drink. But she soon returns carrying a tiny paper cup containing two orange pills, and a large plastic beaker of water. She helps him into a sitting position and he swallows the pills, draining the beaker.

"That should set you up," she says.

"Thank you." He watches as she turns to go. "Please? My friend?"

"Your friend went home last night. After you came out of surgery. She and the other lady will be back this morning."

Wen nods, sorting through her words. Other lady? he wonders. Perhaps he misheard. He lies back against the pillow and closes his eyes. He wishes Angie were here now.

He sleeps again, and is woken some time later when a short Indian woman wearing a pale green uniform over a purple and gold sari brings him a tray of food.

"Breakfast," she says, pulling a table over to his bed and placing the tray down in front of him.

The food looks as if it has been made yesterday: two slices of white toast, a small pool of congealed baked beans and a soggy cooked tomato.

She hands him a cup of milky tea and carries on wheeling

her trolley down the hall. Wen sips at the tea and chews on a slice of cold toast.

What he would really like right now is a steaming bowl of *dou jiang*, the sweet soya milk he loved as a child, together with his stepmother's homemade *you tiao* to dip inside. But such things are part of the person he once was, not who he has become. He eats as much as he is able from the tray, then pushes it to one side. A few minutes later, an older man wearing a dark blue suit and a white lab coat enters the room and pauses, glancing down at the clipboard in his hand. He is tall and thin with greying temples and an air of benign competence, and when he eventually raises his head, it occurs to Wen that perhaps he owes this man his life. The man crosses over to his bedside.

"I'm Doctor Stewart, the head of surgery here. How are you feeling, Mr. Wen?"

"I am very fine." Wen eases himself up gingerly.

"May I take a look at your abdomen?" The doctor waits patiently for him to respond.

"Your stomach," the doctor says, pointing. "Where you were injured last night? May I see?"

"Oh," says Wen. "Yes."

The doctor turns and pulls the curtain closed and steps forward. Wen slides the hospital gown they have given him to one side. The doctor carefully lifts the dressing and peers beneath.

"They've done a good job on the stitches," he says, nodding. "It's already beginning to heal."

"You do this?" asks Wen.

"No. I'm the supervising physician. The registrar on call treated you last night. But the wound looks very clean. I don't think you'll have any problems."

"Thank you. Thank you very much."

"There'll be some scarring. The knife ruptured your abdominal muscle, so you'll have to take it easy for some time. Six weeks, at least. No contact sports. No heavy manual labour. Do you think you can do that for us?"

Wen nods. He has barely understood a word, apart from knife and six weeks. Something is easy, but he is not sure what.

"Thank you," he says again.

"You're very welcome. You were quite lucky, in the end."

"Yes," Wen murmurs. "I understand." He has always been lucky.

Just then the nurse pokes her head around the curtain.

"Excuse me, Doctor, there's a policeman outside. He wants to know if he can have a word with Mr. Wen."

"Yes, of course, we're just finishing." The doctor nods at Wen and turns away. The nurse pulls back the curtain, then motions to a uniformed policeman in the hallway to come forward.

"He's all yours," she says to the policeman, and walks out of the room.

Her words are chilling. Wen has absolutely no idea what to expect from the man now walking towards him. His eyes slide over the uniform: the badge and holstered baton and the radio on his belt. Wen nods to him a little nervously.

"Good morning, Mr. Wen. I was wondering if I could ask you a few questions about the men who attacked you."

"Okay."

"You *knew* them? They were associates of yours?"

Wen considers lying, but does not know what information Angie has given them. Besides, he thinks, he is through with deceit.

"Yes. A little."

"Can you tell me their names?"

"No. I do not know the names."

"But you knew them," says the policeman doubtfully.

"I know only one. But is not real name, I think."

"And this name was...?"

"Little Dog."

The policeman's eyebrows shoot up.

"Little Dog," he repeats.

"Yes," says Wen.

The policeman sighs, then writes the words on a small pad of paper.

"These men. Were they Chinese? Like you?"

Wen nods.

"And you owed them some money?"

"Yes."

"You arranged to meet, to give them the money, and then what? Was there a fight?"

"No." Wen shakes his head.

"So what happened?"

Wen hesitates. What happened was fate, he thinks. It was his destiny. But he must offer some other explanation, one that will make this man think that what happened was an accident, and that it should not concern him any further.

"He drink too much," says Wen finally.

Once again, the policeman's eyebrows shoot up. But then he nods, as if this is an all too familiar response.

"He was drunk?"

"*Verr* drunk," says Wen emphatically.

The policeman scratches the side of his head with the pen.

"So he was drunk. Then what? You had an argument?"

"He get angry."

"About what. Money?"

"Yes. I give him money. But he still not happy."

"Why?"

Wen shrugs. "He is this kind of person. All the time drinking, all the time angry. Just like that."

The policeman sighs. "Okay. I'd like you to look at some photos later, if possible. Perhaps this Little Dog is known to us. We may have him on file."

"Yes," says Wen. "Of course," he adds, trying to seem helpful. He will look at all the photos they want him to. He will look and look and he will find no trace of Little Dog in their files. Because it is finished.

"Could I ask you about your status here, Mr. Wen? Are you working?"

Wen feels a rush of panic inside. "Yes," he says. "I work as gardener."

"How long have you been in the UK?"

"Almost two years."

"And you have a visa?"

Wen freezes. The policeman is staring at him.

"Yes. I have family here. And girlfriend."

The policeman makes a note. "We might need to take a look at your papers later, if that's okay."

"Of course," murmurs Wen, lowering his eyes.

"Thank you," says the policeman. "That's all for now."

"Thank you," replies Wen.

The policeman nods and turns to go, but pauses.

"One more thing," he says. "Your name has come up in a separate police inquiry. A detective from Liverpool would like to have a word with you later, if possible."

Wen nods, his heart pounding. Up until this moment, he had thought luck was on his side.

November 2004

Lili sleeps the sleep of the dead on Angie's sofa, waking only when Angie rouses her late the next morning with a steaming cup of black tea.

"Oh," says Lili, sitting up. "I am sorry. I sleep too long."

"You needed it," says Angie. "But we should probably get going. I'm worried about Wen."

"Yes, of course," says Lili, flushing with embarrassment. She takes a sip of tea: it is strong and hot and her stomach nearly revolts, but she forces herself to drink some anyway.

"I just need to make a call before we go," says Angie.

Lili nods and rises, carrying the tea into the bathroom. Once inside, she hears snatches of conversation through the door. She cannot make out the words, but the tone of Angie's voice is urgent and slightly pleading. When Lili finally emerges, Angie is off the phone.

"Ready?" she asks. Lili nods.

When they arrive at the ward, Wen is sitting up in bed, and a nurse is just removing the cannula from his hand. His face lights up when he sees them. They wait patiently to one side while the nurse finishes.

"That's it for now," she says. "But I'll be back in two minutes to change that dressing, so don't go away." The nurse smiles at them and picks up her tray, hurrying out of the room.

Once she is gone, Lili comes forward eagerly to Wen's bedside.

"Are you all right?" she asks in Mandarin.

"Lili! How did you get here so quickly?"

"I came last night. Before I knew."

Wen frowns slightly. "Why?"

"Jin told me you'd escaped. But I wanted to see for myself."

"It's good you've come," he says.

He reaches for her hand and gives it a squeeze. It is a tiny gesture, but Lili feels as if it contains all their shared history. Wen releases her hand then and his eyes drift to Angie.

"Are you okay?" she asks quietly.

Wen nods. Lili sees a look pass between them, cannot help but feel a small pang of longing.

"I called Ray," Angie says.

"The police come," he replies. "This morning. Another police will come later. From Liverpool."

Angie nods. "Don't worry," she says. "Ray will sort it."

Wen turns back to Lili, forcing a smile. "I have to get

out of here," he says in Mandarin. "The food will kill me."

Lili laughs. Just then the nurse returns, carrying a tray laden with equipment.

"Right. I'm afraid I'll have to borrow Mr. Wen for a few minutes. I need to change his dressing. There's a waiting area in the corridor."

They find some chairs in the hallway just outside the ward. Angie sits down with a sigh, picking up a magazine. After another minute, they hear the lift open and a heavy-set man in his late forties emerges. Something about him looks vaguely familiar. Lili watches as he pauses and scans the corridor. The man wears a faded black leather jacket and brown corduroy trousers. His jaw is broad and square, and his thick brown hair, greying at the temples, is combed straight back. At once Angie rises to her feet and crosses over to him.

"Thanks for coming down."

"Family," he replies with a shrug and a lift of his eyebrow.

Angie turns to Lili. "Lili, this is my brother Ray. This is Wen's sister, Lili."

Ray nods briefly at Lili, then turns back to Angie.

"How's he doing?"

"He's okay. The nurse is changing his dressing. But the police were already here once this morning. And someone else from the Liverpool squad is due later."

Ray raises an eyebrow. "Any idea when?"

"No." Angie shakes her head. Ray sighs and sits down next to her.

"Why don't I get some coffee?" she asks, rising to her feet.

"Coffee would be good," says Ray. He and Lili watch as Angie disappears down the hallway. Ray picks up an old newspaper and opens it to the sports page, ignoring her. After a few minutes, the lift opens and a burly man wearing an ill-fitting suit emerges. Lili watches as he stops a nurse, and her heart starts to race when the nurse points in their direction. The man nods and heads towards them, just as Ray raises his eyes from the newspaper. At once he jumps to his feet and moves towards the man in the suit. The latter laughs and shakes his head.

"Lawrence," says Ray.

"Raymond Wright. What a surprise."

The two men shake hands. Lili sees the man cast his eyes round, taking in her presence.

"Here on business?" asks Ray.

"Afraid so." The man cranes his neck towards the ward where Wen is, then turns back to Ray. "You?"

"Just visiting."

The man raises an eyebrow and gestures towards Wen's bed. "Friend of yours?"

"You could say that."

"You're keeping odd company these days."

Ray smiles and spreads his hands. "That's retirement. I like to mix with all sorts."

"You always did."

The two men regard each other silently. Ray steps forward and lowers his voice.

"I don't suppose... you'd consider backing off this one, Larry?"

Lili sees the man raise an eyebrow.

"Just doing my job, Ray."

"The thing is... this guy's not who you think he is. In fact, he's nothing but a ghost."

"A ghost," repeats the man.

"You know the type: here one minute, gone the next."

The man stares at Ray for a long moment. Lili sees his left eye twitch slightly.

"I know the type," he says eventually.

"Elusive," says Ray, "but harmless. He's not mixed up in anything. Just an honest bloke trying to make his way."

The man frowns. "And you can vouch for that?"

"Absolutely."

The man sighs and scratches his head. Lili's heart beats so hard she is certain both men will hear it.

"Anyway," says Ray looking around. "I'm pretty sure you missed him. Must've been when you stopped for coffee."

The man in the suit nods his head. "I *am* a bit peckish," he says slowly. "Skipped breakfast."

"The most important meal of the day," says Ray.

"How long?"

"Ten minutes?"

"Make it five," says the man.

Lili sees him cast a quick glance in the direction of Wen's bed, then turn and walk down the corridor towards the lift. She looks over at Ray. He does not take his eyes off the other man until the latter disappears from sight, then he turns to her.

"Time to go," he says briskly.

They enter the room just as the nurse is opening the curtains around Wen's bed.

"There you are," she says, smiling. "I'm through with him for the time being."

Ray nods politely to her and steps forward, bending down close to Wen's bed, as she leaves the ward.

"I hope you can walk," he says.

November 2004

The next morning, Wen shows Lili the work he has done in Angie's garden. As he walks around, he wonders how he could have ever left. The garden makes him feel oddly content. It is his oasis, his place of refuge from the outside world. For he is suddenly tired of migration: he would like to plant himself somewhere for good. This is the thought that flashed through his mind when he lay bleeding in the car park at the train station.

He pauses in front of Miriam's roses. They stand bravely in a line against the wall, their spindly stems at odd angles. Though it is late November, the weather has turned slightly warmer in the last few days, and he sees with pride that one of the stalks has sprouted a tiny bright green leaf, in open defiance of the coming winter.

"Rose," he says in English to Lili.

"*Mei gui*," she murmurs, nodding.

"One day I hope they will cover the entire wall," he adds, waving his hands exuberantly.

He feels a flash of pain in his belly from the wound, and winces slightly.

"You should rest," says Lili.

She helps him back inside and settles him on the sofa. They are alone today, as Angie has gone back to work. Lili makes two cups of tea and carries them into the sitting room, sitting down next to him with a sigh.

"What will you do now?" she asks.

"Stay here. Live well. Honour their memory."

"With Angie?"

"Yes," he says. Angie is part of his life now, part of his equation.

"You are not bound here, Wen. Not to this country. Nor to these people."

Wen tilts his head all the way back, staring up at the ceiling.

"Sometimes," he says slowly, "a place chooses a person. Rather than the other way round."

"Are you sure?"

He nods.

"Perhaps you never intended to return," she murmurs.

Once again he places his hand over hers and gives it a small squeeze.

"What of you? Will you go back home?" he asks.

Lili's eyes drift. "I will stay in London," she says uncertainly. "for now."

"London is good for you? You're happy there?"

Lili smiles weakly. "London is OK."

Wen returns her smile, but he can sense that she is withholding something from him. The realisation is a sad one, for she has never done so in the past. But he understands that England has altered her, just as it has him. And while they have both ended up here, their lives no longer run in tandem.

November 2004

Two days later, Lili lets herself quietly into Adrian's house. She had hoped to find the house empty, as she needs to realign herself. But as soon as she steps into the hallway, she sees the tell-tale signs of occupancy: May's schoolbag, shoes and sweatshirt lie in a heap beside the front door, and Adrian's leather satchel sits open on the table, a jumbled stack of papers stuffed inside. Lili looks down at the set of keys in her hand, feeling once again like an intruder. Should she run?

She stands frozen in the hallway, her eyes drawn to the framed photograph on the table. Sian stares at her intently, the infant May perched in her arms, as if there is something she needs to convey from the other side of death. Lili wishes that the spirit of this unfortunate woman could somehow guide her.

Further down the hall, May's bedroom door is closed, but

behind it Lili can hear a quiet murmuring. She strains to listen, thinking that perhaps May has a friend to play. But then she realises that the voice behind the door is alone. May is speaking to herself, straddling two worlds, just as she has always done. The voice ceases after a moment, and Lili hears a shuffling. In the next instant, the bedroom door opens and May stops short, startled. She clutches a stuffed rabbit in each hand.

"You're back."

"Yes."

May looks down at the two rabbits. Their soft heads lollop forward, as if she has just throttled the life from them.

"We thought you'd gone."

"No."

"Are you back for good? I mean, to live? In your room?"

Lili hesitates, unwilling to lie. "I don't know."

May stares at her, her child's mind turning over Lili's words.

"If you wanted, we could paint it," she says tentatively.

"Paint what?"

"Your room. It was Adrian who wanted it white. But we could paint it purple. Purple is your favourite colour, isn't it?" May's voice is full of hope.

Lili takes a deep breath. For an instant, she imagines the baby safely cocooned inside warm purple walls, its breath milky and sweet.

"Purple is good," she says.

"Adrian wouldn't mind. Not if you were staying."

May takes a few steps forward, stopping just in front of her. She transfers both rabbits to one hand, and slips her free hand into Lili's, her small fingers closing tightly.

"Your hand is freezing," she says then.

"Outside is very cold."

"Do you want some cocoa?"

Lili looks down at May, unable to answer even this simple question. May searches her face expectantly.

"I can make it for you," May says earnestly. "I just learned how."

Without waiting for an answer, she turns and walks towards the kitchen, tugging Lili gently in her wake.

"And I could teach you if you like," she adds over her shoulder.

Lili trails silently after May, the words washing over her.

Yes, she thinks. There is so much she needs to learn.

April 2005

Wen pauses to remove his shirt in the late morning sun. It is the first warm day of spring. A breeze stirs the branches overhead, and with it comes the salt off the ocean. High tide, he thinks absently, picking up the spade. Over the past few months, he has internalised the rhythms of the sea. The sea is a part of him now.

The past several weeks have been rainy, but this morning he and Angie woke to a brilliant cobalt sky. When he opened the door to the garden, he was hit by the pungent smell of new growth. The compost heap he started last summer is already rich and dark, seething with tiny life. After breakfast, he roots around in the old shed for a plastic sack and fills it with fresh compost, hoisting the heavy sack to the front of the garden. *For roses need feeding,* he muses, dropping to his knees. *Just as we do.*

He kneels in the moist earth and spreads the peaty matter

evenly across the flower bed. Miraculously, Miriam's roses have survived the winter, weathering several bad frosts and a battery of storms in the early weeks of the new year. Now they look taller and heartier, and have sprouted a profusion of small green leaves. They no longer seem out of place against his garden wall. He peers at one and sees that it has formed a tightly furled, lime-green bud. He smiles. With a bit of luck and trial and error, he will find the one that suits.

On the night of February 5th, 2004, twenty-one illegal Chinese migrant workers drowned in a tragic incident off the coast of Morecambe Bay. A further two went missing, though their bodies were never recovered. Some weeks later, at a memorial service for the deceased, a member of the local community posited the hope of a better outcome for those who had not been found: perhaps one or both had somehow emerged safely from the freezing waters that night, however unlikely this seemed. *Crimson China* picks up that thread of hope and spins it into something more tangible, though sadly it remains a work of fiction: the character Wen is entirely my own creation, and bears no similarity to persons living or dead.

The background to the novel is based largely in fact, but there are a few knowing errors: the cockling incident occurred on a Thursday, not a Sunday, as my story suggests; the one-child policy in China was not introduced until 1978, two years after Wen and Lili's birth; and the vast majority of illegal Chinese workers in Britain come from the south-eastern province of Fujien, rather than from Hebei, as Wen does. The use of Wen's sister as collateral for a loan by snakeheads is an unorthodox, albeit plausible, scenario – but it is not common practice. If there are other inaccuracies, then I apologise.

When I began this book three years ago, one of my objectives was to write about one of the great forgotten tragedies of modern history: the 1976 Tangshan earthquake, in which more than a quarter of a million people perished. But during the course of writing, I was overtaken by events: in the summer of 2008, another terrible earthquake struck China, this time in the south-west province of Szechuan; and in January of this year, a catastrophe on a similar scale occurred in Haiti. Let Tangshan be remembered alongside both of these.

The experience of illegal Chinese living and working in the UK is indeed fraught with hardship: if anything, the conditions they endure are far worse than anything I portray in this book. The Morecambe Bay tragedy resulted in even greater suffering for the victims' families in China, as the latter were forced to carry on repaying their debts to the snakeheads without the benefit of foreign wages. In 2004, the Morecambe Victims Fund was established to help the families of the victims, and thus far it has raised more than £400,000, nearly enough to clear the half-a-million-pound debts outstanding.

In the wake of the tragedy, the UK government instigated the Gangmaster's Licensing Act to regulate those agencies that supply labour to the agricultural and shellfish industries. It aims to reduce the ruthless exploitation of casual workers by requiring employment agencies to carry a licence, but its critics argue that it only serves to drive illegal immigrants and asylum seekers further underground, putting them at even greater risk.

ACKNOWLEDGEMENTS

Huge thanks to all those whose editorial comments helped to shape this book: Margaret Glover, Andy Carl, Clive Brill and Flora Drew (who, together with the vital help of her newborn twins, gamely agreed to vet the Chinese content). Xie xie ni! Big thanks as well to Hsiao-Hung Pai for enthusiastically sharing her hard-earned knowledge of the conditions of illegal Chinese working in Britain; to Bill Grant for his expertise on horticultural history; and to Jane McDonagh for legal advice.

As always, I am indebted to the fabulous gang at Short Books, whose matchless enthusiasm, unerring judgement and sheer bravado continue to prove that small is by no means inferior: Rebecca Nicolson, Aurea Carpenter, Vanessa Webb and Catherine Gibbs.

Huge thanks as well to my extremely loyal and long-serving agents: Felicity Rubinstein and Sarah Lutyens and their team in London, and Kim Witherspoon and David Forrer at Inkwell in New York. If you have not yet patronised the inspired bookshop run by Lutyens & Rubinstein in Notting Hill, then you are missing out on one of the great pleasures of literary London.

And for putting up with my near-constant state of distraction, big hugs to all the gang at home: Peter, Theo, Cody, Maddy and Megan.

A Conversation With Betsy Tobin

What prompted you to write Crimson China?

I was haunted by the tragedy at Morecambe Bay. I followed the aftermath and kept a file of clippings before I eventually embarked upon the novel in 2007, some three years after the disaster. For me it had a particular poignancy: the idea that you could journey to a strange land and perish without any lasting imprint of your presence seemed unimaginably sad. As a writer I've always been drawn to the notion of identity and culture, and the extent to which we locate ourselves in a particular place and time: what happens to our sense of identity when we are displaced, and what impact does rootlessness have on who we become? These are themes I've returned to often in my work, I suppose because I left my own country twenty years ago, and have struggled to define myself in cultural terms ever since. But I never experienced anything like the extreme isolation of the illegal Chinese community in Britain, who really do operate in a parallel world here. In the words of the character Jin, they are like shadows, and when a shadow disappears, nothing remains. In writing this book, I wanted to create a lasting monument to those who died: to carve them into our collective memory so they would not be forgotten. But I also wanted to conjure a tale of hope, rather than despair.

How did you research the book?

I read everything I could about the illegal Chinese community in Britain and the snakeheads who transport them, and I travelled to Morecambe Bay to see for myself where the tragedy happened. It is a starkly beautiful place, and there is a small, makeshift memorial at the edge of the sands to those who died. If there is an expert on this subject, it is Hsiao-Hung Pai, the journalist who covered the Morecambe Bay tragedy for the *Guardian*, and eventually published *Chinese Whispers: the True Story Behind Britain's Hidden Army of Labour*. Her compelling account of the harsh realities of life for undocumented Chinese workers is one of the finest pieces of investigative reporting to emerge in recent years. She was a great help to me in my research.

Were you concerned about accurately representing the Chinese characters?
To a greater or lesser extent, writing fiction is always an imaginative leap of faith. Creating any character is a challenge, but at the end of the day characters must be true to themselves, rather than to some preconceived notion of who we think they should be. I lived in China as a student in the early eighties and speak some Mandarin, so was able to draw upon my own experience. I've also travelled extensively throughout China in the last five years, so have a strong sense of the country and the challenges it faces today. I hope the book and its portrayals are convincing to both Western and Chinese readers alike; certainly it reflects my long-held interest in Chinese culture.

How did you come up with the story?
I set out to write a contemporary ghost story about a Chinese woman who is haunted by the spirit of her dead brother. But as often happens in writing, the tale that emerged took an unexpected turn. I never intended for Wen's relationship with his rescuer Angie to become the central arc of the narrative: it really was a case of the characters quite literally running off with the story. After I wrote the first chapter, I remember being desperate to shove dinner into my children so I could return to work and see where they were going. For a time Angie

and Wen's world became more real to me than my own; it was certainly more engaging.

What about Lili's story?

Lili's story is essentially about a woman who goes in search of one thing and finds another. I wanted Lili to have her own encounters in Britain, and I had been reading about the experiences of Western families who adopt Chinese children. I was very struck by the complexities these families face when trying to reconnect their adoptive children to their Chinese heritage. The Chinese writer Xinran launched a charity in Britain in 2004 to address these issues. Mother's Bridge of Love aims to help the more than 50,000 Western families who have adopted Chinese children, the vast majority of whom are girls. (Chinese families traditionally value boys over girls, and one of the saddest outcomes of the government's one-child policy is that it created a nation of orphaned daughters.) Although Lili endeavours to help May find her Chinese roots, it is really May who ultimately grounds Lili, and shows her that each of us carries the burden of identity within.

What does the title signify?

I am indebted to my friend Andy Carl for the title: he read an early draft and, knowing I don't have much of a green thumb, offered to vet the gardening content. He contacted an American friend who is an expert on rose germination, and it was he who brought the China roses to my attention. I had no idea that the vast majority of our domesticated rose species were actually imported from China in the eighteenth century, particularly since the Chinese do not especially value the rose. (For the record, they prefer chrysanthemums, plum blossoms, peonies, lotus and water lilies.) As transmigration is a central theme of the book, Crimson China seemed an apt image, though not one that is immediately apparent to the reader. I like the idea that the meaning behind the book's title unfolds only gradually, and that the person who conveys this information is Miriam. The Chinese venerate old age enormously, and Miriam acts as a sort of parallel character to Wen's stepmother in the book; both women are conduits, offering advice, history and wisdom from their respective corners of the earth. Crimson also seemed appropriate, as red has enormous cultural importance in China: it symbolises courage, loyalty and success, as well as happiness, fertility and passion; red is traditionally the colour of choice for Chinese brides.

Do you agree with the UK government's policies on illegal immigrants?
This is a thorny problem: from 2001 to 2007 the estimated number of irregular migrants (the official term for illegal immigrants) in the UK nearly doubled from 430,000 to 725,000. While the government purports to not want these workers, even in a recession there remains considerable demand for their labour. Irregular migrants tend to work in low-skilled, low-paid jobs in construction, agriculture, hospitality, cleaning, care and domestic work, often doing jobs that local workers refuse for lower-than-normal wages. They are not entitled to public services, but neither do they pay tax, so while they contribute to the economy, their contribution is reduced by their irregular status. Most illegal Chinese have no intention of staying in Britain permanently: they are here to work hard for a fixed period of time to improve the living standards of their families back home. In recent years, tougher immigration controls have made it more difficult to live and work illegally, but rather than drive illegal immigrants away, they tend to drive them further underground, often keeping them here longer than they intended. While the government needs to exert tougher border

controls on human trafficking and smuggling, perhaps greater flexibility is needed for employers to recruit unskilled labour from abroad, including temporary visas and return packages that do not jeopardise workers' future immigration status. Such policies would encourage greater fluidity between borders and a labour force that is responsive to the needs of the British economy.

Why should this book appeal to Western readers?
I think there's a growing appetite in the West for books that take readers to places within their own culture where they would not otherwise go. Not all readers are prepared to venture into completely foreign territory; the appeal of this novel is that it locates itself firmly on a crossroad where two worlds collide. Each of us could be Angie: an ordinary person whose fate, through chance, is yoked together with that of a stranger from the far side of the world. Many of us seek to broaden our cultural understanding, but we need pathways that intrigue and compel — I set out to write a gripping story with characters that readers would be drawn to from the start.

Betsy Tobin was born in the American Midwest and moved to England in 1989. She is the author of three other novels, *Bone House*, shortlisted for the Commonwealth prize, *The Bounce* and *Ice Land*. She lives in Islington, London with her husband and four children.